All Good Things

The Last SFX Visions

All Good Things

The Last SFX Visions

David Langford

Illustrations by

Andy Watt

Steel Quill Books
An Imprint of NewCon Press

First edition, published in the UK April 2017
by Steel Quill Books,
an Imprint of NewCon Press
41 Wheatsheaf Road, Alconbury Weston, Cambs, PE28 4LF

SQ006 (hardback)
SQ007 (softback)

10 9 8 7 6 5 4 3 2 1

ISBN: 978-1-907035-43-9 (hardback)
ISBN: 978-1-907035-44-6 (softback)

Cover art copyright © by Andy Watt
Cover layout by Andy Bigwood

Minor Editorial Interference by Ian Whates
Text layout by Storm Constantine

What Has Gone Before

I never expected to spend 21 years writing for *SFX*, Future Publishing's glossy magazine about SF. But having cunningly insinuated a Langford column into the first issue, dated June 1995, I somehow continued to appear in all those that followed at monthly (later, four-weekly) intervals until number 274, dated June 2016. Shortly before the deadline for that column, a budget cut was imposed from On High and chief editor Richard Edwards shared the bad news that he could no longer afford what he kindly called "star writers and illustrations". That is, not only I but the other surviving outside columnist (many had fallen by the wayside over the years) and my page's long-time illustrator Andy Watt also got the push. Hence the unsubtle title of this third and last Langford *SFX* collection. The suggestion that I might receive a kill fee for the already-commissioned columns 275, 276 and 277 was greeted with hearty laughter.

A little back story. The first 128 columns, from June 1995 to March 2005, were assembled – with several special features also written for *SFX* – as *The SEX Column and Other Misprints* (Cosmos Books, 2005; Ansible Editions ebook, 2016); the title alludes to the perennial practice of laying out the magazine's front cover with some actor's head obscuring part of the title's F and thus making it *hilariously ambiguous*. Columns 129 to 183 – April 2005 to June 2009 – were then collected along with a mass of other recent Langford non-fiction as *Starcombing* (Cosmos Books, 2009). Earlier, mostly non-*SFX*, critical efforts had already appeared in the big retrospective volume *Up Through an Empty House of Stars: Reviews and Essays 1980-2002* (Cosmos Books, 2003; Ansible Editions ebook 2016). Finally, *The Last SFX Visions* concludes the long colonnade with *SFX* instalments 184 to 274 – July 2009 to June 2016 – plus a handful of extras from the same time period that bring the contents to a round 100 items.

During this last period the elephant in the room of my writing life – mentioned rather too often in what follows – is the third edition of the *Encyclopedia of Science Fiction*, of which John Clute and I are the principal editors. This, launched as a free online reference work in October 2011, has been taking up all too much of my time from about 2004 to the present day. Please forgive the frequent references to this ongoing obsession, which Charles Dickens famously alluded to in *David Copperfield* when the hapless character Mr Dick (distraught from his pink beam experience) kept going on and *on* about King Clute's Head.

Another tradition of the *SFX* page was that each column ended with a silly little italicized tagline about its author: "*David Langford has been watching the gostak distim the doshes*" or whatever. At some stage the *SFX* editors drifted into the habit of slipping these in without telling me; in self-defence I began to supply my own on the theory that I could contrive a slightly better class of pointless and annoying coda. For this collection I've dropped the more boring or self-serving taglines ("buy my new book!") but retained most of those that were more or less intentionally a final twist or capstone of the current column. To compensate for the cuts I have also re-inserted from memory a number of phrases and gags self-censored to meet the magazine's ever-crueller wordcount limits. Apologies too for the (rare, I hope) repetitions that result from writing for different magazines: for example, I became over-excited about the mysterious roots of Eric Frank Russell's story "Allamagoosa".

Now for the traditional round-up of those who deserve a good word. The Future Publishing/*SFX* editors I worked with while writing the columns in this collection (and some reviews that aren't) are Ian Berriman, David Bradley, Richard Edwards, Guy Haley and Russell Lewin. Pleasant times were had; no hard feelings, chaps. Thanks also to the editors who gave their thumbs-up to other articles and columns here: Claire Brialey and Mark Plummer of *Banana Wings*; Kevin J. Maroney of *The New York Review of Science Fiction*; Jim Mowatt of *The Little Book of 42s*; and Steve Davies, Alison Scott and Mike Scott of *Plokta*. Finally, of course, a tip of the hat to Ian Whates of NewCon Press/Steel Quill Books for madly agreeing to publish this collection; and Andy Watt for the cover and interior artwork.

It feels strange to be no longer the Oldest Inhabitant at *SFX*, the weird old guy in the corner who bangs on about cobwebbed SF books that nobody reads any more and has a load of cranky opinions on forgotten causes like prose style, the Hugo Awards and semicolons. I daresay I'll get used to it.

David Langford, February 2017

Behind the Grim Grin

Long before the recession got underway, more and more major SF authors were resorting to small presses. Story collections, according to traditional publishers, are difficult to market because the general public can't face the hideous effort of dealing with new characters every few dozen pages. Reprints are unpopular too, unless you're in the SF Masterworks or Terry Pratchett class. Publishing wisdom is that readers want a shiny new book, not some dusty old palimpsest unearthed from the forgotten twentieth century.

You'd imagine the SF public would be fascinated by the story behind a film as hugely popular and successful as *The Prestige*, told by the author of the novel on which it was based. Big Publishing thought otherwise, though, and Christopher Priest defiantly set up his own small press to produce this book: the enigmatically named GrimGrin Studio.

GrimGrin now offers four Priest titles – in fact four and a bit – all interesting in different ways. The lead title is *The Magic*, Priest's own take on the making of *The Prestige* from his fine novel of the same name. Have you ever wondered what an author thinks about the brutal dismantling and reconstruction needed to transfer a book to the big screen? It's all here, from his first struggle to write the complex story to a detailed analysis of the movie.

Generally, Priest gives the film high marks despite noting a few plot and motivation problems. He even manages not to be bitter about the antics of director Christopher Nolan, who became so infected by the book's central theme – the obsessive secrecy and jealousy of stage magicians – that he kept announcing: "Don't read the novel! It spoils everything!" Just what every novelist wants to hear.

One thing an author expects from his connection with a successful film is to make a few bob from extra book sales. But the important money-spinner, the American tie-in edition, was sabotaged by the film-makers' refusal to allow any movie scene or image on the jacket. (How Gollancz managed to get around this in the UK is a mystery.) Even though they'd drastically changed the ending, and though the novel has been around since 1995, there was this deep-rooted paranoia about spoilers...

The Magic is a good read, full of thoughtful insights. Learn more about this and the others at christopher-priest.co.uk.

Another much-enjoyed GrimGrin book is the cryptically titled *"It" Came from Outer Space*, collecting 56 assorted pieces of Priest non-fiction published from 1973 to 2008. Section titles: "Fragments of a Life", "Lost friends and colleagues", "Things that come along", "An Enthusiasm for H.G. Wells", "Some science fiction", "Writings of War", "Books and Writers" and "Distractions and Occasions". An entertaining, niftily written mix of criticism, polemic, autobiography, weirdness and outright fun... like the laugh-out-loud anecdote about Anne McCaffrey at an SF writers' workshop, which I daren't repeat here.

Real-Time World simply reprints Priest's first SF collection from 1974 – a mixed bag, though with some notable stories, including a gory anticipation of reality TV – and *Real-Time World +2* is the same book with two extras that somehow weren't included first time around. To buy them both would hardly be sensible.

Personally I wouldn't have had the courage to publish *Ersatz Wines*, a collection of still earlier material subtitled "instructive short stories". These are Priest's first attempts at fiction, some never before printed. The "instructive" part consists of a long introduction describing the author's roots as a writer, followed by unsparingly critical "Then" and "Now" commentary about each story's good and (mainly) bad points. It's not often that a leading SF author invites us behind the scenes like this. *Ersatz Wines* teaches more than you might think about the techniques and problems of fiction.

(Nothing to do with GrimGrin, but I can't resist mentioning the how-to-write-serious-fantasy passages in Lin Carter's *Imaginary Worlds*. These assure readers that his own hero's moniker Thongor "has the ring of clashing steel", while a jolly good name for a wizard is Herpes Zoster. His friends probably call him Herp. Well, Priest admits that one savvy editor persuaded him to change a character's name from Arstourd because it sounded somehow rude.)

What about that slightly sinister press name, GrimGrin? Christopher Priest, who's very popular in French translation, has guested at many continental SF conventions and been tickled by how they pronounce one famous British author. *Brighton Rock*, *Our Man in Havana*, *The Power and the Glory*... You know. GrimGrin.

• *SFX #184, July 2009*

The Voices of Ballard

Losing J.G. Ballard was a shock but not a surprise. His 2008 autobiography *Miracles of Life* – a warmly cheerful book, despite his image as guru of entropic doom and near-future mayhem – casually revealed that the cancer was unstoppable. As he wrote in an iconic SF story of 1960: "These are the voices of time, and they're all saying goodbye..."

Once he'd gone, of course, we heard the voices of snobbery explaining that Ballard was too good to have written SF. His US editor Robert Weil said, "His fabulistic style led people to review his work as science fiction. But that's like calling *Brave New World* science fiction, or *1984*." (*New York Times*.) Ursula K. Le Guin, bless her, had fun inventing parallel claims: it's like calling *Don Quixote* a novel, like calling *The Lord of the Rings* a fantasy, like calling *Utopia* a utopia!

Ballard's own approach to SF was iconoclastic and controversial, but he wrote in 1974: "I firmly believe that science fiction, far from being an unimportant minor offshoot, in fact represents the main literary tradition of the 20th century..." In a 2009 BBC interview he stated again that he was an SF writer and proud of it.

Showing how respectable he'd become, both *The Guardian* and *The New Yorker* marked his death with a Last Ballard Story. Two different ones, each published as if brand-new: "The Dying Fall" and "The Autobiography of J.G.B." Though the first of these was indeed his final story, both had been in *Interzone* in 1996, and even then the second was a reprint from *Ambit* (1984). Don't believe everything you read in the papers.

If the *SFX* Book Club department tackled short stories, a strong contender would be Ballard's weirdly haunting "The Voices of Time", already quoted above. Though not at all a trad SF story, this was selected by the traditionalist – indeed, reactionary – Kingsley Amis for his anthology *The Golden Age of Science Fiction*.

No one then knew how and why Ballard injected such an emotional charge into symbols like abandoned buildings and drained swimming pools. Eventually *Empire of the Sun* and *Miracles of Life* showed how these settings had a huge impact on young Jimmy Ballard, wandering as a boy through Japanese-occupied Shanghai. This was an author who'd actually seen civilisation come (if only temporarily) to an end.

"The Voices of Time" opens with a huge mandala carved into the floor of an empty swimming pool. It flaunts defiantly daft ideas like a house built as a geometric model of the square root of minus one. There are cryptic messages from the stars, every one a countdown, ticking towards zero and the heat death of the universe. Surreal new plants and animals seem to be evolution's doomed attempt to fight back. Nonsense science is used as incantation: "NGC9743, somewhere in Canes Venatici. The big spirals there are breaking up, and they're saying goodbye." There are no alien hordes to be defeated, just entropy, cancer, the Second Law of Thermodynamics transformed into bizarre sad poetry. Unforgettable.

Ballard played more tricks with time and psychology in "The Garden of Time", a rare fantasy tale, and "Chronopolis", describing a nightmare anthill city of 24/7 precision timekeeping that seems slightly more prophetic each year.

Surrealist artists were another key to early work like his *Vermilion Sands* sequence. Our man plugged Dali and others to bemused SF fans in 1960s *New Worlds* articles like "The Coming of the Unconscious". Max Ernst's painting *The Eye of Silence* has such a perfectly Ballardian strangeness that it became the cover for his novel *The Crystal World*.

Ballard moved on to tersely cryptic "condensed novels" that manipulated twentieth-century icons in edgy, disturbing ways. Even the titles collected in *The Atrocity Exhibition* were enough to make red-blooded Americans gibber: "Plan for the Assassination of Jacqueline Kennedy", "The Assassination of John Fitzgerald Kennedy Considered as a Downhill Motor Race" (homage to Alfred Jarry's similar title involving Jesus Christ on a bicycle), and – long before its object of desire became President – "Why I Want to Fuck Ronald Reagan". No wonder his US publishers, Doubleday, lost their nerve after printing *The Atrocity Exhibition* and pulped it before release.

Ballard's novels are rightly celebrated, but when a career gets crammed into an obituary there's rarely room for short-story details. These, however, were stories that rewrote the SF map. They literally changed readers' minds.

Now the voices of time have called James Graham Ballard, and they're all saying goodbye...

David Langford is rereading his Ballard collections.

• *SFX* #185, August 2009

Moose in Darkest Berks

What's an SF convention really like? My favourites are the small, eccentric, untypical events. Last year saw Cytricon in Kettering, with much wallowing in arcane nostalgia on the fiftieth anniversary of the last UK Eastercon held in that same town and hotel. No, I didn't attend in 1958, but both Cytricon guests of honour did. That event was... strange. But fun.

The same goes for my favourite so far this year, Plokta.con 4.0. This was masterminded by the dread UK cabal behind the fanzine *Plokta* ("Press Lots Of Keys To Abort"), a regular Hugo nominee which – thanks no doubt to the editors' famous Orbital Mind Control Lasers – bagged the award in 2005 and 2006. They marked their first win by Photoshopping the Hugo rocket into an old *Missile Command* screenshot to form part of a spoof videogames-magazine cover. As one does.

Plokta.con happened in Sunningdale Park, which to the terror of many was once the Civil Service College but has been rehabilitated. It reminded me vaguely of Portmeirion and *The Prisoner*. Mini-Mokes (or modern equivalent) offering thirty-second rides between buildings to save you a tiring thirty-second walk, rhododendrons everywhere, a giant lawn chess set, and random outdoor weirdness like antique agricultural machinery or an old-style red phone box containing a table with a dinner-place setting for one.

However, Sunningdale Park cannot be held guilty of being obsessed with moose. That's one of *Plokta*'s mysterious foibles, explaining the Moose On Road warning triangle (probably nicked from Canada) and the giant black pirate flag with a Moose and Crossbones design that might conceivably relate to International Talk Like a Moose Day. ("Aaaaaarrrrrrrrrrrr!")

The honoured guests were Diana Wynne Jones of *Howl's Moving Castle* fame, who was ill and sadly couldn't make it, and Paul Cornell of *Doctor Who* script fame, who terrified slower performers by improvising his speech on the spot. The Cabal wheedled new stories from both of them for the souvenir book, cunningly disguised as the fortieth issue of *Plokta*. This may already be a collector's item.

What actually happened at Plokta.con? There was a regrettable amount of drinking despite eye-watering bar prices. (One of the bar staff reads this column. Excuse me while I wave to him.) Science fiction was discussed. Fans wandered the Sunningdale Park grounds looking for clues in the manifestly incomprehensible treasure hunt: I was frightened off this by the starter clue in Cyrillic script. In a side room a dedicated party of paper engineers was constructing the official model of Howl's Moving Castle as imagined by Studio Ghibli. I missed the controversial panel on Web 2.0, where someone who felt Twitter was the one true way (since you don't have to interact, just broadcast your important opinions to the masses) stormed out when others dared to interact by inserting their different and clearly less important opinions.

Oh yes, and there was the musical. Perhaps I'd better not try to describe the musical. Well, if you *insist*... The evil genius Ian Sorensen has been producing spoof rock operas at SF conventions for many years. As a joint tribute to Diana Wynne Jones and Paul Cornell he came up with the starkly inevitable title *Harry Plokta and the Half-Cut Prince*. If J.K. Rowling's solicitors are reading this, could they please stop now?

The included *Doctor Who* homage, besides some Slytherin/Slitheen confusion, was extremely practical. Since there was a clear shortage of male fans who could actually sing, the original Harry Plokta was quickly killed off (by Draco Malfoy. With a light-sabre. In the conservatory. Don't ask) and equally quickly regenerated as female and tuneful. Later, an important plot point required Hogwarts school to have been secretly dismantled and, with the help of those famous messenger birds, moved stone by stone to a new location. *Harry/Harriet:* "It's not possible!" *Dumbledore:* "Surely you've heard of owls moving castle?"

Other parts of the production were less sensible. I was tickled by one of Snape Sorensen's deadly incantations: "Ansible!" A Cabal mother fretted that someone would tell her daughter the significance of Hermione's pink vibrator "wand", and was horrified to find her daughter didn't need to be told. The final ensemble piece involved many pelvic thrusts from the whole cast – including a gaggle of *Scream*-masked Dementors – to the somehow vaguely familiar song *"Let's do the Tomb-Walk again..."*

Not all SF conventions are like Plokta.con. For a start, there are usually fewer moose.

• *SFX* #186, September 2009

Dark Side of the Net

Funny business at Amazon.com in June... Patrick Rothfuss's 2007 fantasy debut *The Name of the Wind* had made a terrific splash, winning awards and storming the *New York Times* bestseller list. So why was this mob posting one-star reviews to Amazon, saying in strangely similar phrases that the book was rubbish, and furiously agreeing with each other in a discussion thread titled "rothfuss is a fraud"?

Most had no track record of Amazon reviewing and seemed to have signed up solely to slam a popular book. Here my spies remembered another US author's online habits. Let's not give him the oxygen of publicity; I'll call him Bob Direhack.

Direhack is a self-published writer of woefully inept fantasies. If you believe his Amazon reviews, though, he bestrides the genre like a colossus. When negative comments appeared – complaining of feeling defrauded by the actual books being raved about – Direhack would report them as malicious abuse and have them deleted. Now that particular tactic has worn thin, bad vibes are rapidly pushed out of sight by a fresh surge of five-star reviews, often with strangely similar phrases. Reportedly Direhack uses scores, even hundreds, of Amazon accounts to hype his own books. Or maybe – let us strive to be fair – his hordes of loyal fans all write in the same style.

There's more! Back in 2002, my newsletter *Ansible* noted a rash of oddly similar Amazon reviews that rubbished newer fantasy authors and instead plugged George R.R. Martin, Robert Jordan and Bob Direhack. Or maybe C.S. Lewis, J.R.R. Tolkien and Bob Direhack. Our man's name got dragged into praise of Philip Pullman by several reviewers who independently used the spelling "Phillip". Who could possibly be writing these barely disguised puffs?

Tactfully I let readers guess for themselves, but the wrath of Bob Direhack or of his devoted fandom was roused. In those days the *Ansible* web archive lived at Glasgow University... which soon had threatening email from a supposed US attorney, claiming that evil Langford had "caused continuing material and economic harm" to Direhack and should be suppressed with extreme prejudice. This was transparently fraudulent. Real lawyers don't operate from throwaway Hotmail accounts, conceal

David Langford

their street address, or talk about "malice of forethought". Ignoring such clues, the spineless Glasgow authorities took down the *Ansible* archive. Happily I had a mirror site elsewhere, but it rankled.

Then the Direhack promotional bandwagon hit Wikipedia. Dedicated Wiki editors with curiously similar styles peppered the online encyclopedia with dozens of articles about this author's hugely important fantasy series. His name was thrust into unlikely contexts – the Literacy entry, for example, because Literacy is something what Bob Direhack does real good. There was a purge of all this "non-notable" Wikipedia hype in 2006, and last summer the entry for Direhack himself (already heavily cut) was hurled by popular acclaim into the dustbin of history. Great crocodile tears of sympathy rolled down my face.

What of the recent mass attack on Patrick Rothfuss? This had the flavour of Direhack's co-ordinated team of "sock puppet" identities, but without the usual recommendations of his dismal novels. The mask began to slip when one of the faceless attackers took time out to slag two other authors, who by uncanny coincidence had both blogged disapprovingly about Direhack's relentless self-promotion. Also, several of the attack dogs amended their Amazon profiles, adding tags that steered profile viewers to the books of... well, what a surprise: Bob Direhack! These tags were hastily deleted when someone blew the whistle; but the secret was out.

Direhack-watchers suspect this failed writer may be simply jealous of newer fantasy authors who crash the fame barrier. Rothfuss isn't alone in being blitzed with one-star writealike reviews for no clear reason. Are accusations that Rothfuss wrote all his own positive feedback (with help from friends and family) intended to distract from Direhack's well-known habits: "Hey, *everyone* does it"? Do they expect us to believe that Rothfuss fiddled the bestseller lists by having those sycophantic pals buy untold thousands of books in several countries? Meanwhile at Wikipedia, someone with a cryptic agenda and a fondness for sleazy innuendo tried to get Rothfuss's and our own Joe Abercrombie's entries deleted – like Direhack's – as "non-notable".

It's all terribly sad; and while Amazon keeps turning a blind eye to anonymous hype and anonymous denunciation, it's not going to end any time soon.

David Langford has no secret online identities. Honest.

• *SFX* #187, October 2009

Googled to Death

The perils of trying to be topical: this was all accurate enough when written and sent in, but Google pulled the rug from under me by overhauling, updating and generally improving their wretched Settlement site to make the process less frustrating. Thanks to kindly SFX *editor Dave Bradley, I was able to slip in a couple of changes before the issue finally went to press. See note at end.*

Lately I've been wrestling with the Google Book Settlement, which isn't a summer camp for remedial readers but the hideously complicated result of a US class action brought by the Authors Guild and various publishers against the famous search engine.

Why? Google launched a vast project to scan and digitize whole libraries of books without the fiddling formality of asking permission or clearing rights with mere authors. Years of legal hassle over this led to a not very satisfactory compromise: the October 2008 Settlement, whose terms apply even to writers who've never heard of it and want nothing to do with it.

Though it sounded dreadfully like work, I thought I'd better investigate the website (www.googlebooksettlement.com) for two reasons. First, writers who don't register there get screwed anyway. Second, I was madly curious about whether Google had nefariously converted my books to digital form. Discovering this, it turns out, isn't easy.

As part of the general madness there are three different Settlement deadlines to worry about. If you want to opt out and tell Google *not* to make free with your work, the cutoff date is 4 September 2009 – approaching fast as I write. If you want to claim your dues under the Settlement, a massive cash bonanza of $60-$300, the deadline is 5 January 2010. And if you've signed up, you have until 5 January 2010 to get your titles removed from Google's book database.

Unless you're really paranoid about snippets from your work turning up via Google searches, the best deal – although opinion is strongly divided on this point – seems to be to opt in, grab any

Settlement pittance, and hope Google Books searches will lead to more sales.

So, had the bastards ripped me off? That is: had I, humble and unassuming Langford, been granted this fabulous chance of literary publicity? I signed up at the Settlement website, expecting to search for my name in the catalogue of books scanned without permission. No such luck.

What I actually got was every instance of a David Langford book that Google knew about. (This is where I congratulated myself fervently on not being a John Smith.) Obviously there should be some kind of checkmark against the important titles, the ones Google had digitized? Nope. Before Google will tell you this, you have to click various buttons to assert your right to every title. What with reprints, translations and false alarms like my newsletter *Ansible* being listed as a book, I had to plod through well over sixty items.

Right! After doing all that and making the terrifying declaration of claim, I came to a whole new table presentation of those sixty-odd books. Now at last there'd surely be a convenient, reader-friendly checkmark to identify those digitized by Google? Ha bloody ha. You have to click a separate "Details" link for every single title. Only then do you see one of three fateful phrases that map your future destiny:

(1) "Digitized without authorization." – meaning, you have a winner! There could be $60 in this for you.

(2) "Not digitized, and will not be digitized on or before May 5, 2009, without authorization." – meaning, this title isn't relevant to the Settlement, so why on earth didn't they filter it out of the initial search?

(3) "May be digitized on or before May 5, 2009 without authorization." – meaning, since it still said the same months later, that Google is rubbish at keeping its records up to date.

To my surprise, I found three Langford titles in the first category. One is a recent SF essay collection, one is a small-press fiction chapbook of incredible obscurity, and one is a non-fiction collaboration from the 1980s. This also confirmed that you need to click *every* Details link – if there are many editions, "Digitized without authorization" appears only against the particular ones Google chose to scan.

After which, if you've also contributed short stories/essays to books, it gets more complicated. The Google Settlement calls such puny little things "Inserts", and there's no way to search for your name.

Instead, you must search by title or editor, and (even more fiddly) give the page range of every "Insert" before discovering whether Google scanned this one. My list of such Langford contributions to books runs to 158 items. Life is too short.

The latest is that the US Department of Justice has opened a new investigation of the Settlement that might just overturn the whole thing. In which case my efforts were a total waste of time…

David Langford doesn't feel very settled.

The last-minute revision, besides changing a word or two in the text, replaced the above tagline with:

David Langford discovered, weeks after sending this in, that Google has since overhauled the site, fixed some irritating problems, and admitted they've scanned all those "May be digitized" titles. Argh!

Since then, following the US Department of Justice intervention, the Settlement has been revised, amended several times, agreed in amended form, wrangled about in various US courts and quashed by the US Supreme Court's 2016 rejection of the latest appeal by the US Authors Guild and others. See Wikipedia for breaking news! It would appear that until such time as US law is changed, Google can do whatever it likes with our copyrighted work.

• *SFX* #188, November 2009

Moving the Goalposts

Every year there's another golden shower of SF awards. Every year someone tries to rewrite the rules – because the system isn't perfect, because a decades-old regulation has sprung a terrible leak in the internet era, or because the pig-ignorant punters are *voting wrong*. We must make them get it right!

Cynics suspected this kind of thinking was behind last year's controversy over the *Locus* Awards, run by the SF community's leading newsletter *Locus*. These have vaguely similar categories to the Hugo Awards, but attract more voters since it's free to vote online; no need to buy a World SF Convention membership as with the Hugos. In 2008 the *Locus* masses were guilty of crimethink in the First Novel category, preferring Patrick Rothfuss's *The Name of the Wind* to Joe Hill's *Heart-Shaped Box*; and again in Collection, where Cory Doctorow beat Connie Willis with most overall *and* most first-place votes.

After the polling had ended, though, *Locus* abruptly changed the rules so their paid subscribers' votes counted double – making Hill and Willis the winners after all. Cory Doctorow, they said darkly, "has a large online fan base", which apparently is cheating. *Locus*-pocus! These awards became suddenly less credible, and the 2009 voter turnout fell significantly.

Also in 2009, the SF Writers of America tinkered with their Nebula Awards. The amazingly sensible innovation is that the 2010 Nebulas, presented for fiction published in 2009, will in fact go to 2009 work! Previously there was a "rolling eligibility" arrangement that (to please SFWA members) gave older work an extra chance. Serious weirdness ensued when the 2007 Nebulas, notionally for 2006, went without exception to things published in 2005.

Now the World SF Society is fiddling with Hugo rules again. Last year they voted to abolish the Best Semiprozine award (created to stop the professional newsletter *Locus* winning Best Fanzine) and to add a Graphic Novel category. Most fans expected both changes to be ratified at the 2009 Worldcon. Remembering the Amazon.com "Ministry of Truth" embarrassment, when they remotely deleted countless copies of *Nineteen Eighty-Four* from customers' Kindle ebook readers, I wondered if I'd wake up after Worldcon to find a gap on the mantelpiece where Hugo hitmen had removed my 2005 semiprozine trophy...

In fact there were several surprises. Neil Clarke of *Clarkesworld*, another semiprozine nominee, had organized a "Save the Semiprozine Hugo" campaign. The Worldcon business meeting voted overwhelmingly to keep this category. They also nodded through the Graphic Novel Hugo – no controversy there – and rejected a proposal that would add female nominees to Hugo fiction shortlists if the voters got it wrong by picking only men.

At the Hugo ceremony itself, when everyone expected *Locus* to take Semiprozine as usual, the audience was stunned to hear that *Weird Tales* magazine had won instead. *Locus* came fourth, after Britain's very own *Interzone*. Neil Clarke's high-profile campaign must have made people think harder about their choices; the argument for abolishing this Hugo was, pretty much, that *Locus* (almost) always won and so it was no fun any more. We live in interesting times.

The smart money was also on *Locus* because of the sympathy effect. Its publisher and founding editor Charles N. Brown died unexpectedly this year – on a plane coming home from another convention; what a way to go – so pundits expected the fans to vote him one last Hugo. We'd had a long rivalry, Charles ending up with 29 *Locus* Hugos and me trailing with 28; I'm glad he was ahead when he died. Goodbye, Charles.

More upheavals! A second semiprozine won a Hugo in 2009, only we mustn't call *Electric Velocipede* a semiprozine because the category it won was Best Fanzine. This is traditionally for amateur zines produced out of sheer love; *EV* is a would-be professional fiction magazine that pays contributors, but evaded the semiprozine category since the rules were carefully designed to nobble *Locus* and elsewhere have gaping loopholes. It was darkly rumoured that *EV*'s editor John Klima had targeted and campaigned for the fanzine Hugo because semiprozine competition is much tougher. All within the letter of the law, but one embittered fanzine nominee grumbled that he'd have preferred to lose to a fanzine.

Aftermath: the World SF Society set up a committee to look again at the semiprozine/fanzine Hugo rules, and I'm sure that like all the best committees of inquiry it will report after several gruelling years of investigation that the Metropolitan Police are guiltless of absolutely everything. Watch this space, but don't hold your breath.

David Langford did the Kessel run in less than twelve furlongs.

• *SFX* #189, December 2009

Random Reading
The Spad-Gas and the Offog

In 2008 I attended an unusually time-binding convention, Cytricon V in Kettering, England, held to mark the fiftieth anniversary of Cytricon IV in the same town and hotel. (An event at which the British Science Fiction Association was founded – but that, O Best Beloved, is another story.) The Cytricon V guests of honour were venerable fans who'd been there in 1958. One was Peter Mabey, who during general chatter in the bar urged me to read an Anthony Armstrong story called (he rather thought) "The Spad-Gas", and to ponder its possible influence.

I knew Armstrong (George Anthony Armstrong Willis, 1897-1976) as a one-time regular *Punch* humorist under the byline "A.A." As the *Encyclopedia of Fantasy* records, he wrote a string of amusing spoof fairy-stories collected in *The Prince who Hiccupped and Other Tales* (1932) and *The Pack of Pieces* (1942; reissued as *The Naughty Princess* 1945). "The Spad-Gas" was apparently one of his cheery sketches of army barracks life between the wars, assembled in at least five volumes. After long search I discovered that the Armstrong omnibus *Warriors Paraded* (1938) includes the collection *Captain Bayonet and Others* (1937), whose lead story is "Captain Bayonet and the Spad-Gas."

Spoilers, spoilers! One morning, Captain Ledger the battalion quartermaster checks his inventory and gleefully reports that a forgotten hut containing spare fire-fighting equipment has two important deficiencies. The "Union, Four-Inch, Brass, Fire-hose" is soon found masquerading as a paperweight on Captain Bayonet's own desk, but the "Spad-Gas" is missing. Helpful lieutenants agree that "a spad-gas was terribly expensive and, anyway, the last fellow who lost one had been cashiered." Consternation ensues.

At length a cunning plan is devised. Having established by subtle probes that the quartermaster himself has no idea what a spad-gas actually is, the sergeant-major gets a brand-new one run up in the armoury: "a queer bit of metal with odd corners and a couple of tubes.

It looked like a cross between something in the fourth dimension and an ultra-modern sculpture. – 'Daffodil and tin-opener'." End of problem. Later an ancient inventory sheet comes to light, the original from which generations of copy-typists had mistaken their cue. The significant item proves to be a Spade, G.S. [General Service].

Compare this with Eric Frank Russell's "Allamagoosa" (1955 *Astounding*), winner of a Hugo for best short story. Russell's setting is likewise military, Space Navy rather than Army. A formal inspection is announced. The ship's galley inventory includes an "offog" that can't be found. Gambling that the officious inspector has no idea what an offog actually is, the captain tells his radio officer to manufacture a brand-new one. This has copious dials, switches and flashing lights: "It looked like a radio ham's idea of a fruit machine." End of problem? Some time later it emerges that the inventory item is a typo and should read "off. dog" – the ship's official dog, a friendly mutt named Peaslake. (Dogs of indeterminate breed are endemic in the Armstrong barracks.)

If Armstrong was his inspiration, Russell still deserves much credit for converting the anecdote into a real and funny short story. Replacing that boring spade with the lively Peaslake is a brilliant stroke: *of course* everyone regards the Off. Dog as a crew member, not a piece of equipment. Russell plays fair with clues: Peaslake is prominently visible in the narrative and we learn at different times that checklist item V1098, the offog, is preceded by V1097, Peaslake's drinking-bowl, and followed by V1099, Peaslake's collar. Justice requires me to note that Armstrong prepares the way for his typo surprise with a brief running gag about the "Union, Four-Inch..." being called a Four-inch Onion.

Better still, Russell followed Theodore Sturgeon's advice and asked the next question. What happens now? Armstrong is content with his anecdote; Russell's hapless captain realizes he must get rid of the fake before any future inspection by someone who knows what an offog looks like. Thus he transmits a report that the offog unfortunately "came apart under gravitational stress... Material used as fuel." Only after the resulting interstellar panic – what and who *else* might come apart under such stress? – does he learn the awful truth.

Even the gravitational stress is arguably foreshadowed in *Warriors Paraded*. "Dropping the Cat", in the included volume *Livestock in Barracks* (1929), opens with a heated messroom debate about whether cats always fall on their feet. The Adjutant remarks "that he had never calculated – even roughly – the internal stresses of a cat." On the same page and in the same paragraph, another officer draws "weird diagrams of imaginary cats' supposed passages through space (with and without gravitational attraction)..." Close enough for an eager influence-hunter like Sam Moskowitz to claim a link?

It seems entirely plausible that Eric Frank Russell read this comic omnibus – several times reprinted, until at least 1950 – and saw his opportunity for a science-fictional twist. But perhaps both he and Armstrong are retelling some military ur-story of faking one's way through an inspection, a yarn that might date from the First World War, the nineteenth century, or Caesar's campaigns? Either way, I'm glad to have met Captain Bayonet's outfit at last; and "Allamagoosa" still makes me smile. Thank you, Peter Mabey.

• *The New York Review of Science Fiction* #256, December 2009

The Agony Aunts

Every issue, the infallible SFXperts answer your SF and fantasy queries: "I read this book once that had Martian tripods attacking London with heat rays, but in the end they all died of measles. What was it?" *Langford* replies: "You've remembered several details wrong, but it's obviously Aldous Huxley's *1984*. Not a lot of people know that this author also founded Scientology." Now, to complement the SFXperts, here's a trial run of the *SFX* personal advice column in which genre notables solve problems posted to our online forum.

• "I'm suffering badly from Hogwarts. Is this one of the known symptoms of Swine 'Flu?" – Voldemort13.

Our star panellist *J.K. Rowling*'s lawyers sent an exclusive response which, after translating legal terms like Avada Kedavra, seems to mean: "That's not funny."

• "Our little kid gets bullied a lot at school. Any tips?" – WorriedDad.

Isaac Asimov writes: "A child must protect its own existence as long as such protection does not conflict with the First or Second Law." *Jerry Pournelle* clarifies: "Nuke 'em till they glow, then shoot 'em in the dark." *Ripley* agrees: "Nuke the entire school from orbit. It's the only way to be sure."

• "I am a lonely teenager looking for a serious relationship. How should I start?" – PimpleGirl.

Charlaine Harris says: "Vampire sex! Lots of sex with a really hunky vampire is the way to go!" *Stephenie Meyer*: "But not, of course, until the fourth volume and after the wedding. That's very important." *Charlaine Harris*: "Doing it several times in book one works for me." *Anne McCaffrey*: "Wouldn't it be so much *nicer* if you teamed up with a telepathic, teleporting dragon? You'd be the envy of your friends and save on bus fares. If your house doesn't have a 200-foot nesting chamber or you belong to the lower orders, why not adopt a cute fire lizard instead?"

• "What's a good name for a fire lizard or similar pet?" – AnonymousUser37.

Iain M. Banks writes: "Some particular favourite names for my cats (or General Feline Vehicles as I call them) are *Barbed and Wickedly Ambivalent Phrase*, *I Love the Smell of Royalties in the Morning*, and *No, Mr Bond, I Expect*

You To Die."

• "Our floor is full of tiny holes and makes a ticking noise. We think it may be death-watch beetle. What to do?" – HouseProud.

Gandalf the Grey investigated your problem: "Far, far below the deepest delving of the Dwarves, the world is gnawed by nameless things. Even Rentokil knows them not. They are older than he. Now I have walked there, but I will bring no report to darken the light of day." That should sort you out! *Ripley* adds... but we've heard her advice already.

• "Another Monday morning, another terrible hangover. Any tips?" – MegaBinger.

Count Dracula knows the answer: "I never drink... wine." *H.P. Lovecraft* suggests removing the afflicted brain and sealing it in a shiny metal cylinder as in his self-help manual "The Whisperer in Darkness"; but this old-fashioned cure doesn't agree with everyone.

• "I am about to qualify as a chartered accountant. What is my best career plan?" – YoungFogey.

Conan the Barbarian reckons this is an easy one: "To crush your enemies, see them driven before you, and to hear the lamentation of their women."

• "A real literary question for a change. What's the first thing said by Frankenstein's monster? I think it's 'Arrgh! Kill!' but my friend Tracy says it's 'Gaaah! Maim!'" – SlowReader.

Luckily, *Mary Wollstonecraft Shelley* just joined the panel: "Pardon this intrusion." Absolutely fine, Mary, you're not intruding at all. "That was the answer, you idiot." And so it is.

• "I think I must be gay and am wondering about coming out of the closet. Can you advise?" – ConfusedTeen.

Here to help you is popular spiritual mentor *C.S. Lewis*: "Be very careful, lad! If you come out of the wardrobe for even a few moments you may find that many long centuries have passed while you were away from Narnia." *Baron Vladimir Harkonnen* also made a suggestion, but when the rest of the panel had recovered from uncontrollable nausea we decided not to print it.

• "What is the ultimate answer to Life, the Universe and Everything?" – HitcherFan42.

Now there's a tough one! Space is running out: *HAL 9000* will compute the answer next issue.

David Langford posted several plaintive queries about the pod bay door but was only told, "I can't do that, Dave."

• *SFX* #190, January 2010

Web of Infamy

One happy chore of running an SF website is updating links to conventions. This can be as rewarding as a severe hangover, though without the enjoyable prequel. Let me tell you all about it.

Convention sites inevitably go out of date. A regular sad spectacle, long after the event, is the front page no one got around to changing: "SomethingCon starts tomorrow! Welcome!" Often a little counter helpfully informs you it's now minus 110 days to the convention.

When will they announce next year's SomethingCon? Until then the link gets exiled to my lengthy Convention Limbo List, checked as often as I can face the pain. Convention web designers have various ways of turning the agony up to 11.

A favourite gambit: put no information on the front page, just a huge graphic image. Sometimes secrets like the date or place are lurking further down, findable by patient scrolling. One US convention hides everything behind links titled News, Information, Details, Forums, etc: you need to check all these to confirm that, yes indeed, nothing has changed for a full year since the last con, not even the fact that it's "an annual event". I eventually emailed that committee and found they'd decided to skip 2009 but hadn't thought this interesting enough to be News on their official website.

Graphics also provide a nifty way to present long, hard-to-type names and addresses, so news gatherers can't copy and paste. Make the bastards *work* to give you free publicity!

Simply omitting the year is puzzling enough. Did it happen in July 2009 or will it happen in July 2010? Other disinformation specialists tease us with a cryptic location. Locals know the Grand Fleapit Cinema, venue of this filmfest, is in... well, whatever city it's in. Grumbling outsiders must scour the site for clues.

A very useful trick is to start a fresh website with no link from the old one and no easy way to guess: AnotherConvention.com gives way, with inscrutable logic, to Anothercon2010.org. To be fair, this may happen because someone let the old domain lapse and can't afford the ransom asked by rapacious cybersquatters. Britain's own Novacon lost Novacon.org.uk that way, and only recently got it back.

Confusion – a popular convention name, incidentally – can be effectively increased by combining the front page of SomeDamnCon's website with a blog or bulletin board for the fan group who organize it. The page keeps changing, but people who check it out in hope of information on the next SomeDamnCon find the lead news is a mass of posts about recent parties and pub meetings. Maybe the truth is out there in a six-month-old message now consigned to the "Older Posts" archive, but who knows and who has the time?

Some committees think regular site updates are for wimps. A traditional way to make readers fretful about membership fees they're reading online in November 2009: "These prices will increase on 31 July 2009." (One US site outdoes that with a page saying the next WhatsitCon will be in Fall 2009 on a date to be announced. Still says the same as winter begins.) Other handy pricing ploys to discourage potential members include:

(a) Revealing the cost only after suckers are well into a laborious system of registering a user name and password which will allow them the great privilege of joining the convention. Hiding price information in a bulky PDF download is also popular.

(b) Accepting entrance fees only at the door and not revealing how much – regulars know roughly what to expect but newbies fear it's "If you have to ask, you can't afford it."

(c) Refusing to publish a postal address where old-fashioned fans can send a dear old lavender-scented cheque for membership.

(d) Refusing to accept payment online as preferred by cutting-edge cyberfans. Actual example: "We are a small convention, and cannot afford to take online memberships." Since PayPal accounts are free and it's a doddle to absorb the PayPal commission by charging a little bit extra to join online, this seemed quite remarkably clueless. The convention was cancelled.

Yes, all examples are genuine, and it's only by a heroic feat of self-control – aided by stern advice from our libel lawyers – that I'm managing not to Name Names in aggravated detail. Now it's time to check the accursed Convention Limbo List again...

In next issue's special guest column, a leading convention organizer explains all the ways in which David Langford irritates him.

Footnote. There are in fact three event listings at the *Ansible* site: one covering the British Isles (also including Eurocons and Worldcons) on the home page at news.ansible.uk; one for overseas events at news.ansible.uk/conlisti.html (the page responsible for most of the pain above); and a third for London at news.ansible.uk/london.html. The Limbo List, being full of vulgar abuse and libellous comments, is not on line. Even I sometimes have moments of sanity.

• *SFX* #191, February 2010

Phil Baker – *The Devil is a Gentleman*

• Review of *The Devil is a Gentleman: The Life and Times of Dennis Wheatley* by Phil Baker (Dedalus hardback, 699pp, £25.00, ISBN 978-1-903517-75-8)

A seven-hundred-page literary biography may look all too daunting, but appearances are deceptive. Lazy readers will be glad to know that the text ends much earlier, with the last 90pp devoted to references, bibliographies (remember the Dennis Wheatley Library of the Occult?) and a detailed index. Still better news is that it's lively, racy reading throughout, often echoing Wheatley's own technique of a slightly contrived cliffhanger at each chapter's end. Phil Baker admires his subject, that "notoriously bad prose stylist", not for the pellucid quality of his writing but as a charmer and something of a rogue, a wide boy with dodgy associates who made good – or at least, made the bestseller lists.

The Wheatley books I lapped up as a teenager were of course the celebrated Black Magic potboilers that began with *The Devil Rides Out* (1934). That one has the famous set-piece scene of our heroes in a defensive pentacle besieged by assorted emissaries of Hell, which played well in the 1968 Hammer film and which (as Baker carefully points out) owes a lot to William Hope Hodgson's *Carnacki the Ghost-Finder*, inventor of the Electric Pentacle.

Close your eyes, if you too were exposed at the right age, and the whole Wheatley Black Arts *thing* comes flooding back from deep memory. The desperate use of technology against insidious evil, like the blazing car headlights that disrupt an open-air Sabbat, or the Mills bomb with which one of Wheatley's more robust heroines despatches a congregation of hapless Satanists. The grisly props like the all-potent Talisman of Set, the god's mummified penis, an occult doomsday weapon that somehow didn't make it into the movie.

Above all, Wheatley loved to pull a *deus ex machina* from his luxuriously padded smoking-jacket sleeve. I fondly remember one lot of good guys having a rough time in a Satanic chapel with malignity and ectoplasm oozing everywhere, and a sticky end seeming inevitable until *zapppp!* this lightning bolt streaks through the roof and sunders the evil altar, purging all nastiness with the relentless efficiency of Dyno-Rod clearing a blockage. Our author then explains with fetching simplicity: "God had intervened."

Until Baker reminded me, I had managed to lose the climax of *The Haunting of Toby Jugg* (1948) in merciful amnesia. This one has genuinely creepy passages featuring a shadowy spider-demon, and you could always skip the political lectures about how Satanism and Communism are essentially the same thing, i.e. bad. (Wheatley was later to make the same discovery about Satanism and trade unions; Satanism and Black Power...) At the finale, with all hope gone and the nice girl about to be ritually violated on a bed of stinging-nettles, the mad great-aunt who for many years has been madly digging tunnels suddenly breaks through into an underground lake to release a flood that drowns all the Satanists in their sunken chapel. Even this is outdone by *The Irish Witch* (1973), a late historical Black Magic novel whose hero, as his daughter faces the usual fate worse than death, "can do nothing except watch, when fortunately a gigantic frog suddenly appears and gobbles all the Satanists up."

As indicated by that quote, Phil Baker's book synopses are not suffocatingly reverent. Rather more impressive is the background tapestry of Wheatley's life, researched with great thoroughness. One dubious mentor comes close to stealing the show in the early 1920s: Gordon Tombe, who indoctrinated Wheatley with the aesthetic/decadent world-view of the Naughty Nineties (Wilde and Pater in particular) to such effect that Wheatley's bookplate shows Tombe as a satyr encouraging Wheatley to make free with not one but all the trees of the Garden of Eden. This scene was drawn by Frank C. Papé, best remembered for lavishly illustrated editions of James Branch Cabell. Papé's good taste may have rebelled at Wheatley's initial bookplate sketch – also reproduced – depicting Tombe as the devil deftly holding and pouring a bottle of champagne with his barbed and sinuous tail. Blimey.

This mentor is definitely trouble. Wheatley has to provide an alibi when, wearing exquisite evening dress to give a look of innocence,

Tombe burns down a large house called The Welcomes for the sake of the insurance. Later Tombe disappears, leading to a comedy of embarrassment as Wheatley hires a private detective to trace him but doesn't dare give the sleuth any useful information for fear of incriminating himself. Eventually Tombe's murdered body turns up in a cesspit at The Welcomes...

The cast is crowded with famous and infamous names, and tasty anecdotes abound. Wheatley plans to bootleg the wares of his family wine trade to Prohibition America, only for all the samples to get nicked in Bermuda; is blackmailed for misuse of ration coupons in World War II but manages to turn the tables; bashes out a pro-Islam, anti-Commie propaganda thriller for the Persian market and contrives to get paid for his efforts from UK Secret Funds, tax-free in cash; is embarrassed when an MP demands actual evidence for the Satanic naughtiness our author keeps claiming is rife in England; reproduces the diabolism-loving cleric and horror anthologist Montague Summers as the evil Canon Copely-Syle in *To The Devil – a Daughter* (1953); gives plot advice to Anthony Powell; cannot resist chocolate, champagne or sweet liqueurs even when diabetes and cirrhosis have set in.

No fact or allusion is too obscure for Baker to track down. Even my own brief Wheatley entry in *The Encyclopedia of Fantasy* (1997) is meticulously quoted, referenced and indexed. But Baker never bores and Wheatley, for all his faults, is sufficiently engaging that you can't help liking the old devil who was "arguably the twentieth century's greatest non-literary writer" – rivalled for this dubious honour only by Agatha Christie and Edgar Wallace.

An enjoyable read, especially for those of us who remember all those occult novels as a guilty adolescent pleasure. As David Blundy of the *Observer* once wrote: "Wheatley has been grappling with the Devil for over thirty years now, and frankly, the Devil's been pretty decent about it."

• *Murky Depths* #11, February 2010

Textbooks of the Argonauts

Every so often this page covers a story that hasn't ended, and later I wonder whether to add what happened next. My very first *SFX* column explored the terrors of Harlan Ellison's famously unpublished blockbuster anthology *The Last Dangerous Visions*. Back then in 1995, I had no idea when this would appear. Now it's 2010 and... well, no change on *that* front.

What became of the new edition of the even more monumental *Encyclopedia of Science Fiction*, mentioned here a few years back? The story so far is that I joined the second-edition editors John Clute and Peter Nicholls to sign contracts with Orbit for a third edition that would be published online. Nicholls later dropped out (or rather, retired upstairs as Editor Emeritus) owing to the ravages of Parkinson's disease, but Clute, myself and assorted volunteers beavered away until by late 2009 the work in progress ran to over 10,000 entries and 2.5 million words. The 1993 second edition had 6,571 entries, 1.3 million words. A huge difference.

But it's still an unfinished saga. After years in the gruelling textual wilderness, living on dried lizards and witchetty grubs, the editors no longer saw eye to eye with the publishers about how the *Encyclopedia* should be presented to the public (you). We parted company with Orbit on friendly terms, and found new backers from outside the SF publishing world. Speaking as the general editor who bashes others' entries into usable shape as well as writing new ones, I can reveal that assembling an encyclopedia is bloody hard work. At least half a million more words to go...

Meanwhile, whatever happened to *The Eye of Argon*, that dire sub-Conan fantasy by Jim Theis described on this page in 1998? This has long been an SF fan favourite in the "so bad it's good" category, a prose equivalent of Ed Wood's *Plan 9 from Outer Space*. Tatty umpteenth-generation photocopies are still treasured and read out at conventions. No one expected fresh news on a story whose origins were lost in the 1970s, but the twenty-first century saw amazing advances in Argonological scholarship.

First someone traced the 1970 Missouri fanzine where *The Eye of Argon* first appeared (*OSFAN* #10, journal of the Ozark SF Association), stashed away in a US library archive. This was vaguely exciting, since the original from which all known copies were made didn't include the last page. For over three decades, Grignr the barbarian hero had been stuck in a cliffhanger death-struggle with a blob monster whose initial unfair tactic was "to slooze up his leg." Worse follows: "The Nautous sucking sound became louder, and Grignr felt the blood being drawn from his body. With each hiss of hideous pucker the thing increased in size." Oh dear.

So it was a distinct anticlimax when that library's copy was also found to be missing the last page – *and* the last but one. Our author Jim Theis, who created this epic clunker when only 16, turned out to have died in 2002 aged only 48. He never wrote another story, but gave huge pleasure to generations of fans who strained to read his strangulated and typo-raddled sentences aloud without giggling.

A complete copy of that rare issue of *OSFAN* finally came to light in another US fan collection in 2004. The ending was revealed and published! Whereupon several people declared it must be a hoax because its style was inferior, or not inferior enough.

In 2006 *The Eye of Argon* had its first professional trade paperback edition, from Wildside Press in America, with a learned introduction by researcher Lee Weinstein, and of course the long-lost climax. Of course, perhaps mercifully, Jim Theis wasn't around to see it.

In 2009 it emerged that another complete *OSFAN* #10 had lurked since the 1970s in an old friend's fanzine collection in London, unread. My pal could have solved the mystery of the lost ending decades ago, but gave his collection away without ever realizing it was in there. The *Argon* finale was exactly as reported in 2004 – definitely no hoax – and the inheritor of this priceless document arranged for scans to be made. True fanatics, or Argonauts as we call them, can now read an exact facsimile of the original. There's glory for you.

So, as "the weary, scarred barbarian trotted slowly off into the horizon to become a tiny pinpoint in a filtered filed of swirling blue mists," the full story of *The Eye of Argon* has at last been told.

Thinks: should Jim Theis get an entry in the *SF Encyclopedia*?

• *SFX* #192, March 2010

A Short History of
The Eye of Argon

David Langford and Sandra Bond

"From where do you come barbarian, and by what are you called?" Gasped the complying wench, as Grignr smothered her lips with the blazing touch of his flaming mouth.

The engrossed titan ignored the queries of the inquisitive female, pulling her towards him and crushing her sagging nipples to his yearning chest. Without struggle she gave in, winding her soft arms around the harshly bronzedhide of Grignr corded shoulder blades, as his calloused hands caressed her firm protruding busts.

Now that we have your attention... Jim Theis's "The Eye of Argon", that notorious sub-Conan adventure embellished with strange typos and purple patches stolen from Clark Ashton Smith's thesaurus, has been circulating in science fiction fandom since the early 1970s. It's a perennial favourite at convention turkey readings, regarded as worthy to appear in the same sentence as Pel Torro, Bron Fane, Leo Brett or even Lionel Fanthorpe. The challenge is to read more than a single page aloud without giggling. The challenge of death – reportedly introduced by Jon Singer – is to do the same with a squeaky voice caused by inhaling helium. Further cultural spinoffs include the Eye of Argon Players at San Francisco's annual BayCon, who use impromptu props to act out the story. As Don Simpson notes, "This really brings out the author's inability to keep track of what object is being held in which hand..."

To prove that there's absolutely nothing which fannish scholars won't investigate, researches in recent years have disclosed more than you could possibly wish to know about the immortal (as so many of us fear) creation of Jim Theis. Here is a brief timeline.

9 August 1953. Birth of the author, James F. Theis, as recorded in the US Social Security Death Index. His surname is pronounced "Tice".

21 August 1970. *OSFAN*, the journal of the US Ozark SF Association, publishes its tenth issue from St Louis, Missouri. Pages 27 to 49 – the latter

being the inside back cover – are devoted to "The Eye of Argon" by Missouri fan Jim Theis, with illustrations. Despite a fairly dreadful front cover the fanzine isn't *that* badly reproduced, but the typing and proofreading leave much to be desired. Early in the story, "Small rodents scampered about, occupying themselves in the daily accomplishments of their dismal lives." Sentences of this quality abound.

21 November 1970. *OSFAN* interviews its star author for issue #13. Jim Theis is fetchingly modest about his success: "... it is nothing to be proud of and yet it is. Because how many people have had their first story published at sixteen – even if it is in a fanzine or a club-zine? How many professional writers have written a complete story at so early an age? Even so, 'Eye of Argon' isn't great. I basically don't know much about structure or composition."

1971 and onward. SF author Thomas N. Scortia loves the rich badness of "Argon" so much that he sends a copy for amusement to fellow-writer Chelsea Quinn Yarbro: "Dear Quinn, Here is an example of FINE writing that we might all enjoy. This must be a nom de plume of L.S. de Camp. – Tom." (Annotation preserved on Darrell Schweitzer's photocopy.) Yarbro is not only entertained but shows the story around and loans it out on request. The last page has gone astray, though, and since the Yarbro Codex is the source of all later recopyings and retypings in fandom prior to 2005, the ending has "always" been missing. Does Grignr the barbarian survive his death struggle with the blob monster whose first devilish move is to "slooze up his leg" and begin sucking, with many a "hiss of hideous pucker"? It is a mystery. Nevertheless, Tom Whitmore and Stephen Goldin work assiduously to spread the story's fame. It becomes a fannish institution. At some stage Chelsea Quinn Yarbro's then husband Don Simpson makes a particularly careful transcription of the text, checked against the original to ensure all typos and mispunctuation are preserved. The "Transcriber's note" describes his high-minded purpose:

> But as a labor of love for those whose 3rd-generation copies have now suscummed to the bitter vicissitudes of time and entropy, worn away by the ravages of countelss re-readings before entralled audiances, yet who have found that the the heady flavor of its stylistic paragraphs has seeped into their soul and still grips it with a fervid grasp, I dedicate this readable version of the inimitable *The Eye of Argon*.

16 May 1983 The Don Simpson ASCII transcript reaches its best-known

form: "ARGON.DOC - 05/16/83 - Version 01", stored on what he proudly recalls as "an 8-inch floppy disk formatted for my S-100 bus CP/M computer (maximum system memory of 64 kilobytes)." This is eventually uploaded to the Internet by Doug Faunt, who rarely receives his due share of the blame. In some later copies the final "Transcriber's note" is slightly changed, with "readable" becoming "machine-readable". We notice everything.

8 March 1984. Jim Theis is interviewed on the Californian radio talk show *Hour 25*, which has featured regular readings of "The Eye of Argon". He declares himself unhappy that his youthful folly continues to be mocked, and says he'll never write anything again. (Source: Wikipedia.)

1987. "The Eye of Argon" is reprinted in chapbook form by Hypatia Press of Eugene, Oregon ("Socialogical [*sic*] Explorations series, issue 1"), with new illustrations and a new byline, G. Ecordian for our protagonist Grignr the Ecordian. Inspired by the story's first line of dialogue – "Prepare to embrace your creators in the stygian haunts of hell, barbarian" – Darrell Schweitzer publishes a learned appraisal in *Fantasy Review* 10:6 (July/August) with the self-explanatory title "One Fine Day in the Stygian Haunts of Hell: Being the Whole Truth About the Fabled 'The Eye of Argon'."

1995. The Hypatia Press chapbook is reissued or relaunched. Quizzed online about the lack of credit to Jim Theis, publisher Alan Bard Newcomer explains in lower case: "the legends surrounding [eye] were such that we chose to credit the book to grigner the ecordian / it was not possible to ascertain mr.theis's feeling regarding the traveling of his story across america" (rec.arts.books.marketplace, 27 August). But if we leave his name off, it is implied, he may not notice. Elsewhere, Dave Langford takes over the updating of the UK SF Fandom Archive created by Naveed Khan on the Glasgow University website, and is unable to resist converting the included ARGON.DOC's plain ASCII text – as originally digitized by Don Simpson and now replicated all over cyberspace like some ravening von Neumann machine – to an easier-on-the-eye HTML web page.

1997 Darrell Schweitzer's essay is reprinted in his collection *Windows of the Imagination*. Just to keep Argonologists – or should it be Argonauts? – on their toes, the title is subtly changed to "One Fine Day in the Stygian Haunts of Hell: Being the Lore and Legend of the Fabled 'The Eye of Argon'." By 2009, even Schweitzer has wholly forgotten that the original title was different.

26 March 2002. Death of James F. Theis, recorded in Missouri – again from the US Social Security Death Index. Birth and death dates match well

enough to confirm that this is "our" Jim Theis. His seventeenth birthday was twelve days before the front-cover date of *OSFAN* #10, so the story would have been written and accepted rather than published when he was sixteen. As Darrell Schweitzer also observes below, he died at only 48.

November 2003. After all this time, the actual source of the story is widely unremembered. Samuel R. Delany has somehow come to believe that it was thrown together as a group joke by a Clarion workshop class. Darrell Schweitzer sets him right in *Ansible* #196: "My colleague Lee Weinstein cracked the 'mystery' of 'The Eye of Argon' recently. The story was originally published in the fanzine *OSFAN* (the journal of the Ozark SF Society) #7 *[sic]*, 1970. There is a copy of this priceless publication in the Paskow Collection at the library of Temple University in Philadelphia. Mr Weinstein has actually held this amazing artifact in his trembling hands. A subsequent issue interviews the author. This interview has been posted online. The story really *is* by Jim Theis, who was a well-known Kansas City fan, something of a local celebrity. In KC, his authorship was common knowledge. He was not a Clarion student... Alas, Theis died a couple years ago at age 48." Another alas: this library copy of *OSFAN* is also missing the last page. And, indeed, the last page but one. Stapling technology was poorly understood in 1970s Missouri.

November 2004. Lee Weinstein enters the lists of published Theis scholarship with "In Search of 'The Eye of Argon'" (*The New York Review of Science Fiction* #195). One thing leads to another: Gene Bundy, administrator of the Jack Williamson SF Library at Eastern New Mexico University, reads this article and is moved to investigate. His lithe opaque nose (phrase © Jim Theis, 1970) twitches at the discovery that the collection includes an intact *OSFAN* #10, back cover and all. The story's final paragraphs have come to light at last – and a photocopy is very soon on its way to Lee Weinstein.

10 December 2004. The no longer lost ending has its first public outing in 34 years, as the climax of the traditional "Eye of Argon" reading at Philcon in Philadelphia. At long last "the weary, scarred barbarian trooted slowly off into the horizon to become a tiny pinpoint in a filtered filed of swirling blue mists..."

February 2005. Lee Weinstein follows up his previous *NYRSF* article with "In Search of 'The Eye of Argon': a Postscript" (*The New York Review of Science Fiction* #198), featuring a transcription of the ending. "It is only three paragraphs long, but a friend of mine noted, 'It does not disappoint.'" Perhaps the most poignant sentence describes the fate of the blob monster into which the Eye of Argon – that "scintillating, many fauceted scarlet emerald" – has transformed, leaving fandom with a 34-year cliffhanger: "All that remained was a dark red blotch upon the face of the earth, blotching things up." But who is Jay T. Rikosh? His accolade appears after Jim Theis's byline on the long-sought final page: "winner of the Jay T. Rikosh award for excellence!" Even Lee Weinstein is baffled. Meanwhile, Langford and others make morbid haste to update their online versions of the story.

2006. John Betancourt of Wildside Press publishes the first trade paperback edition of the complete text, including the newly discovered ending and an introduction by (that man again) Lee Weinstein, based on his *NYRSF* material and titled "In Search of Jim Theis". Only one small enigma remains: "Who Rikosh is or was or what the significance of the award was, I have no idea."

September 2009. Sandra Bond has acquired Ian Maule's fanzine collection, and unearths a treasure:

> I have an Important Announcement to make.
> One which may shake fandom to it's bones and leave it quavering in a moist blob of gore on the ornately pattened floor of its oppulent throne rooms while saucy wenches laugh in scorne.
> I have an original copy of "The Eye of Argon", by Jim Theis.

Yes, the collection contains a virgin *OSFAN* #10! This was originally sent to antipodean fan Mervyn Barrett, then living in London. Sceptics who believed the rediscovered ending to be a fake or hoax are crushingly refuted: Sandra writes, "I may also add that the last page is extant in this copy and the ending as reported a few years ago is definitely canonical." Jay T. Rikosh, awarder of excellence, proves to be the story's illustrator; three of the awful drawings carry his signature. It is a sobering thought that the secret of the elusive ending could have been cleared up decades earlier if only Ian Maule could be bothered to look at his own fanzine collection. More from Sandra:

> This wasn't Theis's only appearance in the fanzine; for good measure he also contributes a two-page report of a local fannish party on August 7th 1970. This will never be read aloud at conventions. However, some of the poetry in the fanzine is definitely on Argon level; though none is by Theis, one is by Rikosh –

IYCK! by Jay T. Rikosh

In the dark a scurrying, scuttling, slithering creature is heard.
Nervously you emblazon the room in light seeking it uselessly.
After a toal inspectic, with renewed courage, extinguish the light.
The pad, pad, tail dragging hiss has returrned impossibly in the dark.
Relax my friend, tis merely the visit of the lonely timid Iyck; yycckk!

Who shall deny this its place alongside Theis's masterpiece?

All things are intertwingled. The "Eye of Argon" illustrations include a tiny picture of this beastie, identifiable not so much from that poetic description as from its subtly meaningful caption "IYCK!!"

24 October 2009. Sandra Bond emails Langford with 26 massive attached files: "THE EYE OF ARGON is scanned, thanks to a session with Alice Dryden's scanner!" And continues in more appropriate vein:

"Do what thou wilt with them, for they are palimpsests of an earlier time than this, when warrier barbarians wandered abroad on the earth with no mind to the future or to what we laughingly call civilisation." Quoth Grignr to the wench who delivered a sigh of pathos.

"But stay," Interjected Carthina bustily. "Would it not be wise to give credit to those whose talents commingled to form a melange of skill that gave birth to this epic tale and to the fanzine that went forth to display the story to the assembled and wandering multitudes of readers?"

"Aye, that it would," rejoindered Grignr. "So let it be known that *OSFAN* #10 was edited by Chester H. Malon Jr and Sally D. Watson, yet was it published by Douglas O. Clark. Furthermore I vouchsafe, that Charles Prokopp drew the cover which graced the fanzine, whilst the pen of Francis X. N. Weyerich limned the full page that precedes the saga, and the back cover which follows hard upon its heels. And verily did Jay T. Rikosh create the five illustrations to the epic itself, of which I must give greatest place to the stout calliph on page 32 who doth appear to be smoking a big fat joint."

But the whilst Grignr was delivering this catalog of credits, the wench had made good her getaway and left the barbarian standing alone...

November 2009. After rather too much obsessive labour, including careful repair to patches of badly faded duplicating on page 32, a PDF facsimile of "The Eye of Argon" – plus the fanzine's front and back covers for the sake of context – comes into existence. Be afraid. Be very afraid.

1 December 2009. The facsimile "The Eye of Argon" goes online (see Links below) and the Ansible.uk website version is enhanced, or otherwise, by the addition of Jay T. Rikosh's illustrations. Thirty-nine years. That's not

too many.

29 December 2009. Now Don Simpson has scrutinized the facsimile and informs Langford: "As the person responsible for the original ASCII transcription of The Eye of Argon (and author of the Transcriber's Note) it is my embarrassed duty to point out my errors." One is trifling; one restores a seduction long lost to literary history but slightly reduces the narrative weirdness "because without the missing bit both Agaphim and Agafnd die twice during the story, while with it only Agafnd does." Like the fabled ending, the italicized words below were long omitted from the best-known transcript:

> "Aye; I was at one time a slave of prince Agaphim. His clammy touch sent a sour swill through my belly, but my efforts reaped a harvest. I gained the pig's liking whereby he allowed me the freedom of the palace. It was through this means that I eventually managed escape *of the palace... It was a simple matter to seduce the sentry* at the western gate. His trust found him with a dagger thrust his ribs," the wench stated whimsicoracally.

Do we have closure at last? We fervently hope so, because the fan world should be spared another article like this.

Links

For more than you could possibly wish to know, see ansible.uk/misc/eyeargon.html for "The Eye of Argon" itself, a web-page conversion of Don Simpson's transcript, to which the lost ending was added in 2005 and the illustrations in 2009. An almost as sanity-eroding companion page to the above, with links to the digital text, trade paperback, PDF facsimile, variorum readings and sundry other learned references too appalling to summarize here, can be found at ansible.uk/misc/eyeargon-intro.html.

• *Banana Wings* #41, March 2010

Mythago Man

It doesn't feel possible that Robert Holdstock can have died. He always seemed the fittest, most energetic person at any SF convention or writers' workshop. "Larger than life" is a cliché but he genuinely was. Flabbier authors struggled, panting, to keep up with Rob's huge strides on his favourite any-weather woodland walks: as he once said, "The slap of a wet oak leaf is one of the things I love most." Traditional frisbee sessions at Milford workshops often ended with a mighty Holdstock throw that defied Olympic records to land deep in some impenetrable bramble-thicket. Laughs all round, from Rob most of all...

Impenetrable thickets and secret heartwoods became his great theme. I was there at Milford in 1980 when he shyly offered his breakthrough story to the massed critics: the first part of *Mythago Wood*, which as a novel won multiple awards and had its 25th-anniversary edition in 2009. Even the novella version was compulsive, with mythic archetypes haunting an ancient wood infinitely larger inside than out, sucking in twentieth-century investigators until they too become part of myth. Jungian psychology meets the Matter of Britain! The revelation of Ryhope Wood's primal monster is still breathtaking – one of the most shiver-inducing moments in modern fantasy.

I could write far more about Rob's novels, and indeed I already have at vast length for a US reference book: *Supernatural Fiction Writers* ed. Richard Bleiler. To my relief, Rob liked that essay and quoted a little bit on his website. What I couldn't say there, and what doesn't show in high-fantasy writing, was how exuberant, funny and lovable he was in person.

Early in his career, like so many other authors, Rob dashed off potboilers to pay the rent, and his sense of humour would sneak into these – often by sending up fellow-writers. As Robert Black he produced the film novelization *Legend of the Werewolf*, set in a Paris where wolf casualties are rushed to the Sacre Bleu Hospital; one victim, an unspeakably filthy sewer-scavenger who collects cigarette-ends from the slurry to dry and enjoy, was named for the unamused author Michael Scott Rohan. As Steven Eisler, Rob did the SF art book *Space Wars: Worlds and Weapons* and gave the painted hardware unlikely captions – such as, commemorating two hearing-challenged contemporaries, "The Rohan-Langford 'Deaf Ear'

Subspace Jamming System."

Among the funniest things Rob ever wrote was a fanzine piece on another dire book-of-the-film assignment, *The Satanists*. Eight days to write 180 pages, with the script dialogue only a tiny fraction of the required wordage! Delirium soon set in:

"Story flags a bit as Black Mass proceeds, so flip to priest slumped in a corner and have Satanist come over and kick him a few times. 'Vomit rose to his lips as the foot thudded into his groin, then smashed into his mouth.' This sounds familiar so I check back and find I've used exactly the same expression twice in the same chapter. How many times can one be kicked in the mouth and lose the same teeth? I am reminded [...] that last year in three consecutive SF stories I wrote 'The screams of the time travellers were terrible to behold.' Just for the hell of it I write 'Simon's screams were terrible to behold.'"

The Satanists was duly published as the book of the Tyburn Films movie, which was to star Peter Cushing (with Telly Savalas as the bad guy) but never in fact got made. Hoots of laughter from our author...

Tall, bouncy and enthusiastic, Rob had a reputation for social gaffes – or at least for worrying obsessively about having made them. Cronies think he knew exactly what he was saying at the long-ago pub meeting where an attractive lady editor, Jo Fletcher, presented him with his first World Fantasy Award. The trophy was a sinister-looking head of H.P. Lovecraft, sculpted by cartoonist Gahan Wilson. "Gosh," Rob babbled, "This is going to be an amazing day in my diary! Got up – went to the pub – had a great time – was given head by Jo Fletcher..." The screams of the audience were terrible to behold.

Rob died on 29 November 2009 after a short, unexpected illness. His non-religious funeral was hugely crowded, with both moving and comic speeches from family and friends – too many to list. Malcolm Edwards of Orion/Gollancz did a fine job as MC. There were photos of Rob everywhere, generally wearing a huge smile. Most appropriately, he had a holly-shrouded wicker coffin.

One of the shining lights of British fantasy has gone out. It's still hard to believe.

David Langford once invented an alternate physics of oscillating time for Rob's novel Earthwind.

• *SFX* #193, April 2010

Elementary, My Dear Watson

It's fun to watch lawyers crawling from the woodwork when someone scents a big pot of money. Philip K. Dick didn't sue the British SF Association for titling one of its magazines *Nexus* in 1980, and his heirs weren't bothered about Nexus the 1980s comics character, or *Nexus* the 1996 online gameworld... but when Google called its new phone Nexus One, this triggered a shock-horror threat of lawsuits to defend the Nexus 6 replicant brand name in Dick's *Do Androids Dream of Electric Sheep?* (1968) and the film *Blade Runner*. Because – note the subtle legal difference – Google has a big pot of money.

No one is likely to prove their ownership of a Latin word that's been part of the English language for centuries, but maybe the Dickoids hope for a nuisance-value settlement. Who knows? Meanwhile, some pundits are frothing about the number of familiar SF ideas in James Cameron's *Avatar*, and never mind that you can't copyright ideas. The film's smoking-gun equivalent of Nexus is the magic antigravity element unobtanium. A Hugo-winning SF novel, *Startide Rising* by David Brin, used unobtainium (note the slightly different spelling) for an arcane weapons system back in 1983. Could Brin be consulting his lawyers?

No: he has more sense. Unobtainium is a traditional physics/engineering joke dating from the mid-twentieth century. It's the stuff you use to make massless levers and frictionless bearings for ideal lab experiments. It gets another SF namecheck in Wil McCarthy's *The Collapsium* (2000), where the programmable quantum-tech material called "wellstone" can simulate any conceivable element including "imaginary substances like unobtainium, impossibilium, and rainbow kryptonite." Of course unobtainium has long been part of the *Star Trek* universe, wearing false whiskers and pretending its name is dilithium.

The most famous antigravity element – unobtainium's first incarnation – is Cavorite (actually an alloy), which in H.G. Wells's *The First Men in the Moon* acts as a gravity screen allowing his spacecraft to float free of Earth. Though Einstein's general relativity made it clear that Cavorite is indeed impossibilium, the idea is so tempting that a US crank set up the Gravity Research Foundation in 1948 to find a "gravity shield" alloy. Eventually the GRF became all respectable and switched to awarding gravitational-physics essay prizes, several to Stephen Hawking.

Cavorite rip-offs are common, as in Joseph Kitchell's 1924 *The Earl of Hell*, which subtly disguises Germany as Hunovia and the magic element as Nilgrav. More imaginative names include Disney's flubber and the *Rocky and Bullwinkle* cartoon show's upsidaisium. Magellanium, from David Duncan's *Dark Dominion* (1954), has a nice name but unusually daft properties: it's gravitationally attracted only to the dwarf companion of the star Sirius, so a spaceship built of Magellanium automatically falls off Earth and continues falling in the general direction of Sirius. I forget exactly how they get it home again.

The most plausible imaginary elements tend to lurk in hoped-for "islands of stability" somewhere beyond the end of the known Periodic Table, and are usually mindboggling power sources – like the "trans-Plutonian isotopes" making up the doomsday explosive PyrE in Alfred Bester's *The Stars My Destination* (1956), or the "trans-three-hundred elements" of the ultimate fuel Illyrion in Samuel R. Delany's *Nova* (1968).

Some other elements that never were:

Celestium, in a forgotten 1907 SF novel called *The Mystery*, explains the puzzle of the *Mary Celeste* – this dangerous stuff emits a highly specialized radiation that makes sailors jump overboard. Tell that, as they say, to the marines.

Nipponanium, a Japanese discovery in Margery Allingham's detective novel *The Mind Readers* (1965), causes telepathy and lets schoolkids trawl the minds of classmates for information – just like downloading your essay from the web.

Orichalcum, the fabulous metal mentioned in such ancient texts as Plato's story of doomed Atlantis, is rediscovered by a famous fictional airman in *Biggles – Charter Pilot* (1943) by Captain W.E. Johns. But *this* orichalcum spontaneously catches fire when exposed to air, a point that Plato didn't mention, and Biggles fails to get rich.

Lastly: George O. Smith's short "Pandora's Millions" (1945) features a slew of brand-new elements created by tinkering with the settings of a matter-duplicator, and named after assorted story characters. We never learn what these are good for, but the great discovery is identium – a synthetic element that can't be matter-duplicated. This instantly replaces gold as an ideal currency standard, saving the solar system's economy from rapacious bankers. If only! So we end as we began, with a big pot of money.

David Langford hopes to acquire wealth and fame by discovering Langfordium.

Later: this column must have been written too late to allow a mention of Tom Holt's imaginary element aposiderium in *Blonde Bombshell*. Or maybe, since an important property of aposiderium is that it mysteriously causes amnesia, I just forgot.

• *SFX* #194, May 2010

Random Reading
The Pervasion of Lint

What is the occult significance of navel lint? Avram Davidson's short story "The Singular Events Which Occurred in the Hovel on the Alley Off of Eye Street" (*F&SF* February 1962) is a gallimaufry of oddities set in a singularly odd alternate 1961, whose hero George – an industrial alchemist by profession – has passed his finals in the Deep School and won "the right to wear the Navel Plug, with two Pips". Which may be a liability, for when he's ensorcelled and abducted by a seeming Drum Majorette 1/c, she torments him with the pretext of being about to "withdraw George's Plug, two Pips or no two Pips." He protests strongly: "without the Plug I should swell up with lint in simply no time; funny thing about me, I'm very susceptible to navel lint, always was, from a child."

Let us leave George to his fate, which he escapes via both dexterity and *deus ex machina*, and remember that the wondrously erudite Avram Davidson was a literary eclectic who like Borges had seemingly read everything that the rest of the world had forgotten – see in particular his 1993 *Adventures in Unhistory*. Was the navel-lint horror a flight of fancy or an obscure allusion? Without comment, here are some extracts from a contemporary document of the English Civil War, *The Diary of Ralph Josselin (1616-1683)* (Royal Historical Society, 1908; Oxford University Press, 1976):

> *22 April 1649:* This week the Lord was good and merciful to me and mine in our peace, plenty and health; my navel hath continued well through God's goodness about 6 weeks...
>
> *5 May 1649:* I feared my navel this day, there was some lint that stick in it; I think it was by reason of my former sweating; I meddled not with it, but I look up to my God perfectly to heal me...
>
> *26 May 1650:* My navel continued well this week, for which I bless God; my bile grew sorer, and my kernels [glands] in my

flank...

20 April 1651: My navel continued somewhat moist; I did not yet dress it. I leave myself to my God who knoweth what is best for me, and I trust he will direct me for the best, and will be health to my navel and marrow to my bones.

If only the Rev. Ralph Josselin had enjoyed the secure comfort of a Plug, with two Pips!

Invoking the little-researched theme of lint in genre fiction leads with a certain inevitability to Steve Aylett's characteristically deranged *Lint* (2005), a purported biography of SF author Jeff Lint – who is not Philip K. Dick but has frequent eerie resemblances. His life, for example, is changed forever by his "Fantastic Lemon" Experience of 1973, although "Lint never could explain to anyone what was so 'fantastic' about the lemon." There are almost believable full-colour illustrations of Lint's terrible book jackets, inscrutably scripted comics (*The Caterer*, a whole "reprint" issue of which has since been published), nightmare-inducing TV animations, etc. etc., all spun out in inventive detail. The whole farrago is crammed with intensely silly one-liners: "In 1949 Lint managed to convince the hapless Alan Rouch [a fictional fellow-author] that he could win the Nobel Prize by disguising his head as a giant eyeball." 144 pages later, when you'd swear that Aylett must have forgotten that throwaway line, we get the authentically tatty cover of *J-LINT*, a fanzine devoted to Lint and featuring an interview with Rouch illustrated with a photo of someone whose head is disguised as a giant eyeball. I laughed a great deal while reading this – often embarrassingly, on trains – and wish I'd tackled it when a review would have been timely. If you need any further commendation, there are enthusiastic back-jacket plugs from both Michael Moorcock and Alan Moore.

"Eh? Lint Paean?" some reader may by now have remarked, which is of course an anagram of Elephantina – and Andrew Drummond's *Elephantina* (2008) is a highly quirky period novel with genre resonances. Its hero ought to be Dr Patrick Blair, who truly did dissect the unfortunate elephant that foundered and died in 1706 Dundee. But it's narrated by a humbler character, Gilbert Orum, the local engraver who illustrates Blair's treatise (Royal Society, 1710) and has misgivings about being required to observe and take part in the prolonged, gruesome dissection of a very large and latterly very putrefied carcase. His journal is presented, edited and footnoted by the quarrelsome 1830 commentator "Senex", who views Orum's foibles and financial difficulties with deep disdain but somehow manages to swallow his dislike of Blair's whimsically subversive comparisons of Elephantina to the body politic, and her various decaying organs to assorted Scots worthies expecting corrupt personal gain from the imminent Act of Union with England. Towards the end, with an editorial arrogance reminiscent of Kinbote in Nabokov's *Pale Fire*, "Senex" angrily asserts total control over the text and banishes Orum to the footnotes. There are fantastic elements: Orum may be an unreliable narrator, and may be hallucinating when he hears the Elephant enumerate the detailed tally of her bones, but even "Senex" is unable to explain how this mere artisan (whose Latin isn't equal to Blair's gag about naming one bone the *Ossiculum Orumiculum Inutilum*) has somehow set down the exact technical osteology which Blair was not to publish until four years later. Tasty, with a decided charnel-house whiff; darkly funny and very odd. The publishers, Polygon of Edinburgh, have presented the book as a nice facsimile of the supposed 1830 edition, with 2008 copyright details tucked away at the rear. Drummond's previous novels, we learn, were *An Abridged History of the Construction of the Railway Line between Garve, Ullapool and Lochinver* (2004) and *A Handbook of Volapük* (2006).

No doubt the great Avram Davidson knew all about Dr Patrick Blair's monograph, and would have appreciated lines like this from the *Elephantina* introduction's paean to Blair, *Great Son of Dundee*: "Had he not corresponded with the esteemed botanist M. Tournefort of Paris, whose death was declared by Dr. Patrick Blair to be 'a general loss to the vegetable kingdom'?" Indeed.

• *The New York Review of Science Fiction* #261, May 2010

Amazon Ate My Hamster

This column has occasionally been rude about Amazon.com, but only in a spirit of fair comment, free speech, and friendly give-and-take. Beneath our rugged, sardonic exteriors, Amazon and I were buddies... until one day they pulled my book from sale.

It wasn't just me: Amazon.com believes in overkill. In late January they removed their Buy buttons for virtually every book published by Macmillan companies, including the major SF/fantasy imprint Tor Books (and thus me). Adding to the pain, Amazon kept the Buy links in place for used copies: they didn't mind selling the book and taking their cut, so long as Tor and starving author Langford got nothing.

What happened? Macmillan was negotiating a new deal with Amazon. They demanded an "agency model" giving them more control over pricing, particularly of cheap ebooks which (Macmillan thought, though maybe wrongly) could sabotage the first sales rush of a hardback bestseller – a vital earner for publishers. The idea was that cheaper ebooks could come later, like cheap paperback releases, but not immediately. Amazon, to maybe oversimplify, wanted those ebooks heavily discounted from the outset as loss-leaders for their famous Kindle reader.

The complex rights and wrongs could be debated at vast length, but Amazon soon tired of mere negotiation. They threw a hissy fit and went nuclear by delisting Macmillan's titles – yanking a significant percentage of the total stock on their virtual shelves. The idea was to terrify Macmillan into surrendering quickly, as Hachette (Orion/Gollancz, Orbit, etc.) did when Amazon hit them with this tactic in 2008. This time it didn't work as well.

This time, the online SF world reacted like a wasps' nest poked with a stick. Authors who check their Amazon sales ranking hourly felt it wasn't Macmillan that was being targeted but *them*. Us. Worst hit were writers with new books just launched or just beginning to take off – until Amazon.com merrily crippled their chances. It's an amazingly efficient way to lose goodwill.

In this publicity war, Macmillan scored by quickly releasing a calm-seeming official statement from the CEO. Amazon's top management stayed quiet. Two days after the uproar began, though, the Amazon Kindle team explained on their web forum that they'd kicked all those authors in the groin to express "strong disagreement" with Macmillan. They grumbled that "we will have to capitulate and accept Macmillan's terms because Macmillan has a monopoly over their own titles". So it was all over?

Despite talk of capitulation, Macmillan authors continued to suffer for further long days. The Buy buttons didn't return until a full week after their removal. Meanwhile that whiny remark about Macmillan's monopoly was much mocked. Authors were fascinated to realize they too are evil monopolists. I myself, for example, have a brutal monopoly on prose by David Langford, and hadn't previously understood just how disgraceful this was. Conversely, of course, Amazon's monopoly of the Kindle ebook reader must be a Good Thing.

The bottom line for what was nicknamed Amazonfail is that influential SF authors/bloggers acquired a deep dark grudge against Amazon and its bully-boy tactics. Many SF websites removed Amazon affiliate links, including the mighty web presences of the SF Writers of America and even (agreeing with SFWA for once in a blue moon) me.

And is the publishing world on its knees? Far from it. Two other biggies, Hachette and HarperCollins, have since joined Macmillan in demanding "agency model" terms. Maybe one day we'll wake up to find that – a few small presses excepted – Amazon is petulantly refusing to sell any books at all.

David Langford switched his links to The Book Depository, who haven't been evil yet.

Later: Trying to be principled is usually bad for the bank balance, but I seem to be making a somewhat larger pittance from The Book Depository's affiliate fees than I did from Amazon. The rewards of virtue...

Later still: A loud "Oh bugger!" burst spontaneously from my lips when The Book Depository was bought up by – you saw this coming, didn't you? – Amazon.

• *SFX* #195, June 2010

49

Protons and Simile

In the interestingly skewed language of John Barnes's fantasy *One for the Morning Glory*, protons and simile are a famous ethnic dish consisting of roast protons in a sludge of simile made from boiled piecemeal. Elsewhere in the genre, similes are tasty figures of speech which can be spoiled by clumsy cooking. Some favourite examples follow.

Over-the-top: "They were lifted off the ground like salmon plucked out of the Kushiro River as they headed upstream to spawn in the mountains of Hokkaido." (Alexander Besher, *Rim*.) "A swirling lava lamp of colors boiled on the screen like a hallucination that the cat had dragged in." (*Rim* again.) "Now at last Vera Verovna knew what she felt like: the mouse before the cat, the bee before the bear, the frog before the snake, the child before the dinosaur, the leaf before the wind, the beauty before the beast." (Uri Geller, *Shawn*.) Perhaps also the cart before the horse.

Earthy: "The sound of water grew louder, and the gusting of the wind was like the eerie farting of a giant animal." (G.P. Taylor, *The Curse of Salamander Street*). "When he was yet a million miles away the bright ring of fire that marked its portal filled the sky in front of him, flexing and twisting like the devil's anus in spasms of immortal agony." (Alan Glasser, *The Demon Cosmos*.) "The thought felt like a tapeworm lodged in the gut of his mind." (Brian Ruckley, *Winterbirth*.) As a certain SF critic once put it, this is a concept which the mind cannot stomach.

Interestingly mistyped: "...the abbot watched dazedly as they rushed like lemurs towards destruction." (Frank Corsaro, *Kunma*.)

Sexy: "Her nipples were still pink like goldfish snouts..." (Robert Wells, *Right-Handed Wilderness*.) "Excitement leaped like a trout in the public trousers." (Thomas Harris, *Hannibal*.) Maybe that isn't meant to be sexy, but I have a persistent vision of this high-class tailor murmuring, "On which side does sir keep his trout?"

Cryptic: "From Ujuk, however, a heavy, misshapen umbrage fell and lay like a prone incubus beside his chair." (Clark Ashton Smith, *Zothique*.) "The sun set, like a fried egg sliding over a pan and being lost in the fire." (R.L. Fanthorpe, "Face of Evil".) "Pieces of a jigsaw puzzle began to pop into place like rabbits into holes at the sound of dog." (Peter Hawkins, "The Edge of Oblivion".) "He sounded like a dead child discovering that eternity is some buzzing, languorous dream of Bath." (M. John Harrison, "Running Down".) "...tears coursed hot streaks down his cheeks, falling like mercury snowdrops..." (Andy Remic, *War Machine*.) Mercury snowdrops must be rather like small lead balloons.

A tasty gourmet image: "Lydia flapped around on the ground like a wounded fish as Flag tried to fry her." (Kris Greene, *The Dark Storm*.) Could she be flapping like a trout in the public trousers?

Impossible to argue with... describing a space elevator: "Just to the south of them, the new Socket was like a titanic concrete bunker, the new elevator cable rising out of it like an elevator cable..." (Kim Stanley Robinson, *Green Mars*.)

If aspiring authors need more examples, do please avoid the "Striking Similes" section of Grenville Kleiser's deadly serious compilation *Fifteen Thousand Useful Phrases* (1917) – designed to improve your paltry prose style beyond all recognition. I wish I knew where he found this fine specimen: "She flounders like a huge conger-eel in an ocean of dingy morality." Or, as the case may be, in the public trousers.

David Langford flung these words at the keyboard like a madman shaking a dead geranium.

• *SFX* #196, July 2010

Secret Histories II

Over in the reviews pages, *SFX* struggles to cover the major genre publishers' endless flood of books. Herewith some recent treats from small presses that you won't find over there...

Ernest Bramah still has a cult following for his ornate fantasies about – and told by – the ingenious Chinese storyteller Kai Lung. Dorothy Sayers was a particular fan, and often quoted Kai Lung in her Lord Peter Wimsey novels. The great thing is Bramah's mock-Oriental dialogue, which drips with elaborate, deadpan politeness as shown by this encounter in a dark dungeon: "If it is not absolutely necessary for your refined convenience that you should stand on this superfluous person's unprepossessing face, he would, for his part, willingly forgo the gratifying pleasure."

Kai Lung Raises His Voice (Durrant Publishing) is a new collection of the seven rarest Kai Lung stories, plus four long, previously unpublished ones unearthed from a Texas archive of this very English author's papers. For lovers of refined, jewel-like and subtly silly prose, it's quite a publishing event.

Eric Frank Russell is another author fondly remembered by older readers. Though British, he specialized in slick American-styled SF full of wisecracks and fast-talking heroes outwitting not terribly bright aliens, as in *Wasp* ("I can't imagine a funnier terrorists' handbook" – Terry Pratchett). He anticipated *Star Trek*'s mixed-race spaceship crew by several years in *Men, Martians and Machines* (1955), whose boldly going team includes a black surgeon and several cantankerous, tentacled Martian chess fanatics, although (because *some* things were still unthinkable) no women.

Now comes a relentlessly detailed biography of Russell: *Into Your Tent* by John L. Ingham (Plantech UK), who's researched every detail of a life Russell tried rather hard to keep private. No shock revelations, but some small surprises. Two quick grumbles: the first chapter's desert waste of family history will make outsiders' eyes glaze over; and though any literary biography needs one, there's no index. To compensate, we get a useful 56-page bibliography. Meanwhile, it's fascinating to learn what Russell did between stories – such as studying Charles Fort's compilations of bizarre events that eventually inspired the *Fortean Times* – and how this influenced him. RAF service in World War II helped fill his later work with satire of pompous brasshats. Essential reading for fans interested in knowing what made Russell tick. The title comes from his short story "Into Your Tent I'll Creep..."

What makes all the other SF writers tick? In 1989, a convention not held in Mexico and therefore called Mexicon asked ten probing questions of many UK authors; long answers were encouraged and the results were published. In 2009 the British SF Association repeated the survey, with added authors and a new question about twenty years of change. The annotated results of both surveys make a substantial, instructive paperback: *British Science Fiction & Fantasy: Twenty Years, Two Surveys* (BSFA), edited by Paul Kincaid and Niall Harrison. It's crammed with insider information.

Lastly... If you loved Jorge Luis Borges's classic *The Book of Imaginary Beings* but were frustrated by its lack of any recipes or culinary advice, be sure to try *The Kosher Guide to Imaginary Animals* by Ann and Jeff VanderMeer (Tachyon Publications). Taking their cue from Borges and often arguing with him, the intrepid VanderMeers not only describe a bizarre menagerie of apocryphal beasties but debate the vital issue of whether they're kosher. Concerning the Bakir or dream-devouring tapir, for example – He: "So Jews can eat dreams." She: "So long as they're not dreams of pork."

There are many more profound insights, and I'm sure it's very wrong of me to giggle. "What if a dragon asks politely to be eaten?" "Jews don't take suggestions from non-kosher food." "Does that mean you take suggestions from kosher food?" "Shut. Up." A tasty little book.

David Langford has long admired Bramah and Russell, took part in both those BSFA surveys, and is not kosher.

• *SFX* #197, Summer 2010

Election Fever

In "The Law", a mildly noted SF story by Robert M. Coates, the law of the land breaks down – the law of averages. Symptoms include massive traffic jams as everyone impulsively goes for a drive at the same time. Maybe that same law was misbehaving when our 2010 General Election managed against the odds to produce a (briefly) hung Parliament. We tossed the electoral coin and – as in high-magic regions of Discworld – it fell balanced on its edge.

This year's election coverage was also the most science-fictional in history. Countless spoofs of David Cameron's posters included a green Cameron ("We can't go on like this. Puny humans."), a blue *Avatar* native ("No digital effects have been used...") and the inevitable Dalek ("We will soon exterminate all hope you have."). In France, *Le Monde* offered another Tory-*Avatar* connection by identifying the leader of England's blue tribes as James Cameron.

The quirkiest alternative Cameron poster was aimed at "Song of Ice and Fire" fans who are frustrated – some quite abusively so – by George R.R. Martin's delays in finishing his next volume. Hence the pledge: "Vote for us and we will ensure *A Dance with Dragons* is released in 2010."

Meanwhile, following the trend of mash-up novels like *Pride and Prejudice and Zombies*, the weary government became New Labour with Zombies. Literally, according to a senior minister quoted in Andrew Rawnsley's *The End of the Party*, who detected worryingly zomboid symptoms in Gordon Brown: "He looked absolutely terrible. The shoulders were hunched. The flesh was literally dripping off his face..."

How about the Lib Dems? Nick Clegg had solid SF credentials as great-great-nephew of exotic Moura Budberg, one of the many mistresses of H.G. Wells. *The Guardian* ran a ten-point comparison of the Kleggs – green, scaly alien mercenaries who plagued Judge Dredd in *2000 AD* – and the Cleggs who plagued marginal seats with their "Orange, smooth skin". Amazing similarities were claimed: Kleggs are outlawed from Mega-City One, while Cleggs are outlawed from the electoral system. *Not* very prophetic.

Lib Dem MP Lembit Opik (who lost his seat, perhaps not because of this) praised his Cleggoid leader as a high-fantasy saviour with hairy feet: "He's like Frodo. He arrived in Middle Earth all innocent, but ready to take on the forces of evil. He is the only one capable of wearing the ring of power without being corrupted. Vince Cable is our very own Gandalf." Which set Tolkien fans wondering who, in this analogy, could be Sauron. Or Saruman, or Gollum. Non-Tories suspected that Tolkien's Morgoth, the ancient foe who was overcome in a past age of the world, had to be Margaret Thatcher.

If SF/fantasy celebrity endorsements won elections, Labour would have surged ahead. Patrick Stewart campaigned for them, though Gordon Brown spurned his offer of performance tips for the TV debates. ("Don't let the flesh literally drip off your face.") David Tennant starred in a party political broadcast. J.K. Rowling not only endorsed Labour but published a *Times* polemic about her past woes as that ultimate Tory hate-figure, a single mother. The Harry Potter vote was split when Potter actor Daniel Radcliffe came out of the closet to admit he rather fancied Clegg's lot. Dumbledore's voting preferences remained unclear. A belated report of a UFO hovering over Michael Howard's house may or may not have persuaded illegal aliens to favour the Conservatives...

Afterwards, hearing the stories of closed polling stations and turned-away voters, I remembered the election in E.E. Smith's *First Lensman* which was closely supervised by the Galactic Patrol, ran perfectly, and gave a clear-cut, popular result. But that's science fiction.

David Langford is the man who put the Ess Eph into psephology.

• *SFX* #198, August 2010

The Mathemagician

Another of my heroes has gone, but he had a good long run: Martin Gardner, celebrated for his highly influential "Mathematical Games" column in *Scientific American*, died this May aged 95. Until the end, he was still writing and publishing new articles.

The creaking Langford shelves hold forty-odd of his many books, including all fifteen collections of "Mathematical Games". Gardner reliably made maths fascinating and fun by highlighting the weird stuff. Impossible objects, magic squares, mind-bending paradoxes, infinity, fractals, peculiar folded-paper constructs like hexaflexagons and hypercards... the list went on. And became trickier with time as Gardner got steadily deeper into his subject. Serious gibbering ensued when a roomful of SF fans tried to play the card game Eleusis (first described in his June 1959 column, with a revised version appearing in July 1977), whose rules change with every hand. You win by being the first to deduce what on earth the rules are.

In the days before desktop PCs, mainframe computer sysops learned to dread Gardner's *Scientific American* revelations – like the 1970 column on "Life", a playerless game of cell-patterns that mutate according to set rules and demand to be programmed into a computer. Although machine time then cost serious money, vast amounts (mostly at universities) were furtively stolen for Life simulations and the discovery of strange, self-reproducing Life-forms. The game crept into SF too, in Piers Anthony's fairly dire novel *OX* and Greg Egan's far more ingenious *Permutation City*.

Gardner had many other enthusiasms, most famously the clobbering of pseudoscience. His early book on this subject, *Fads and Fallacies in the Name of Science*, is highly entertaining but led to trouble in SF circles. Once he turned on the radio at 3am to hear John W. Campbell, editor of *Astounding SF* and a firm believer in both L. Ron Hubbard's Dianetics and assorted mysterious mental powers, tell the world: "Mr Gardner is a liar!" Another hefty debunking volume is *Science: Good, Bad and Bogus*. He was a founder member of CSICOP, the Committee for the Scientific Investigation of Claims of the Paranormal, and wrote many, many essays for its journal *The Skeptic*. (Note to subeditor: Americans insist on spelling it that way.)

There's more. Gardner's loves included fantasy and SF. He wrote little fiction – his best stories are collected as *The No-Sided Professor* – but for years contributed maths puzzles with a genre flavour to *Isaac Asimov's SF Magazine*. He was the first critic to write seriously appreciative essays on the Oz books by L. Frank Baum; he even produced an Oz novel of his own, *Visitors from Oz*. In his masterly editions of Lewis Carroll, *The Annotated Alice* and *The Annotated Snark*, the unravelling of buried jokes and forgotten allusions can sometimes be more entertaining than Carroll himself.

Also fond of G.K. Chesterton's fantasies and Father Brown detective stories, Gardner wrote extensively about both. Indeed he repeated his footnoting efforts, rather less successfully, with *The Annotated Innocence of Father Brown*. Stephen Fry gave this a critical kicking in a *Listener* review that spelt its victim's surname "Gardiner".

When asked to write an alternate-history story in which the development of the SF genre itself was radically different, I invented a timeline where pulp-mag science fiction started on *this* side of the Atlantic with *G.K. Chesterton's SF Magazine**, and everyone contributed to a vast franchise of spacegoing Father Brown stories. In this world, a scholarly footnote explained, Martin Gardner published the learned treatise *Flambeau, Boskone and Ming the Merciless: The Annotated Father Brown Villains*. That made him chuckle; but I should have included Stephen Fry.

David Langford still cherishes his typewritten letters from Martin Gardner, who didn't use computers.

* There really was a Chesterton magazine, *G.K.'s Weekly*, launched in 1925 – the year before Hugo Gernsback's pioneering SF magazine *Amazing Stories*.

• *SFX* #199, September 2010

Bicentennial

Two hundred issues of *SFX*! I think my carefully hoarded sense of wonder just exploded. Hardly anyone now remembers those early days when publishing technology was so primitive that J.K. Rowling had yet to be invented; when email attachments were carried by cleft stick; when burly typesetters assembled *SFX* pages one letter at a time and never had enough X's to spell out the more exotic alien names. Not a lot of people know that Klingons were originally Xlinxons but had to be changed owing to the shortage of type.

There'd be a terrific flutter of quill pens as our interviewers raced to record the latest epigram from H.G. Wells: "No, dammit, I do *not* write sci-fi and most certainly not steampunk. I am an author of Scientific Romance." Stanley Kubrick responded to a typically cheeky film review titled "The Milky Bar Kid" with a telegram that's still framed in a place of honour on the office wall: YOU BASTARDS STOP AM BANNING A CLOCKWORK ORANGE FROM EVER BEING SCREENED AGAIN STOP LOVE STAN. Who said this magazine wasn't influential?

SFX coverage of the first ever science fiction convention – January 1937, in the Leeds Theosophical Hall – set the tone for later hard-hitting reports by focusing on the unforgivable lack of a bar for Langford to hang out in. Future cons took heed. The Couch Potato department was also very different in its early days, with the team listening intently to a huge-horned gramophone playing scratchy 78 rpm records of BBC Radio's *Journey into Space* or the more science-fictional episodes of *The Goon Show*.

As for the famous guests we've had in these pages... Mary Shelley's editorial was a slight disappointment, banging on about feminism when everyone hoped for her candid opinions on the Hammer classic *Frankenstein and the Wolfman Meet Dracula's Mummy*, and Lewis Carroll's artistic photos of naked child stars (including early *Doctor Who* companions) couldn't be published because the subjects' toenails were all exquisitely trimmed – *SFX* feared a tabloid witch-hunt against pedicure. But guest editor Russell T. Davies was bitingly funny about how Terry Pratchett's Discworld is total pants as SF, and Isaac Asimov also gave great value. Celebrated as the author who crammed the history of the entire world into one volume and his own autobiography into two, he granted *SFX* an exclusive 250,000-word interview that had to be run in microdot form. The souvenir fridge magnet on which it appeared is a highly coveted collectible.

Our most iconic front cover must be the photo of Philip K. Dick, who was having a Pink Beam or possibly a White Powder experience and lurched sideways so that, hilariously, his head covered a letter of the title and it looked as though the magazine was called *SF*. San Francisco! How we all laughed. But one of our designers was inspired: "We could *adapt* this concept..." Yet again, Dick had profoundly and prophetically influenced the future.

Now at issue 200, *SFX* continues to narrow the lead of my own newsletter *Ansible*, which has 277 issues as I write. Since this appears monthly and *SFX* can squeeze in thirteen editions a year by inventing new months like Summer or Christmas, my days of supremacy are numbered. The two publications should be neck-and-neck in a mere 71 years, by which time *SFX* will have celebrated its 1000th and indeed 1100th issues. More parties – I can hardly wait.

David Langford, on the occasion of his 200th column, has been promised a champagne breakfast. He merely has to bring the champagne. And the cornflakes.

• *SFX* #200, October 2010

In Your Dreams

Some rash person had to ask: did Christopher Nolan steal the idea for *Inception?* Shiny "new" SF concepts always turn out to have been done before, and bloggers quickly found the smoking ray-gun: a 2002 Scrooge McDuck comic titled "The Dream of a Lifetime!" In this highly science-fictional drama, Scrooge's arch-foes the Beagle Boys break into his bedroom and use a special mind-link device to enter, manipulate and steal information from his dreams – all suspiciously like the film.

Now there's no copyright in mere ideas, and anyway Nolan says he's been mulling over this one since he was sixteen. That would be 1986. Obviously the McDuck scriptwriter invaded Nolan's dreams on a post-1986 mission of pilferage. So presumably did Greg Bear, whose *Queen of Angels* (1990) has disturbing sequences in which researchers use a special nanotechnological hook-up to enter and explore a psychopath's internal "Country of the Mind". This blasted landscape, stinking of burnt sanity, isn't easy to escape from...

Or perhaps Bear swiped the idea from Pat Cadigan's *Mindplayers* (1988), or Kim Newman's *The Night Mayor* (1989) with its professional Dreamers. Aided by a special machine, two Dreamers must walk the mean streets of a crime lord's noir-movie dreams and halt his naughty activities.

As a media expert, Newman knows every episode of TV's legendary *The Prisoner* by heart, including "A, B and C" (1967). Here the sinister Village authorities, trying as always to find what makes Patrick McGoohan tick, bring in a special gizmo to interrogate him through his dreams. A giant video screen displays the dream action as our hero tangles with dubious characters (codenamed A, B and C) fed from data-tapes into his sleeping mind. Eventually he manages to seize control of dreamland and leave his tormentors with egg all over their faces.

Now the writer of that *Prisoner* story might well have lifted the notion of dream invasion from Roger Zelazny's 1966 SF novel *The Dream Master* – based on his Nebula-winning novella "He Who Shapes"

(1965). The Master or Shaper is a future psychiatrist using a special widget, linked via "a crown of Medusa-hair leads and microminiature circuitry", to enter and rearrange his patients' dreams with a view to sorting out their neuroses. Big trouble comes when he takes on someone with a stronger mind than his own.

Zelazny was savvy enough to know that a closely similar problem features in John Brunner's 1958 "City of the Tiger", which became the novel *Telepathist* (US title *The Whole Man*). Although for once there's no special contraption – it's all done by then-fashionable mental powers – this is a classic treatment of the theme. The undersized, physically crippled hero is a high-powered "curative telepathist" who projects himself into psychotics' obsessive dream-fantasies and breaks them down, hauling the unwilling patient back to sanity like a kid torn brutally away from Xbox addiction.

Naturally Brunner had pinched the idea; or rather, openly admitted his homage to the pioneering "Dreams are Sacred" by another British writer, Peter Phillips. This 1948 *Astounding* magazine story was adapted for BBC's *Out of the Unknown* SF anthology series as "Get Off My Cloud" (1969). A fantasy author has gone into a coma-like fugue state, acting out a gaudy dream version of his own sagas. Scientists use a special souped-up encephalograph link to insert the hard-boiled hero into the dream, where he attacks wish-fulfilment with douches of cold common sense.

I'm told Peter Phillips is still with us, aged 90. Think of the royalties he could collect from all the above, if only authors were allowed to copyright their ideas...

David Langford is applying for a special trademark on the word "dream".

Footnote: Several further film antecedents like Paprika *were omitted because (a) the magazine doesn't allow me all that much space, and (b) I'm far more interested in the books, which invariably got there first.*

• *SFX* #201, November 2010

The Weediest Link

For those who love a glittering intellectual display of erudition and repartee, there are dozens of TV quiz shows to avoid. Nevertheless my spies keep reporting SF highlights. On *Eggheads* in August, someone had to name the world's bestselling SF novel. To make this easy, they dropped a hint: it was by Frank Herbert. The contestant said with quiet confidence, *"2001: A Space Odyssey."*

Who researches these questions, I wonder? Wikipedia's page on all-time bestsellers shows an estimated 12 million copies for *Dune*. Less than *The Hitch-Hiker's Guide to the Galaxy* with 14 million, and far below the 25 million for *Nineteen Eighty-Four*. At a guess, they either forgot *Hitcher* altogether or ruled it out on the flimsy excuse that it's based on a radio series; while Orwell's masterpiece was all too likely excluded through the familiar snobby reasoning, "It's good so it can't be SF." Now read on if you dare...

A £16,000 question on *Who Wants to Be a Millionaire*: "Who wrote the Discworld series of science fiction *[sic]* novels? (a) Frank Herbert; (b) Douglas Adams; (c) Isaac Asimov; (d) Terry Pratchett." The contestant toyed with Herbert before eventually giving up.

On Birmingham local radio: "Who wrote *Charlie and the Chocolate Factory?*" Caller: "Was it H.G. Wells?"

In It to Win It: "Which fictional character was also called Lord Greystoke?" Contestant, who has never heard of Tarzan: "Lawrence of Arabia."

Radio Clyde: "Which famous detective features in the Agatha Christie *[sic]* novel *The Hound of the Baskervilles?*" Contestant: "Is it Harry Potter?"

Are You Smarter Than A Ten-Year-Old?: "Who wrote the story of Peter Pan? A.A. Milne, J.M. Barrie or T.S. Eliot?' Contestant, a teacher: "Okay. I've read the story. I've saw the films. I've not saw the panto. I'm pretty sure it's T.S. Eliot."

The Weakest Link is a rich source. "Who wrote the 1951 novel *The Sands of Mars...?*" Not one of Arthur C. Clarke's best-known efforts, but the long-delayed answer caused general surprise: "John Betjeman?" More questions from the dread Anne Robinson follow.

"What is the name of the London club that marks the start/finish point in Jules Verne's *Around the World in 80 Days*?" Contestant, allegedly an English teacher: "Ronnie Scott's."

"The writer of the graphic novels *Watchmen* and *V for Vendetta* is Alan who?" Contestant: "Er... Ginsberg."

"The 17th-century physician who discovered the true nature of the circulation of blood within the human body was William who?" Contestant: "Shatner."

"In which sci-fi sitcom did the computer, Holly, change sex when the actress Hattie Hayridge replaced Norman Lovett?" Contestant: "*The Hitchhiker's Guide to the Galaxy*."

"A lycanthrope traditionally turns from a human into what kind of animal?" Contestant: "Lion." Now that doesn't really deserve all-out mockery – "lycanthrope" is something of a specialist word. Speaking of big cats, though, hidden clues in character names are apparently no help: "In *Winnie-the-Pooh*, what type of animal is Tigger?" Contestant: "A rabbit." Suppose, as a daring thought experiment, they'd asked "What type of animal is Rabbit?"

More beastly fun on Century Radio Northeast: "In which book is Room 101 a place to be feared?" Caller: "*The Hundred and One Dalmatians*."

Years back, ITV Teletext ran a challenging *Watership Down* quiz including tough questions like "Who wrote *Watership Down*?" To which their own answer, as you may already have guessed, was Douglas Adams.

I live in fear of a *Weekendest Link* game at the next *SFX* Weekender convention. "The columnist who's written for every issue since #1 is David who?" Then an excruciating pause while our contender hesitates between Bowie, Cameron, Duchovny, or Tennant.

• *SFX* #202, December 2010

Serial Thriller

Most SF readers have a certain guilty nostalgia for books they gobbled up in their teens or earlier. As the cynical quotation goes, "The Golden Age of science fiction is twelve." (This is attributed to many people but was coined by Peter Graham. Another exciting trivia-quiz factoid.)

One series I kept buying in my salad days was E.C. Tubb's endless "Dumarest" space-opera saga, in which rough, tough spacefarer Earl Dumarest gets into deep trouble on planet after planet while questing for his home world, which has faded into mythology. No one believes it exists. Even while trying to kill or seduce Dumarest, villains and hot-eyed temptresses would pause to say something incredulous like: "Earth? As well call a planet Dirt, or Soil!"

All action-packed stuff, set in a seedy galaxy of generally brutal and feudal worlds. Dumarest hardly has a moment to recover from the agonies of his latest long interstellar haul in a cryogenic coffin before it's time for more fisticuffs, knife-fighting or all-out combat in the local arena.

Enemies pursue him, especially the sinisterly emotionless Cybers of the dread Cyclan, who Know Everything because they regularly connect to their shared galactic consciousness – a vast hive-mind of cyborg brains hidden underground on some secret planet which series addicts just knew would turn out to be Earth. There are gorgeous girls for Dumarest too, usually one per book, usually (as another sequel looms) ending up either tragically parted from our hero or tragically dead. Onward!

The novels tended to have one-word titles, often the name of the current luscious lady: Derai, Kalin, Lallia, Mayenne, Eloise, Veruchia... Some of these had mysterious mutant psi powers; Veruchia, presumably, had a hideous growth on the foot.

It's easy to mock the repeating formula elements in Tubb's series. Star-travel in High mode (first class, drug-assisted) or Low (steerage in a frozen coffin) is described again and again in similar phrases. Each instalment's evil Cyber ecstatically links with the Cyclan Mind in almost *exactly* the same words. Someone else usually scoffs about a planet called Dirt or Soil. Nevertheless, these are reliably entertaining action-adventures, written by a skilled wordsmith – short, gripping, punchy novels with no word-processor bloat. Dumarest had a huge following in his day.

The saga began in 1967 with *The Winds of Gath* (UK hardback title just *Gath*) and was dumped by US publisher DAW Books at volume 31 in 1985, with our hero's quest still unfinished. Donald A. Wollheim, founder of DAW, loved Dumarest and always wanted more; but after his death, the new management disagreed. For the last two episodes, readers had to wait until 1997 (with a 1992 preview in French translation) and then 2009.

Ted Tubb, as he was known to friends and fans, was still steadily writing and publishing novels when he died in September 2010, aged 90. His first SF story – in *New Worlds* magazine, long before its takeover by Michael Moorcock – and first novel both appeared in 1951. He edited the British magazine *Authentic SF* from 1956 to its demise in 1957, and was a legendary figure in fandom. A founder member, for example, of the British SF Association in 1958, and a charismatic, brass-throated fundraiser at innumerable convention charity auctions. Even the tattiest magazine was "worth the price in paper alone!"

Tubb was the last survivor of what the *SF Encyclopedia* calls "the extraordinary conditions (low pay, fixed lengths, huge productivity demands) of early 1950s SF in the UK". None of those fifties magazine-hack colleagues could attend his funeral; he'd outlived them all. But he was well loved.

• *SFX* #203, January 2011

Hidden Messages

An unexpected bottle of champagne is always welcome. One of my secret weekend vices is doing insanely difficult newspaper crosswords, and *The Independent* rewards winners with bubbly. Cheers!

Though SF-themed crosswords are quite common, few SF stories involve cruciverbalism. Evelyn E. Smith's "BAXBR/DAXBR" is one, with a puzzle-obsessed protagonist who's so excited by fitting shiny new Martian words like *baxbr* and *daxbr* into crossword grids that he doesn't grasp their context, the planned Martian annihilation of our puny species. I know that feeling.

In Arthur Sellings's "One Across", the hapless hero solves a crossword with no diagram – slowly realizing the words connect in multiple dimensions. Across, down, through and *out*. Unfortunately, visualizing the fourth dimension sucks him into it (as so often happens in SF) and a terrible fate looms... Clive Barker's "The Hellbound Heart" mentions a crossword that opens another dread portal.

Addicts automatically read words backwards, just in case. The city in Ursula Le Guin's "The Ones Who Walk Away from Omelas" was inspired by a Salem, Oregon road sign. *Under Milk Wood*'s fabulous Welsh town was originally Llareggub, later toned down to Llaregyb for sensitive BBC listeners. When Terry Pratchett invented the Discworld version of Wales, he followed Dylan Thomas's lead and called it Llamedos. Robert Heinlein's *Tunnel in the Sky* lays a trap with a dire warning against "stobor", which are not what smartarse readers expect. Obscure SF author Robert C. Givins also wrote as Snivig C. Trebor. Not a lot of people wanted to know that.

Backward-readers particularly love Edward P. Bradbury's *Barbarians of Mars*, an imitation Edgar Rice Burroughs adventure dotted with oddly familiar names: Drallab, Golana, S'sidla, Nosirrah, even K'cocroom. Yes, "Bradbury" was really Michael Moorcock. As a treat for SF fandom, he threw in the Flowers of Modnaf: "Their scent from here is pleasant, but when approached more closely it induces first a lethargy, then a creeping madness..."

Anagrams are stealthier and less obvious. Practically the only *Star Wars* trivia answer I know is that Lando Calrissian rearranges as Carolina Islands. Master parodist John Sladek signed his cruel Arthur C. Clarke spoof "Carl Truhacker". Hugo Gernsback, SF magazine pioneer, used three subtle pseudonyms in a single issue of his *Science Fiction Plus*: Greno Gashbock, Kars Gugenchob and Gus N. Habergock. Another major editor, the eccentric John W. Campbell, appears in *Barbarians of Mars* as Blemplac the Mad. James Lovegrove's alternate-world novel *Provender Gleed* features Anagrammatic Detectives, juggling people's names to learn their secrets: "*Honestly*? Or *on the Sly*? We can tell you which!"

More devious still are acrostics. One volume of James Branch Cabell's "Life of Manuel" fantasy sequence includes a high-flown sonnet whose lines' first letters spell THIS IS NONSENSE. Vladimir Nabokov's "The Vane Sisters" becomes a ghost story only if you notice that, unknown to the narrator, those two dead sisters have left their acrostic mark on his closing paragraph. Ramsey Campbell's "The Words that Count" plays a similar trick to encode a satanic message. A favourite example comes from the *Man from U.N.C.L.E.* novelizations published long ago by A.A. Wyn of Ace Books. Unhappy with the miserable pay, David McDaniel caused the first letters of chapters in his U.N.C.L.E. spinoff *The Monster Wheel Affair* to spell out A A WYN IS A TIGHTWAD.

Finally: Max Beerbohm, author of *Zuleika Dobson* and other literary fantasies, hatched a 1940 plot to drive Britons insane via the *Times* crossword. His puzzle had six laughably easy answers to hook the reader; all other clues were meaningless, impossible. *The Times* printed it... but nervously published Beerbohm's devilish explanation next to the grid. Thus England was saved from total wartime demoralization, and we won after all.

"David Langford" was once an answer in the Telegraph general knowledge crossword.

Later: a November 2010 *Independent* cryptic crossword (which I completed but failed to keep) demonstrated that Ursula Le Guin's name has entered the English language. A clue whose answer had to be a kind of weapon featured the phrase "SF author": solvers were expected to think of LE GUIN, which (minus the I) formed part of NEEDLE GUN.

• *SFX* #204, February 2011

Seven Year Itch

You know that irresistible urge to scratch an itchy spot that ought to be left alone? For several whole issues this column has managed to ignore journalists being unspeakably patronizing about genre fiction readers, but the recent outbreak from The Celebrity Channel/Eleven (who?) is a classic of our time: "Eleven have never attended a sci-fi convention (honest), but if we ever did, we'd imagine it to be a rather tame affair. You know – lots of geeks dressed as Wookies and Dr. Who, mingling around quietly with one hand on their inhaler and the other in their Mum or Dad's palm." Oh, *thanks*.

More of the g-word at Comic-Con: "It's the Cannes of geekdom, where everyone's a critic but nobody needs to see more than a minute of new footage to cast their verdict. They're the type of people who'd queue for a month just to smell one of Han Solo's socks, but their judgment now dictates the flow of billions of dollars." (*Guardian*.) I promise that I have never, not even through my inhaler, smelled Han Solo's socks.

Even worse is the fashion stigma of tie-dye socks, or anything else tie-dyed. Because: "It's Terry Pratchett books and Games Workshop. It's the implication that elsewhere in your wardrobe there may lurk a T-shirt that says 'SMEG HEAD' and that, on occasion, when someone asks what you're having in the pub, you smirkingly ask for a Pan-Galactic Gargle Blaster." (*Guardian.*)

Yes, games fans are no better: "If you go to a games convention in the UK, you're generally surrounded by fat, smelly people with no social skills." (*Financial Times.*) All male, all unmarried: "Two science fiction films are up for Oscars, much to the delight of single men with a penchant for multi-sided dice." (*Guardian* Sport.)

The official *Guardian* style guide even explains how to annoy the terminally sad: "Trekkers... how to refer to Star Trek fans unless you want to make fun of them, in which case they are Trekkies."

Maybe the problem with us geeks is the company we keep: "Like paedophiles and science fiction fans, the far right were quick to wise up to the internet..." (*Guardian.*)

When it came to mockery of Alastair Reynolds's million-pound Gollancz deal, you could detect a whiff of sour grapes in the *Bookseller* gossip blog: "Twitterers also tell me that the Al Reynolds mega book deal has been misreported too – that doesn't surprise me as no one would give a science fiction writer a million pounds for 10 books. I mean how many anoraks does a geek need? My spy tells me that it was actually an advance of £10 for a million books and not vice versa." Ho ho, jolly satirical.

Once in a blue moon, though, someone sees the other side – like Jason Solomons of the much-cited-above *Guardian*, after agreeing to talk about *Avatar* at what he thought was a technical conference but proved to be "a weekend-long gathering of slavering sci-fi fans [...] something beyond my worst nightmare." He bit the bullet, though, and on the day found those strange people with blue skinpaint, stripes, tails, etc. "were all very pleasant and went round hugging each other. And me. Embrace your nightmare, is today's lesson." Then Solomons moved on to watch Arsenal vs West Ham, surrounded by hordes of slavering footie enthusiasts of whom many were weirdly dressed or perhaps even face-painted, and had his epiphany: "I realized these two worlds were really just the same." Which is rather a commonplace insight in SF circles, but rare indeed for journalists. I wonder why?

David Langford is now feeling almost mellow, even about Grauniad *hacks.*

• *SFX* #205, March 2011

Ten Foot Pole

One benefit of a writing career used to be that we were too puny a minority to be spam targets. No offers of amazing drugs that greatly enlarge your huge throbbing royalty statements and make your literary agent scream hoarsely for more. No Nigerian-style opportunities to get rich (after paying a few routine bribes and handling charges) by acquiring the 500,000 Harry Potter first editions stashed in a secret bunker by Saddam Hussein.

It's started now, with email to me personally from "a Marketing Specialist of Bookwhirl.com" – a name chosen to sound like the established Bookworld.com search engine when cold-calling. His irresistible offer: "I came across your book entitled, 'What It Is We Do When We Read Science Fiction'. We are interested to promote it and we'd like to help post your book up to 1,000 highly traffic websites and increase online book exposure." All this for mere undisclosed sums of money!

It wasn't so much the slightly fractured English ("interested to"... "highly traffic") that caught my eye, as the fact that I didn't write that book. It's a collection of SF criticism by Paul Kincaid, which happens to have a Langford introduction. Marketing specialists are supposed to notice these subtleties. When Bookwhirl cold-called the SFSite.com comics reviewer, their sales expert was similarly confused: "*The X-Men* is not your book?"

As usual, a little research online revealed that others had already done lots of such research. Bookwhirl reps have pestered every author whose email or phone number they can trace, from famous Piers Anthony down to lowlifes like me. Claiming to be based in Wisconsin or sometimes Iowa, they're actually a Philippines outfit that fondly hopes naive authors will pay them to spam people. For $3499 they'll ensure your name is mud by annoying a claimed 10,000,000 recipients with ill-written plugs for your work. Sounds like a great way to ruin a career.

Thanks to the net, dodgy promoters, publishers and agents can be checked at sites like Absolutewrite.com and SFWA's Writer Beware at www.sfwa.org/Beware. It's always useful to share information... which brings me via an incredibly contrived transition to the big question that no-one has yet asked the SFXperts panel: "Did any SF writer predict the great Wikileaks scandal?"

Well, John Brunner came amazingly close in 1975 with his novel *The Shockwave Rider*. This features an early SF vision of the Internet, and a hacker hero who – more for having a bad attitude than for any actual crime – is captured by a US government agency, held without trial in a secret place and savagely interrogated. Innocents like his girlfriend get the same treatment, with no chance of legal representation or due process. Cruelly unfair, of course: such things could never happen in law-abiding America.

When loose again, our hacker's revenge on the system that gave him such a bad time is to unleash a net "worm" that ransacks secure databanks and publicly reports *everything the public ought to know*. Corporate scams, political corruption, dubious food ingredients, criminal sources of income, fake medical treatments, and much more. All this was 35 years before the current Wikileaks fuss began.

Of course *The Shockwave Rider* – and the even earlier story in which data also leaks uncontrollably, Murray Leinster's 1946 "A Logic Named Joe" – couldn't get everything right. Neither predicted that the utopian free flow of information on the net would consist mainly of spam, spam, spam, phishing bots and spam.

David Langford wishes his own emails didn't get spam-blocked for mentioning Philip K. Dick, without even promising to greatly enlarge him.

• *SFX* #206, April 2011

Load of Balls

Contribution to a symposium titled "The History of Fandom in 37 Objects".

Ah, nostalgia. The small object of desire that I fondled most repeatedly in the glory years from 1978 to 1985 was that miracle of rare device, the IBM Selectric II typeball. Not just one, of course – I ended up with twenty-four.

Tell young fans the Selectric procedure, and they won't believe you. One typed along merrily in Courier 12, good for cutting stencils (don't even try to tell young fans about duplicator stencils) until some *emphasis* was needed, and with a deft flip Courier 12 would be whipped out of the machine and Courier 12 Italic clipped into place. When thinking big, I could switch from elite to pica pitch with Courier 10, though there was no Courier 10 Italic ball. But a handy stopgap called Light Italic worked at either pitch, and went with more or less anything.

Ansible moved from stencils to litho printing (which it may still be possible to tell young fans about): Delegate and Light Italic with occasional Symbol 12 smartarsery when I felt typographically exotic, or mathematical, or Greek. Did I really do headlines in the dread Script face, the moral equivalent of Comic Sans?

It seemed like betrayal when after years of dextrous ball-fingering I moved the whole operation to a daisywheel printer (tell young fans...) and then a laser printer. The golf balls still gaze reproachfully from their case. Orator – that was the huge tall one that would never cut stencils properly. Adjutant, Artisan, Diplomat, Dual Gothic, Letter Gothic, Manifold, Polygo, Prestige: I don't even remember what all these looked like. A nostalgic favourite is Olde English, acquired on my 1980 TransAtlantic Fan Fund trip and used approximately once a year to type things like Merry Christmas.

All useless now, without a Selectric to put them in. But I can't bear to throw them away.

• *Plokta* #41, April 2011

Exuberant Verbosity

Abnegation. Anadems. Argence. Bartizans. Bedizened. Benignant. Benison. Brume. It's an addiction: I can't read Stephen R. Donaldson without jotting down his latest researches into the Ultra-Complete Maximegalon Dictionary. In the new Thomas Covenant epic, *Against All Things Ending*, he mingles new discoveries with old favourites...

Caducity. Caliginous. Carious. Cataphract. Cerulean. Charlock. Chlamys. Chrism. Chthonic. Circadian. Clinquant. Cloacal. Condign. Condyles. Cymar. Cynosure. Deflagration. Deliriancy. Demesne. Despoilage. Destrier. Devoir. Dromonds.

I love SF's weird words, not so much invented languages like Klingon as bizarre one-offs. In John Brunner's *The Shockwave Rider*, future people don't say "okay" but "Sweedack", supposedly from the French "Je suis d'accord" – a likely story. Larry Niven offers the feeblest ever swear word with "Tanj!", standing for "There ain't no justice!"

(Ebon. Ecru. Effluvium. Eidolons. Eldritch. Embrasure. Exigent. Formication. Frangible. Friable. Fug. Fuligin. Fulvous. Galvanic. Gangrel. Gavotte. Gelid. Glaive. Glode. Gravid. Guerdon. Gyre.)

SF technospeak is crammed with silliness. When someone in Neal Stephenson's *Anathem* says, "I have to counter-strafe the new clanex recompensators...", the reply is a huge relief: "I have no idea what this means." I never grasped the scientific units in Arn Romilus's *Brain Palaeo*: "As you know, the Masters possess a positive potential of several thousand bratilgrovits on which they depend for motivation." Even when you substitute "Laws of Robotics" for the jargon in the following, there still seems to be some problem: "Robots were constructed with an inbuilt verboter unit, preventing them from either doing or not doing an action that might result in harm to a human." (Gardner F. Fox, *Escape Across the Cosmos*.)

(Ichor. Illucid. Illusive. Immanence. Immedicable. Immiscible. Incarnadine. Incondign. Incused. Ineluctable. Innominate. Irenic. Irrefragable. Irrefusable. Jerrid. Knaggy. Knurls. Lambent. Lealty. Lenitive. Louring. Lucence.)

Some words aren't meant to be understood. The tragedy of future humanity in Brian Aldiss's "The Failed Men" is the maddeningly untranslatable "struback". Diana Wynne Jones's *Fire and Hemlock* features a McGuffin of which nothing is known but its name, the Obah Cypt. A similar problem bedevils the quest for the Throme (the what?) in Patricia McKillip's *The Throme of the Erril of Sherill*. An alien Platonian in John Brunner's story "Out of Order" reveals that his idea of fun involves pretonsuling and incoblapsimine, whose meaning we mercifully never learn. And in Alfred Bester's "Of Time and Third Avenue" who could argue with the profound saying reverently quoted by a visiting time-traveller: "The Future is Tekon"?

(Malefic. Mansuetude. Marge. Marmoreal. Marrow-meld. Metatarsus. Moil. Muricated. Nacre. Nascent. Nitid. Niveous. Oneiric. Oriflamme. Orogeny. Paresthesis. Pearlescence. Pediment. Percipience. Phalanges. Plash. Puissance. Rachitic. Rapine. Ribbands. Roborant. Rugose.)

Before *Hitchhiker*, Robert Sheckley was the acknowledged master of silly SF terms. In "Bad Medicine", the hero's psychotherapy machine proves to be a Martian model which diagnoses feem desire – a vile perversion – and urgently insists that he try to remember his goricae. Another hapless Sheckley hero in "Protection" is adopted by a gronish (that is, invisible) validusian derg, whose friendly help unfortunately makes him vulnerable to nastier beings like the gamper, grailers, leeps, feegs, melgerizer and thang. To avoid the dreaded thang, it's vital *not to lesnerize*. Our man has no idea what this means. The story ends on an ominous note as he's about to sneeze. Or in Thomas Covenant phrasing, to sternutate.

Sacral. Salvific. Sapid. Scaur. Scrannel. Scrog. Scurf. Sempiternal. Sendaline. Siccant. Soilures. Spilth. Spume. Stricture. Surquedry. Susurrus. Suzerainty. Swales. Talus. Tarsal. Theurgy – the most frequently appearing of all these words. Threnody. Tocsins. Tumid. Utile. Verdigris. Verdure. Viridian. Virtu. Vitriol. Wight. Writhen.

Oh, Mr Donaldson's wonderful vocabulary always sets me off. Now I feel all argute, inchoate and refulgent.

David Langford knows which politician said that another was inebriated with the exuberance of his own wossname.

• *SFX* #207, May 2011

Sanity Clause

Early in my career, a publisher sent me a book contract which I ungratefully didn't sign but showed to a friend who already wrote for a living. He wasn't impressed: "The only thing this lacks is the clause specifying that the Author shall deliver his wife, suitably garbed in see-through chiffon gown, for a period of full copyright." Another literary pal was reminded of the old Dobson Books contract, which he swore had conditions like "in ye euent of tardie Deliuerie, ye Scribe shall be flogg'd."

After negotiation, that contract was rewritten for author-friendliness – but I'd been terribly tempted to sign the dodgy version anyway, for fear of missing out. Publishers, splendid folk though they are, can't resist trying it on.

There was a fuss when HarperCollins slipped a new clause into their standard contract this year, giving them the right to cancel if "Author's conduct evidences a lack of due regard for public conventions and morals, or if Author commits a crime or any other act that will tend to bring Author into serious contempt..." Involved in a scandal that stirs up colossal publicity for your book? You may have to pay the advance back; pure-minded HarperCollins doesn't like the wrong kind of fame.

The great Ursula K. Le Guin responded with a tongue-in-cheek confession addressed to HC bossman Rupert Murdoch: "Before I wrote my book *Emily Brontë and the Vampires of Lustbaden*, which you published this fall and which has been on the Times Best Seller List for five straight months, I committed bad behavior and said bad words in public that brought me into serious contempt in my home town of Blitzen, Oregon. In fact the people there found me so seriously contemptible that I am now living in Maine under the name of Trespassers W..."

More funny business came to light when an outraged US literary agent reported on Macmillan's new contract, in which clause 6b allows the publisher to create "derivative works" based on the author's book –

rehashing its characters and settings. Who owns the copyright to these "new works"? Why, the publisher, of course! Just imagine if J.K. Rowling had signed a deal like that when new and inexperienced. "Don't worry, Ms Rowling, our soft-porn series beginning with *Harry Potter and the Suspenders of Enticement* is totally legitimate. It's simply a derivative work that we've created and own all the rights to, just like it says in your contract."

Sometimes, alas, spotting the nasty clause doesn't help. A few years back, a minor imprint of a major publisher wanted me to write this non-fiction book in a hurry. They offered a modest sum up front, with more when the text was delivered and approved. That's normal. What wasn't normal, as my agent spotted, was the clause saying that if they didn't like the result of my months of toil – or if they changed their mind for any reason or none at all – even that first miserly instalment of advance money must be repaid in full. Ridiculous, said my agent. Deal's off, retorted the publisher: "We cannot work with an author who refuses to accept editorial direction." No, not when the directive is "Shut your eyes, Luke, and sign the Clause!"

Long ago, SF author Damon Knight offered three maxims for young writers: "love your work; read your contracts; make friends when you can." Wise advice still, but today we need a fourth: read that contract *again*.

David Langford still feels grumpy about flightless Antarctic birds in evening dress.

• *SFX* #208, June 2011

Hidden Secrets

Story ideas I'll probably never get around to writing, number 5,271,009: What if Edgar Allan Poe deciphered the Voynich Manuscript?

He'd certainly have loved to try. Poe was fascinated by cipher messages – look at his story "The Gold-Bug". In his 1839-40 US magazine column, he challenged readers to submit a cryptogram he couldn't crack. One man defeated him... or so it seemed, until Poe scholars started wondering whether this mysterious master-cryptographer "W.B. Tyler" was a pseudonym of Poe himself. But that's another story.

One good reason why Poe never tested his skill on the Voynich Manuscript is that, although the latest radiocarbon dating places it in the early 15th century, it didn't come to light until book-dealer Wilfrid Voynich got hold of it in 1912. Shame.

The manuscript, written in an unknown alphabet, is a prime example of historical weirdness. What *language* is it in? What are all those unidentifiable plants and cosmological diagrams? Who are the naked ladies bathing in green gunge that flows through Heath Robinson lash-ups of arcane plumbing? Before the date was nailed down, many people hoped the author was famed proto-scientist Bacon – either Roger the futurologist monk (13th century: too early) or Francis the essayist and cipher fan (16th century: too late). Is the MS alchemical? Complex insanity? Could it be science fiction?

A useful, entertaining round-up of theories is *The Voynich Manuscript* (2004) by Gerry Kennedy and Rob Churchill. They report that crypto expert William F. Friedman, who famously broke the Japanese "Purple" code in World War II, decided the manuscript was an experiment in creating an imaginary language. Just like Tolkien, really, except that Tolkien's illustrations are sadly deficient in naked ladies bathing.

(By the way, Friedman and his wife Elizebeth also wrote *The Shakespearean Ciphers Examined*, mercilessly dissecting efforts to extract the secret messages – usually from Francis Bacon – hidden in

Shakespeare's plays. Like so many attempted Voynich translations, the results tended to be surreal gibberish.)

My favourite book inspired by the Voynich MS is Luigi Serafini's amazing *Codex Seraphinianus*, also written in an unknown script and even more crammed with bizarre illustrations. But I first read about the Voynich codex in Colin Wilson's novel *The Philosopher's Stone*, a heady mix of Lovecraftian and paranormal themes. What else, said Wilson, could the ancient, undecipherable Voynich text be but H.P. Lovecraft's *Necronomicon*, the dread grimoire whose merest semicolon is a shuddering threat to sanity?

One thing led to another. Some Voynich scholars had suspected the manuscript was a modern hoax, and some Lovecraft scholars thought it would be fun to, ahem, reconstruct the *Necronomicon* from first principles. Which is how I found myself working on this mighty project with George Hay (whose idea it was), Robert Turner and Colin Wilson. My contribution was a Poe-like essay on cipher-breaking, which cited Francis Bacon and other pioneers of secret writing, and "explained" how the *Necronomicon* had been cunningly encoded in the occult book *Liber Logaeth* by another 16th-century savant: Doctor John Dee. Who, until the 15th-century dating was established, was frequently suspected of having perpetrated the Voynich Manuscript. "Our" version of the *Necronomicon* appeared in 1978, and is of course definitive. Unless it turns out to be a 15th-century hoax.

One last true fact. Colin Wilson – once misleadingly lumped together with Kingsley Amis and other 1950s UK novelists as the "Angry Young Men" – will be 80 around the time this *SFX* appears, in June 2011. I've enjoyed his writing for many years. Happy birthday!

David Langford, though undecipherable, is always ready to raise a glass.

Later: My own title for this one was "Unbreakable Code". I have no idea why *SFX* changed it to the equally uninspiring header above: maybe the original contains a filthy innuendo that I missed.

• *SFX* #209, July 2011

Jones Disagrees

Diana Wynne Jones, who wrote some of the twentieth century's finest children's/YA fantasies and died this March, never seemed quite grown-up. Rather than being a dignified Major Author and Living National Treasure, she had the air of a mischievous teenager who just happened to have wrinkles (like the age-cursed heroine of her *Howl's Moving Castle*) and might at any moment do something outrageous. I remember Diana chatting at a convention, wearing a neck-brace – her health jinx had struck again – decorated, with permission, with a frieze of dancing nymphs by an artist from the *Encyclopedia of Fantasy* team. This seemed entirely logical.

As an expert fantasy practitioner she gave the *Encyclopedia* a helping hand, mainly through trenchant notes in the margins of overly pretentious drafts: "Bollocks!" Her favourite critical quote came from a student thesis about her: "Jones disagrees." This became a household catchphrase, frequently addressed to the cat.

You must know her wonderful books: the Chrestomanci and Howl series, the Dalemark quartet, the hilariously daft *Archer's Goon* (adapted for BBC television), the genre-crossing *Deep Secret* (a fan favourite, containing a wickedly plausible SF convention) and many more... Critics tried to pin down Diana's elusive magic; she read the results with fascination and was delighted by the tasty bits: "My favourite is the assertion that I am 'rooted in fluidity'. Obviously hydroponic, probably a lettuce, possibly a cabbage. A new light is cast." The critic, I'm told, was mortified.

It wasn't only Diana's health that was jinxed. She was convinced that disasters escaped from her books into real life. For example, there's a goddess in *Drowned Ammet* whose power is to raise islands: "The first time I went on a boat after writing that book, an island grew up out of the sea and stranded us." Even a visit to 10 Downing Street, when Tony Blair threw a party for top children's authors, included cursed canapés ("I took a rice thing from one of the small ladies and it came open and rice went all up my sleeve, like gummy little beetles.")

and the dire political embarrassment of *nearly* getting trapped in the Number Ten loo.

Likewise the joy of publicity: "Did you know that the *Daily Mail* insists that all women have to be photographed in a skirt? And not in black. I had to buy a skirt." And again: "The feisty photographer from *SFX* decided that the best and most typical pose for me was halfway down the stairs to the hotel toilets, where she had me leaning against the wall idly toying with a beer bottle. Now what gave her that idea?" Some of my happiest memories of Diana are from convention bars...

Jones was still Disagreeing in her last email to me. She'd seen the proceedings of a learned seminar on her work, which she'd been too ill to attend: "the whole set of speeches from the DWJ conference (that I most miserably failed to get to; now I am glad: I would have shot upright from the audience and announced 'Jones disagrees' like anything). Anyway, these speeches had now been tidied into articles and I read them and found myself most thoroughly Derridaed and Foucaulted and always referred to as 'the Text'. In future I shall have to say 'The Text disagrees'." And she signed off in a Welsh sort of way, as Jones the Text.

Now the memories and the highly rereadable texts are all we have. If only Diana were here to disagree.

David Langford isn't much consoled to know that two final books (one short fantasy, one essay collection) are awaited.

• *SFX* #210, Summer 2011

Tribal Rites

I've been doing it since 1974, you know, despite medical evidence that it makes you go blind – or at least causes terminal anorexia of the wallet. It's one of the arcane rituals of binding in the UK fan world; if you've read Jorge Luis Borges's "The Sect of the Phoenix" you'll suspect it of being a sordid euphemism. Yes, I went to Eastercon.

This year's was in a Birmingham (i.e. Solihull) National Exhibition Centre hotel, surrounded by stark NEC building-block architecture to represent the Future, bluebell-infested woods to symbolize Fantasy, and swarms of horrible black mating flies from the nearby lake as a reminder of what happens in convention bedrooms.

What's Eastercon, apart from Britain's national SF convention? The gathering of the SF tribes, Brian Aldiss once put it, meaning that you meet all sorts of riffraff. Young fans drool over the guests of honour, this year including David Weber of Honor Harrington fame (see my *SFX* #104 column, "Hornblower in Space") and Peter F. "Tree-Slayer" Hamilton of enormous great fat trilogy fame. Boozy fans flock to the real ale bar, also featuring real cider with that toxic hue known to pathologists as "Mrs Blenkinsop's Specimen". Greying old fans appear on panels titled "Is Fandom Getting Old and Grey?" and bang on about this troubling question until another of them drops dead.

A newer tradition is that the tribes unite for the one and only programme item that's so sacred that nothing else can be scheduled against it, the Saturday evening showing of *Doctor Who*. Sometimes the Chair of the convention is rebranded as the Sofa and sits at the front so the entire audience can hide behind this iconic piece of furniture.

Alas, I'm not much of a programme-goer: the official pose is that I've heard it all before, which is a fib because my hearing was always terrible. Now it's even worse and I've given up pretending to follow those damned panels where writers persuasively argue that the most significant cultural aspect of steampunk (or zombies, vampires, space opera, slipstream, New Weird) is that you should buy their latest book.

Instead, the dealers' room is a great place for chat as well as acquiring SF treasures you really really can't afford.

Eastercon's art show brought me serious payola, with that splendidly Gothic fantasy artist Anne Sudworth slipping me a copy of her artbook *Gothic Fantasies*, perhaps hoping I'd mention her marvellously lit landscapes here. But I am incorruptible. David A. Hardy, the artist guest of honour, does fine space and SF pictures (including one Langford book cover) but failed to offer any interesting bribes and doesn't get a namecheck.

Nor can I describe the lavish secret parties, because the Hotel Police are still trying to track down the hosts and charge them 500% corkage. Further attractions included book launches (I'm too modest to plug Ian Whates's Arthur C. Clarke-homage anthology *Fables from the Fountain*, which I'm in), multi-author signing sessions (I was part of the one to which *no one at all* came; the Guinness Book of Records is aghast), the BSFA Awards (Ian McDonald's *The Dervish House* won as best novel), a voting session to choose who runs the 2013 Eastercon and where (decision embarrassedly deferred to next year since there were absolutely no volunteers), and – for the non-photogenic – the uplifting opportunity to be photographed with your head inside a replica satellite. SF fans, keen-eyed peerers into the future, will not be fobbed off with paper bags.

Scandalous conversations were plentiful, and I'd reveal countless tasty titbits if it weren't for the super-injunctions. Like caviar or root canal therapy, Eastercon is an unforgettable experience.

• *SFX* #211, August 2011

Random Reading
Old Stuff

Nelson Bond, *The Thirty-First of February* (1949). A vaguely familiar title once announced as an episode in James Branch Cabell's "Witch-Woman" fantasy sequence, only three of whose ten planned stories were written. Bond persuaded Cabell to grant him a "Conveyance of Title in Fee Simple" (reproduced on the back jacket and within), giving permission in doggerel to use the title. How could a Cabell enthusiast resist? The thirteen tales here are mainly slick fantasies, but include some rougher-hewn SF like the classic shaggy-god story "The Cunning of the Beast" (1942 *Bluebook* as "Another World Begins") and the alien-nasty yarn "The Monster from Nowhere" (1939 *Fantastic Adventures*). Kingsley Amis had quoted and deplored the latter's "repulsive style" in *New Maps of Hell*, so one passage was eerily familiar. The interesting thing about the monster is that it's four-dimensional, manifesting to puny humans as a number of separate, shifting 3D cross-sections as its various appendages intersect our space. Should this be added to the *SF Encyclopedia* theme entry DIMENSIONS? Yes and no: the title was already cited there, but with a different date and credited to Donald Wandrei. Next question: is Wandrei's "The Monster from Nowhere" (1935 *Argosy Weekly*) *also* about a 4D horror? No, according to the collective erudition of the Fictionmags mailing list, where I learned the source of this mix-up: the Bond story was collected in Groff Conklin's *Best of Science Fiction* (1946), whose first edition wrongly credited it to Wandrei. Another *Encyclopedia* error corrected! This is how I spend my days.

Ernest Bramah, *A Little Flutter* (1930). Mildly fantastic comedy whose sole genre element is the existence of that unlikely giant bird, the Patagonian Groo-Groo. This is initially described as an alarming "five yards two feet in height", which must be a typo or a joke since it's central to the plot that the thing is man-sized. All that actually remains of this prodigy by the time the story gets underway is the skin, and our hero – who for purposes of conditional inheritance must feign an interest in ornithology, and for reasons of mindboggling auctorial manipulation has an unwanted guest (in fact an escaped criminal) on his hands – finds it convenient to have the Groo-Groo skin inhabited. But how long can this impersonation fool the bird experts, including a learned Scot of such caricatured awfulness that modern British readers are likely to have a nervous sense that the Race Relations Act is looking over their shoulder? A very minor Bramah fiction, whose deep obscurity I now understand.

Eric Linklater, *The Pirates in the Deep Green Sea* (1949), a children's fantasy of undersea adventure featuring magical breathing-under-water oil, a fellowship of immortal ex-sailors led by Davy Jones, and a pleasing reification of the lines of latitude and longitude as actual ropes which are knotted at their intersections and must remain so for the safety of the world. Naturally the dastardly pirates of the title have plans (somewhat poorly motivated, but never mind) to "improve" on the existing knots, at risk of rendering everything *utterly higgledy-piggledy*. Whimsical fun – Cully the Talking and indeed Singing Octopus is a notable character – but it could have used a trifle more piratical menace. The two main buccaneer leaders huff and puff and plot at length, but (unlike, say, the sinister Abner Brown of John Masefield's not dissimilarly toned *The Midnight Folk* and *The Box of Delights*) don't seem to have it in them to *do* anything truly dastardly. Linklater's previous juvenile venture *The Wind on the Moon* (1944) won him a Carnegie Medal; this non-sequel didn't.

Richard C. Meredith, *We All Died at Breakaway Station* (1969). This was the launch title for the 1980s UK reprint series "Venture SF", a Hamlyn imprint that promised good old-fashioned space opera: "DO YOU REMEMBER when humans were heroes, androids didn't have social hang-ups and the only good alien was a dead one?" Like most Venture titles, *We All Died at Breakaway Station* is a reprint from Robert Hale Ltd (motto: "it doesn't have to be good, we have a guaranteed UK library sale"). Not that this is a seriously bad novel. Meredith works hard to put across the story of a heroically doomed rearguard action in space, but can't quite deliver his prologue's promise of an epic to rival Thermopylae, Horatius at the Bridge, and the Alamo. The alien Jillies are adequately nasty, and certainly the only good one is a dead one, but they're coming in overwhelming force. Holding the pass, as it were, are two starships crewed by ruined, cyborgized human casualties of too many past defeats. Can they delay a Jillie breakthrough long enough for the vital FTL message to be relayed by Breakaway Station? This could have worked well had Meredith engineered a steady, inexorable build-up of narrative momentum towards his foretold end. Unfortunately it suffers from twitchy jitters in the form of many flashbacks and cross-cuts, generating a perpetual sense of confusion about time and place – ah, *now* we're back in the present, or are we? Quite an interesting failure.

A.A. Milne, *Toad of Toad Hall* (1929). Acquired partly for completism and partly out of sheer curiosity as to how Milne, a competent playwright and popular as such in his day, had adapted Kenneth Grahame's *The Wind in the Willows* for the stage. As expected, the more mystical bits ("Wayfarers All", "The Piper at the Gates of Dawn") had to go, and what remains works well. But I found myself just a tiny bit shocked that, for the sake of a rousing finale, Milne allows the supposedly reformed Toad to sing his vainglorious "Last Little Song" not as a private fling in his bedroom but as the closing party's central attraction – and not only with every evidence of non-reformation but so seductively as to lure all the rest of the cast into an impromptu song-and-dance of unadulterated Toad-worship. Stage direction: "The incense of their adoration streams up to the be-laurelled TOAD..." At the very last, even the hitherto reliable curmudgeon Badger succumbs. Even Badger! The pillars of reason topple.

J.B. Priestley, *Adam in Moonshine* (1927). His first novel, which according to the 1993 *Encyclopedia of Science Fiction* is driven by "sf concerns". Hardly more so, though, than *The Prisoner of Zenda*. On mentioning his surname to chance companions on a train, our hero Adam Stewart is Ruritanianly mistaken for the Pretender awaited by conspirators who hope to restore England's Stuart monarchy in place of boring old Parliament. This ineffectual revolutionary movement, already well known to the police, includes three gorgeous young ladies with whom Adam enjoys romantic but chaste mini-adventures while evading the dogged constabulary. There are hints that Priestley had, like so many others, got drunk on G.K. Chesterton's *The Man Who Was Thursday* (1908): the huge and mysterious Baron who leads the "Companions of the Rose" is a Chestertonian Sunday figure without the undertow of menace, delighting in grand gestures like ordering thirty pairs of false whiskers or – when the police swoop at last – sending Adam and his number-three love interest (she drives the getaway car) on a headlong moonlit escape with a case of "secret papers" that proves to contain only the makings of an excellent picnic. Light-hearted silliness.

• *The New York Review of Science Fiction* #276, August 2011

Respect At Last

Remember how the world ended on 21 May, starting with an earthquake and (by Hollywood tradition) working up to a climax? Neither do I – another dud prophecy. But if science fiction fans watched for signs of the End Times, we'd have felt a superstitious thrill when the ultra-respectable British Library launched its 'Out of This World' SF exhibition on the 20th. Like the Pope giving equal time to Scientology.

Hordes of familiar faces thronged the St Pancras library for the 19th May launch party. I'd never had my company requested by a Baroness before: Baroness Blackstone, British Library Chair. Her introduction and China Miéville's thematic pep-talk reverberated through the vast echoing foyer, while free wine evaporated with magical speed and experts on alien biosystems tried to analyse the strange nibbles. Mike Ashley, author of the official exhibition book, stared nervously at a gob of Godzilla snot – delicious purée of wild asparagus, allegedly. I selected a tiny *2001* monolith that proved to consist of solid fish gristle. We front-line SF correspondents take many risks.

The unexpected star of the launch was Charles Chilton MBE, who kick-started British radio SF with his 1950s *Journey into Space* series for the BBC and was cheerily looking forward to his 94th birthday. Wide-eyed youths like Brian Aldiss (85), and a range of even younger writers who remembered the repeats, were deeply awed.

The exhibition itself, guest-curated by Andy Sawyer of the SF Foundation Library, is loosely themed for SF "worlds" – Alien, Time and Parallel, Virtual, Future, End Of and Perfect. Despite arty set-pieces like a flying saucer crashed into a wall of library shelves, it focuses unashamedly on actual books. One reviewer seemed dismayed by this unexpected emphasis on old-fashioned print media from, as it happens, the British Library. Surprises include a fantastically obscure Spanish volume from 1887 featuring SF's first time machine, a year before the earliest version of Wells's masterpiece appeared as "The Chronic Argonauts"... a title Wells wisely abandoned.

It's good to see what famous SF novels looked like in their first editions. As I gaped at unaffordable (by me) treasures behind glass, eminent critic John Clute grumbled about the BL's old bad habit of removing dustjackets and sending them to the Victoria & Albert Museum to be stored – uncatalogued and unfindable. Which is why the exhibition had to borrow many Clute and Foundation copies.

But there are all sorts of visual thrills; not just book illustrations, garish magazine covers, comics artwork, the first typescript page of *The Day of the Triffids* with unworthy opening paragraphs crossed out... The literal high point is a *War of the Worlds* Martian tripod, looming over the gallery and missed by all those who failed to look up. Gestures to bibliophobes and kids include a "design your own alien" computer setup that projects the current repertoire of badly drawn aliens on the wall. Also a traditional dark-blue police box has crept in, possibly under its own power. None of us could get the door open.

Several party-goers looked properly smug at being part of the exhibition, like Christopher Priest with his novel *The Affirmation* or David Pringle with many issues of *Interzone* magazine from his editorial reign. I never expected to make the cut, and indeed went home without noticing that the doom-and-gloom section includes a copy of the greatest disaster novel (or literary disaster) of all time: Earthdoom by myself and John Grant. Fame and official respect at last! I must visit again, just to gloat.

• *SFX* #212, September 2011

Panic Stations

Once in a while I've mentioned working on the new *Encyclopedia of Science Fiction*, something that's been chugging along in the background of my life – and not just mine – for years and years. It's like that long idyll of university coursework that seems to drift on forever until you hear the stark news that your final exams are just six weeks away. Where did the time go?

Suddenly it's all happening! Contracts have been signed, and Gollancz are publishing the *Encyclopedia*! It's to be free of charge, online, with the first "skeleton" version going up at the end of September 2011, and we still haven't written the all-important entry for Charles Stross! (Just joking, Charlie. Well, not really. Pretend you didn't see that.) This is the time of testing, as hardened *Encyclopedia* workers summon their last reserves of strength while Langford runs gibbering into the distant sunset...

The Gollancz announcement would have appeared on 4th July, but America was celebrating the making of *Independence Day* (I think it was) and our publicity chaps kept their big splash for the 5th. Like every titbit of SF information these days, this news was Facebooked and BoingBoinged and Twittered in all directions. Probably the biggest publicity boost within the SF community came from the Mighty Tweet of Neil Gaiman, bless him, who opined: "The best news of the week, unless Earth is Saved from a Martian invasion on Friday: The @SFencyclopedia is coming back..."

Am I, and John Clute and the other editors, really panicking? Yes and no. We have a mass of boring old statistics to comfort us. The 1993 second edition of the Great Big Fat Book – which like the 1979 first edition won a Hugo award – contained 6571 entries and about 1.3 million words. This third edition-in-progress keeps growing, and as I write is pushing close to 12,000 entries and 3 million words. That's... quite a bit. When will it be finished? Technically, never. After the beta version goes online, we have another million words to add in monthly instalments before declaring victory. Even then, regular updates should continue until the exhausted editors topple with a final sigh of relief into the grave. Tickets for this spectacle will be available through the hyperefficient outlets used by the 2012 Olympics.

Interestingly, some prospective readers are already saying they don't want to consult such a vast reference work on a website. Some fancy having a real book – but the massive second edition ran to 1320 pages of tiny print, before corrections and addenda were stuffed in for a paperback reissue. The third would be over 3000 pages for only the current text, rising to a likely 4000; not even Peter F. Hamilton's publishers could cope. Would a CD/DVD alternative be so much different from a website? Other would-be punters fancy installing the *Encyclopedia* as an app for their smartphone or iPricy. Maybe Gollancz's experts will find a way to keep them happy.

Meanwhile, our stern copyeditor keeps spotting typos and administering short sharp shocks: "Another time traveller who died before he was born!" Oops. And several of the contributing editors, hugely knowledgeable experts on various facets of SF to whose vast knowledge I grovelingly defer, have so far expertly failed to deliver anything. Closing time approaches in the Last Chance Saloon.

Must stop now. I have entries to write, ever so many entries. I may be gone for some time.

David Langford nervously invites all of you to take a look at www.sf-encyclopedia.com. Except Charlie Stross.

• *SFX* #213, October 2011

Naughty, Naughty

Because our language keeps changing, yesterday's writing can read very strangely today. There's a famous line about teenage lust in Jane Austen's mock-Gothic melodrama *Northanger Abbey*: "At fifteen, appearances were mending; she began to curl her hair and long for balls..." Likewise, strait-laced Emily Dickinson wrote a poem about a dying tiger that startles modern readers with "His Mighty Balls – in death were thick". To everyone's ill-concealed relief, she meant eyeballs.

Naturally this happens in SF too. Vibrators make several worrying appearances in older stories. The specimen confiscated from a US cop in Algis Budrys's "The Edge of the Sea" proves to be merely part of his radio. More often they're weapons, as in T.H. White's *The Master*, whose supervillain plans to impose world peace with the threat of his massive vibrator. A Moral Dialogue about spanking ensues: "If you can't make people be good with a hair brush, you can't with a vibrator, can you?" (Don't answer that.) A.E. van Vogt's *The Voyage of the Space Beagle* features a catlike alien predator which Earthmen naturally call pussy: "I'm going to ask various experts to give their suggestions for fighting pussy." Suitable hand-weapons are duly deployed for an assault on pussy: "Vibrators fumed and fussed."

More seeming kinkiness appears in E.E. Smith's *Masters of the Vortex*, whose hero thinks about his (late) wife "flagellantly". Experts agree the author meant something slightly different, with no actual flagellation involved.

Only the filthy-minded will cringe at the exhibitionism in David Lindsay's fantasy *The Violet Apple*: "He exhibited his seed, of which Grace had already spoken to her half-sister. "What do you want done with it?' inquired Virginia, holding it to the light between her thin thumb and finger." Likewise: "Sternly, he kept his hands away from her. No sense making it harder than it was." (Sheri S. Tepper, *After Long Silence*.) Then there's the "Queen of the Argzoon" chapter in Edward P. Bradbury's *Blades of Mars*: "That was another reason why we should not expose ourselves! The Argzoon would enjoy taking revenge on members of the race that had defeated them." Ooh – in a Kenneth Williams voice – painful.

Clues in *Private Eye*'s crossword often trade shamelessly on the fact that "members" has various meanings, some of them not rude. The great SF example is the Lens-wearing hero's wedding in E.E. Smith's *Second Stage Lensmen*: "Then, as Kinnison kissed his wife, half a million Lensed members were thrust upward in silent salute."

Larry Niven's entirely logical title for a ramdrive starship pilot can still look a mite peculiar, depending on context: "You know what to do with a woman but you are one of those men fortunate enough not to need one. Otherwise you could not be a rammer." (*A World Out of Time*.)

Some authors go the other way, keeping things excessively clean. Despite impeccable Dirty Old Man credentials later in life, the young Isaac Asimov couldn't bring himself to describe a well-endowed lady as stacked like a brick shithouse, but crafted a cunning future-tech alternative: "Wow! Isn't she built like a force-field latrine, though?" (*The End of Eternity*.)

You can't be too careful. An Australian newspaper competition setter was recently sacked for a trivia quiz whose final question asked who wrote *Do Androids Dream of Electric Sheep?* Unfortunately all the answers ("What is the official currency of Vietnam?") were slang terms for, ahem, the male member. And some Australians, despite the tough talk and corks round their hats, are terrible prudes.

David Langford was taking pencil notes at an American convention and asked if he could borrow a rubber.

• *SFX* #214, November 2011

Who's In Charge?

When banks totter and stock markets do kamikaze impersonations, some SF fans remember the 1970 R.A. Lafferty story that begins: "There is a secret society of seven men that controls the finances of the world. This is known to everyone but the details are not known. There are some who believe that it would be better if one of those seven were a financier." ("About a Secret Crocodile", August 1970 *Galaxy*.)

All the best conspiracy theories agree that Secret Masters run the world. According to David Icke they're giant space lizards posing as the Royal Family, though there's the worrying possibility that Icke doesn't think he's writing science fiction. More traditionally it's the Bavarian Illuminati, as deliriously revealed, complicated, refuted and disinformationed in Robert Shea's and Robert Anton Wilson's *Illuminatus!* trilogy. (They even managed to sneak one of their eldritch Masonic symbols onto the dollar bill!) In *Little, Big* by John Crowley, US politics is controlled by a cabal of men in suits called the Noisy Bridge Rod and Gun Club, which is maybe too plausible to be funny. Even more convincing, until the sinister organization was abolished in 2002, was Tom Holt's dark suggestion that we're all puppets of the Milk Marketing Board.

I have a weakness for ultra-dotty conspiracies that turn out to be shaggy dog stories, like G.K. Chesterton's *The Man Who Was Thursday* and A.E. van Vogt's *Weapon Shops of Isher* books. What these have in common is that the two opposed sides (anarchist bombers versus police, libertarian gun merchants versus oppressive Empire) are secretly run by the same godlike puppet-master. Oops, forgot to say "spoiler warning" there.

Speaking of dottiness, there's an *Illuminati* card game where everyone gets to play a conspiratorial power-group: the Servants of Cthulhu, the Bermuda Triangle, the Gnomes of Zurich... Thus, after complex alliances and double-crosses, the International Communist Conspiracy – aided by the Orbital Mind Control Lasers – may well end up as the power behind the CIA. Or, conversely, behind *Star Trek* fandom.

Sometimes secret masters are literal chess-players, moving us like pawns on the board and giggling at our silly delusions of free will. When this is revealed to the manipulated hero of John Brunner's *The Squares of the City*, he's only slightly cheered to be told he's not a pawn but a knight.

Still more ego-deflating is the idea that mere animals are in charge. Eric Frank Russell wrote this story twice, with dogs running the show in "Into Your Tent I'll Creep" and camels in "Homo Saps". Camels are also famously hyperintelligent in Terry Pratchett's *Pyramids*, and so of course are mice in *The Hitchhiker's Guide to the Galaxy*. When the protagonist of Fredric Brown's "Come and Go Mad" learns that the black, red and white factions that secretly control Earth are the ants, he goes... oh, you guessed.

Not all authors take Secret Masters seriously. William Tenn mocked the idea of a hidden power behind the throne in "The Servant Problem", where supreme ruler A is secretly controlled by B, a puppet of C, who's unknowingly in the power of D – and D is helplessly loyal to A. In John Sladek's *The Muller-Fokker Effect*, dedicated conspiracy theorists struggle to decipher messages they're sure were embedded by devious Commies in the endless decimal places of *pi*. Jorge Luis Borges's very short "The Sect of the Phoenix" describes a furtive and slightly disgusting cult which (readers gradually come to realize) includes the entire human race. With the possible exception of the Milk Marketing Board.

David Langford denies being a Secret Master of Fandom. Well, he would, wouldn't he?

• *SFX* #215, December 2011

Carnacki Brings Home the Bacon

One day in October 2011, SFX freelancer William Salmon asked me for a text-bite about my favourite tale starring William Hope Hodgson's classic occult investigator Carnacki the Ghost-Finder. Although my response below was greeted with ecstatic thanks, I have no idea whether it appeared in the relevant feature in SFX Special #53 (not part of the usual numbering sequence), of which I did not receive a complimentary copy).

Surely everyone's favourite Carnacki episode must be "The Hog", for its trans-Lovecraftian evocation of, well, pigging out. "The howling, squealing, grunting, rolling clamour of swinish noise coming up out of that place, and then the monstrous GRUNT rising up from it all, an ever-recurring beat out of the depth – the voice of the swine-mother of monstrosity beating up from below through that chorus of mad swine hunger..." So compelling that even the victim can't stop himself from grunting back. As with the swarming, terrifying and deliciously tasty hordes of swine-things in Hodgson's *The House on the Borderland*, this was a brilliant feat of product placement by the Pork Marketing Board.

• *SFX Special* #53, 2011(?)

Triffid Pursuit

I'm writing in the final throes of *SF Encyclopedia* madness. The online "beta text" version should be well launched by the time this *SFX* sees print, but right now I have regular small-hours paranoia about the need to know – or pretend to know – absolutely everything about SF. Imaginary quizmasters haunt my nightmares.

Eva D. Fanglord (looking horribly like Anne Robinson): Name an SF author who collaborated with himself.

Myself: Er um how about Lester del Rey? He gave his own pseudonym Erik van Lhin equal billing on his novel *Police Your Planet*. Not a lot of people wanted to know that.

Q: While we're on the subject, who wrote *Siege Perilous* by Lester del Rey?

A: I think that's a trick question. I think it was ghost-written by Paul W. Fairman.

Q: What do the first *Terminator* movie, AOL and the 2011 film *In Time* have in common? A short answer, please.

A: Harlan Ellison. He filed copyright lawsuits against them all.

Q: Lee Barton, Thornton Bell, Noel Bertram, Leo Brett, Bron Fane, Trebor Thorpe, Neil Thanet, Pel Torro... which is the odd one out?

A: Um. They're all pseudonyms of Robert Lionel Fanthorpe made up from various letters from his name. Can I phone a friend? No, wait, there's no M in Fanthorpe! Noel Bertram wrote for the same publisher but was someone else.

Q: Indeed. Which SF god, featuring in many mighty space-oaths, has golden gills, gadolinium guts, iridium intestines, tungsten teeth and curving carballoy claws?

A: L. Ron Hubbard. I take that back, it's Klono in Doc Smith's *Lensman* series. He had an emerald-filled gizzard too.

Q: I don't wish to know that... Of which SF novel did the stern critic James Blish say that when it won a Nebula award, "I stepped quietly out into the kitchen and bit my cat"?

A: Easy-peasy. Samuel R. Delany's *The Einstein Intersection*.

Q: Correct, but I'm deducting one point for smugness. Which famous SF author was deeply embarrassed to have written in a novel, "There are no mountains on Mars"?

A: Arthur C. Clarke, in *The Sands of Mars*. I say this very humbly.

Q: Correct, but I'm deducting a point for grovelling. Your next question is on imaginary books: G.K. Chesterton's short story "The Blast of the Book" has one that apparently causes its readers to vanish from the earth, and Frederik Pohl's *Gateway* sequence has one about his inscrutable aliens called *Everything We Know about the Heechee*. What do they have in common?

A: Both of them are all blank pages.

Q. Which SF author was born Edward Hamilton Waldo but wrote his books under a more plausible name?

A: Kilgore Trout... no no no, I mean Theodore Sturgeon.

Q. Anthony Boucher wrote three short fantasy stories titled for the demons who appear in them: Sribidegibit, Snulbug and Nellthu. What do *they* have in common?

A (polishing fingernails modestly): They're all dodgy words from the "Bad Quarto" edition of Shakespeare's *King Lear*.

Q: Lose five points for being too clever by half. And the last question, for £64,000 or a hot date with the *Doctor Who* companion of your choice: What are the sinister walking, stinging vegetables that overrun Britain in John Wyndham's classic disaster novel *The Day of the* –?

A: Tribbles! Oh, hang on, was it Tripods? Trillions? Er, I need to phone a friend...

Q: David Langford, You Are The Weakest Link.

Then I wake up screaming.

• *SFX* #216, January 2012

Deep Impact

Forget the jet-packs and flying cars. What we want is that medical nanotechnology they have in SF, the stuff that magically, painlessly restores our damaged bits a molecule at a time. Instead...

Wheeeeeeeee

It happened when the madness of launching the *SF Encyclopedia* was at its height. Brian Aldiss's quickie definition of SF is "Hubris clobbered by nemesis." Which means that in my hour of glory I broke a tooth. And the nice man with the white coat and the very high-pitched drill says it needs to be crowned.

Wheeeeeeeee

Think of something else. Great SF About Dentists. There's a proud genre tradition that Earth's dentists are so superior that they get abducted by aliens desperate for their skills. Like the unfortunate Goldpepper in Avram Davidson's "Help! I Am Dr Morris Goldpepper", held captive by toothless humanoids within whose dentures he cunningly conceals his messages for help. The dentist hero of Piers Anthony's *Prostho Plus* is also kidnapped and forced to cruise the galaxy fixing weird sets of teeth, including one cavity so gigantic that he nearly gets lost inside. The one in my jaw feels about that size now.

Wheeeeeeeee

Happier thought. The Phillips radiation treatment in Doc Smith's *Lensman* books. One dose and your missing parts start to regrow, whereupon elderly test subjects rediscover the prolonged agonies of cutting new teeth while their comrades laugh heartily. Maybe not such a good wish-fulfilment after all.

Wheeeeeeeee

Who else in SF has dental peculiarities? Ah: the doomed Duke Leto in *Dune* gets a replacement tooth (inserted without anaesthetic, argh argh) which, once bitten, releases enough poison gas to kill everyone in the room. Roars of laughter, breaks the ice at parties. Cute, but as a fashion accessory it'll never catch on. Gully Foyle in *The Stars My*

Destination is rewired as a cyborg superman, with his teeth as the operating switchboard for amazing new powers. Must have been so embarrassing when he bit into a gristly steak, flipped a tooth and caused his eyes to light up, or accelerated by accident into a superspeed killing frenzy.

Wheeeeeeeee

SF conventions are mysteriously bad for the teeth. I had one snap off at Novacon way back. Another proved unequal to the struggle with a water-chestnut mere hours before my first onstage appearance as a convention guest in Portland, Oregon. While everyone else was having fun in the bar, hapless Langford was stretched out in another of those torture chairs trying to avoid the deeply philosophical thought: "I am having root canal work at American prices." (The convention, bless them, paid for it.)

Wheeeeeeeee

Frankly, it's a personal phobia. The nastiest horror story I ever wrote was cribbed directly from bad dreams about bicuspids. Even the huge pile of harmless teeth accumulated by the Tooth Fairy in Terry Pratchett's *Hogfather* gave me the creeps on first reading. And I'm trying really hard, while helpless in the dentist's chair, not to think of the story in Christopher Fowler's collection *Uncut* about a chap with a split tooth who (no don't think about it) slowly discovers the man in the white coat is a lunatic dental impersonator who argh argh argh...

Wheeeeeeeee.

Can he really be finished? Rinse, spit, credit card. Stagger into the street, nostalgic for SF stories where teeth are restored by nanotechnological magic. Of course, with my luck I'd get a batch of defective nano that dissolved me into grey goo or restructured my whole head into a single giant molar.

David Langford is haunted by the knowledge, gleaned from The X-Files, that The Tooth Is Out There.

• *SFX* #217, February 2012

The Dragon Lady

One long-ago Eastercon saw a surprise entertainment – a fan version of the Oz story masterminded by Judy and James Blish (he played the Great and Terrible Wizard) and titled *The Wizard of Ozimov*. Robert Holdstock wore a hideously uncomfortable metallic spray-painted costume as the Tin Woodman. The show was stolen by a cameo part, the madly overacting Wicked Witch with green make-up and the only professionally trained voice in the cast: Anne McCaffrey. Unforgettable.

Very sadly, James Blish died in 1975, Rob Holdstock in 2009; and in November 2011 we lost Anne McCaffrey.

She'd been active a long time, publishing her first story in Hugo Gernsback's final SF magazine in 1953 and her first novel in 1967. *Restoree* has a typically tough, feisty heroine who not only rescues the male lead from durance vile but, since he's useless at sea, sails the getaway boat more or less single-handed.

There are glints of autobiography in McCaffrey's best-loved works. Though she most definitely wasn't a cyborg, her operatic training resonates through *The Ship Who Sang* (whose opening story, which she could never read aloud without tears, mourns the death of her father) and again in *The Crystal Singer* – whose heroine has to deal with learning that she has a good singing voice and not, as she'd passionately wanted, a great one.

McCaffrey's favourite hobby was horse-breeding, and her neatest literary coup was translating the traditional horse-mania of teenage girls into a loving telepathic pair-bonding with dragons – for girls and boys alike – in the Dragonriders of Pern sequence. Its first two stories won her the Hugo and Nebula. The series may have stretched out too long (a writer has to live, after all), but there's real magic in the early volumes.

Though of course it's not magic but psi powers that can be given sciencey names like telepathy and teleportation, acceptable to the "hard SF" magazine *Analog* where Pern debuted in 1967-1968. Science fantasy, critics call it. The world of Pern has the romantic air of adventure fantasy but is underpinned by science: the dragons are genetically engineered, the riders' ancestors arrived by spaceship, catchy ballads are mnemonics that hide scientific clues, and there's a great deal of Old Technology to be rediscovered. Lovers of boys' toys were won over too. The series gained a huge, admiring readership.

A digression that I can't resist: the SF author Richard Cowper had a favourite anecdote about his first writers' conference, where an exuberant woman he'd never seen before (guess who) seized him and cried, "*You have the eyes of a prune!*" Well, he did have twinkly eyes, and it seemed Anne McCaffrey was irresistibly reminded of one of her characters whose name sounded a bit like...

She wasn't the first SF author to give us catlike aliens, but the ones in *Decision at Doona* have a certain memorable charm. This story also features a pesky and unspeakably irritating human brat who for some inscrutable reason is called Todd. Now read on...

More recently, Anne McCaffrey received two of SF's major life-achievement honours, the SF Writers of America Grand Master Award in 2005 and the Science Fiction Hall of Fame in 2006. A frequent convention guest, she was always voluble, generous, witty and hard-working, signing books for eager readers until her hand seized up with cramp. She kept on writing, and answering the fans' online messages, until the end. Her son and (latterly) collaborator Todd repeated her apology to an SF convention she wasn't well enough to attend: "Sorry that old age came up and bit me on the a**!" It bites us all in the end.

Somewhere in imaginative space, the cyborg spaceship Helva is singing a lament for the Dragon Lady.

David Langford found "The Wizard of Ozimov" online: see efanzines.com/Prolapse, issue 5.

• *SFX* #218, March 2012

Still Barmy

"After all, isn't science fiction supposed to be barmy?" wrote an *Independent* reviewer. Over at the *New Yorker*, "Science fiction is so inherently close to the absurd that the toughest challenge is not to lampoon it." Steve Jobs died and *Macleans* magazine explained that before Macs, "Computers were for geeks, science fiction enthusiasts and others even further beyond the pale."

Fantasy gets no more respect, especially when it's big on TV. Contemplating *Merlin*, the *Telegraph* wondered: "When did epic fantasy switch from being the nerdy stuff that the Dungeons & Dragons kids played at break time to something that is currently asking for consideration as serious television?" Maybe when it was made respectable by Sir Thomas Malory in 1485.

Clearly *A Game of Thrones* was too popular to be any good. Salman Rushdie sniffed: "It was garbage, yet very addictive garbage – because there's lots of violence, all the women take their clothes off all the time, and it's kind of fun. In the end, it's well-produced trash...' (*Haaretz.*) At the *New York Times*, one female pundit found it too depressing, like Tolkien and C.S. Lewis: "the same predictably doomed battles between factions – armies from the north, east, south, and west, clashing into the night." Another played the D&D card: "If you are not averse to the Dungeons & Dragons aesthetic, the series might be worth the effort." Asked whether the naughty bits were "historically accurate", *Esquire*'s sex columnist explained: "The *Game of Thrones* franchise has its hooves firmly dug into the genre known as 'fantasy', which [...] relies on supernatural phenomena as a primary element of plot, theme, or setting, and permits the creator to put in as many tits as he wants."

What would newspapers do without SF and fantasy, though? They're always pillaging the genre for similes. One political fellow resembles a hobbit (and so according to the *Indie* does George R.R. Martin), another is nicknamed Gollum, the *Guardian* describes Ken Livingstone and Boris Johnson as rivals for the role of Batman, John Redwood is a Vulcan like the chap journalists tend to call Dr Spock, and – in a hideous ethnic slur on *Doctor Who*'s chubbiest villains – any notably squat, corpulent Tory is dubbed a Sontaran. Which reminds me of the spine-chilling prophecy of political coalition in David Whitaker's 1965 novelization *Doctor Who and The Crusaders*: "No decision was more difficult for Susan or easier for her grandfather [the Doctor], who knew in his heart that she must share her future with David Cameron."

As in countless B-movies, the *News of the World* phone-hacking scandal erupted like "the moment when the monster, created in a secret laboratory, finally breaks free of any restraint and goes rampaging off amid a trail of mayhem." (*Sunday Telegraph*.) The embattled James Murdoch, by way of role model, once had "a life-sized cardboard cut-out of Darth Vader outside his office". (*Independent*.) World finance can be described only in terms of shuddering horror: "Enter a terrifying procession of ghouls. The US economy has started to stumble lethargically, as if bitten by a zombie. The eurozone countries, one by one, are being drained of lifeblood by a swift and merciless vampire." (*Financial Times*.)

The genre infection has even reached the *Evening Standard* beauty column. After a pricy eyelash treatment, it seems, "your lashes will darken and fatten and seem to multiply like triffids." Stumping around on their three little legs, inflicting cutely poisonous stings – we've all met people with eyelashes like that...

• *SFX* #219, April 2012

Hello, Lobachevsky

Once again Hollywood hosts an explosion of creative talent that stretches the bounds of imagination in its tireless quest for the perfect, lucrative lawsuit.

Because *Avatar* played such merry music on the cash register, the favourite legal target is James Cameron. Surely Harlan Ellison couldn't resist after successfully suing for use of his story ideas in *Terminator*? Instead, he irrepressibly went after the makers of *In Time* – apparently on the basis of reviews explaining that the plot has people's allotted time monitored and cut short by cruelly bureaucratic Timekeepers, as in *Logan's Run*. Sorry, I'll read that again... as in Ellison's even older "'Repent, Harlequin!' said the Ticktockman".

The legal crunch point came when our author actually saw the film for himself, said something not a million light-years from "Oops," and cancelled the lawsuit as suddenly as he'd launched it.

Meanwhile, to greedy eyes, *Avatar* seems a soft target because it's reminiscent of so much past SF. Poul Anderson's 1957 story "Call Me Joe" is a plausible influence, featuring a paraplegic whose personality is projected into a hunky artificial body to explore Jupiter, which he enjoys so much that he goes native. But wait – Anderson's story surely owes something to Clifford Simak's 1944 "Desertion", where explorers transformed into natives of Jupiter find their new bodies and senses so wonderful that they can't face being changed back to mere men.

Again, Cameron's theme of brutal colonial oppressors versus tree-hugging natives recalls many other works including Ursula Le Guin's "The Word for World is Forest". Something like *Avatar*'s Tree of Souls was an alien communications nexus in James Blish's *A Case of Conscience*. Unobtainium, variously spelt, is a jokey reference in several SF tales (see my *SFX* #194 column "Elementary, My Dear Watson") and features in the film *The Core*. Floating mountains sail the sky in Philip José Farmer's *The Lavalite World* and – of course – Roger Dean's iconic artwork. Dean himself complained that *Avatar* "had the look and feel of my work for sure. [...] It was like they had access to my DNA." Or maybe they had access to old Yes albums.

As the saying goes: steal from one source and it's plagiarism, but borrow little bits from all over and that's research. *Avatar* is full of basic SF mulch, traditional narrative elements (the writing-workshop term for clichés) that have percolated through dozens of stories. You can't copyright general ideas.

So now we're seeing a new approach by optimists seeking that legendary pot of gold at the lawsuit's end: James Cameron fiendishly stole their *unpublished* story which is exactly like the movie!

Allegedly he pinched *Avatar* from two screenplays by a chap called Bryant Moore, allegedly submitted to Cameron's Lightstorm Entertainment in 1994 and 2003. In December 2012 Moore sued Cameron and 20th Century Fox, asking $2.5 billion damages since "Cameron stole his idea for the movie..."

He's not alone. SF author Eric Ryder claims he worked for two years with Cameron on a film based on his own "KRZ 2068", with "striking similarities" to *Avatar*. He's suing too. So is Gerald Morawski, who just knows that *Avatar* is modelled on his pitch to Cameron for the unfilmed *Guardians of Eden*.

The great mystery is how, uninfluenced by such high concepts as heaps of money, three different people came up with the same scenario so that cunning devil James Cameron could pinch it from all of them.

David Langford likes the suit against Cowboys and Aliens by someone who used the theme in 1994. Little does he know that Howard Waldrop did it in 1987, perhaps homaging the 1950s magazine Space Western Comics...

• *SFX* #220, May 2012

Revenge of the Eyeballs

"The Eyeballs in the Sky!" That catchphrase from the late great Maurice Dodd's *Perishers* cartoon makes regular appearances in my SF newsletter when I record the peculiar things that fictional eyes get up to. Such as: "Marley's great, popping black eyes bounced around the room..." (James L. Swanson, *The Stuff That Dreams Are Made Of.*) "It was as though his eyes were two planets that had suddenly broken free from gravity and got whirled off – victims of centrifugal force." (R.L. Fanthorpe, *Out of the Darkness*.) Or, more moistly intimate, "I saw a pair of beautiful blue eyes caressing my face." (Jocelynn Drake, *Wait for Dusk*.)

This year the eyeballs, as it were, bit back. There's a horrific moment in Brian Aldiss's story "The Moment of Eclipse" where our hero's eyesight is slowly eclipsed from within. The culprit turns out to be a parasitic worm in his eye, a memory I wished I didn't have crawling through my head when the shadow started to grow in my own field of vision. It was a good time to panic.

"His eyes ran, literally, across the whole of the upper portion of his face..." (Richard Marsh, *The Beetle.*)

On Monday the dark patch in my right eye was merely worrying, on Tuesday the optician made soothing noises but sight seemed worse, on Wednesday the doctor was highly alarmed and referred me to our local hospital, and on Thursday the surgeon decided he'd better operate next day. By then the eclipse had expanded into central vision: I couldn't read with that eye any more. Grim thoughts followed, about Jorge Luis Borges, famous blind writer and librarian, and the characters based on him in Umberto Eco's *The Name of the Rose* and Gene Wolfe's *The Book of the New Sun*, book-lovers unable to see the page... It was a long, sleepless night before the operation.

"Everard finished a night's sleep and a breakfast which Deirdre's eyes had made miserable by standing on deck...' (Poul Anderson, *Guardians of Time*.)

So what's retina surgery under local anaesthetic like for the person behind the eyeball? In SF terms it's reminiscent of having an eye wired open as in the film of *A Clockwork Orange*, and being forced to watch all the bits of the famous *2001* light-show that landed on the cutting-room floor because they weren't pretty or psychedelic enough. *Readers:* "Stop! Stop! Too much information already!" NHS nurses, bless them, know how to deal with post-op trauma. They give you tea and buttered toast.

"Slowly his right eye lidded itself and then rolled back on a moist optic." (Frank Belknap Long, "Willie".) "The porcine little eyes widened just a bit and then settled elastically back to half-mast." (Jeff Somers, *The Electric Church*.)

Successful operation, the surgeon said at once, but it took me a while to bounce elastically back. For cunning therapeutic reasons they put a big bubble of gas in your eye – sulphur hexafluoride, who'd have guessed? The resulting Bionic Langford couldn't actually see much until that slowly dissolving bubble had shrunk a lot.

"The woman took her eyes from him languorously and placed them, in a delicate fashion, on Mosely." (Jane Jensen, *Sins of the Fathers*.) "...abandoned buildings where the homeless hide and hungry eyes that will take your cigarettes and your wallet." (Joseph S. Pulver, "To Live and Die in Arkham".)

Maybe I should queasily stop collecting those eyeball quotes. Or maybe, now I'm almost back to normal, I won't.

David Langford is hugely grateful to the eye departments at the Royal Berks Hospital (Reading) and Edward VII Hospital (Windsor).

• *SFX* #221, June 2012

Round Number

I may be one of the oldest inhabitants of this magazine, but I bet you never realized I'm staring three hundred in the face. Unless the vast Langford publishing operation is wiped out by a well-judged meteor impact on Reading, July 2012 sees the 300th issue of my vile SF gossip-sheet *Ansible*. Would that round number be a good place to stop?

If I drove a stake through my accursed creation's heart and buried it in an unmarked grave, I could say goodbye to formatting long boring award listings... the Hugo shortlist now has sixteen categories with five or more nominees in each. Even more heart-warming would be a rest from writing short but painful obituaries. In the early months of 2012 *Ansible* ran over sixty of these, including venerable authors John Christopher (remember the TV version of his *Tripods* series?) and Russell Hoban, plus game designer M.A.R. Barker and artists Jean "Moebius" Giraud, Ralph McQuarrie of *Star Wars* fame and Darrell K. Sweet. All very gloom-inducing.

Some good news for a change, if you like World SF Conventions: because no rival bid emerged by the March deadline, the London Worldcon bid for 2014 is unopposed and doomed to succeed. See www.londonin2014.org. Unless London is wiped out by a well-judged meteor impact, we should be having another UK Worldcon. I'll be in the bar.

Meanwhile, the sillier *Ansible* departments also cheer me up. Some newspaper hack always has a new sneer at genre fiction, like this horrified *Guardian* summary of the ebook market: "Sci-fi and self-help. Even paranormal romance, where vampires seduce virgins and elves bonk trolls." Other tasty stories of strange bedfellows include a recent *Financial Times* piece that tantalizingly began: "Harry Potter and Viagra have more in common than you may imagine." Ever since I quoted Margaret Atwood explaining that *Oryx and Crake*, her future-dystopian novel of rampant genetic engineering, isn't nasty old SF because it contains no "talking squids in outer space", we've had regular talking-squid sightings, and this major SF theme (though not yet an *SF*

Encyclopedia entry) acquired its own website at: talkingsquidsinouterspace.com.

Authors grumble entertainingly, like Terry Pratchett reporting his fanmail during the Harry Potter boom: "Did you get the name Hogswatch from Hogwarts?" Terry: "I'm inclined to say yes." He also invented a specialist *Ansible* acronym often found in his email: NFA,YB. This stands for "Not For *Ansible*, You Bastard." It became such a well-used synonym for the regular fannish DNQ (Do Not Quote) that on one surreal occasion I found myself writing in deadly confidence: "Terry, this is NFA,YB..."

Where are the bastards of yesteryear? Long ago I got into copious hot water for quoting the Major SF Author who'd ranted, "Not only did that bastard Kubrick fire me, he hired my enemy to adapt my story!" – my lips are still sealed, but Google knows all. But there was no problem with William Gibson's uninhibited description of rude bits censored from his *Count Zero* magazine serial: "a special Lite version with reduced *motherfucker*-count and no graphic but intensely poetic and moving descriptions of oral sex. 'At IASFM,' I was told, 'you can't come in anybody's mouth.'" If I published *that* today, *Ansible*'s email edition would be blocked by the net-nanny filters that tag "bastards" as Pornographic Language. Pornography, I feel, should be made of sterner stuff.

Then there's the thrill of recognition. Hugo awards are exciting enough (*Ansible* has won six), but I was gobsmacked by email from the *Big Brother* 2012 organizers, urging my readers to volunteer for in-house humiliation. Because BB is "keen to represent all aspects of society" and make equal fun of us all, even the talking squid in outer space.

It is a proud and lonely thing to run an SF newsletter.

David Langford suspects he has to keep going, or the subscribers expecting paper copies way beyond issue 300 may band together and kill him.

• *SFX* #222, July 2012

Puppies & Ray-Guns

The SF award season traditionally kicks off with grumbling about the lame-brained judges who picked the wrong books for the latest Arthur C. Clarke Award shortlist. This year was no exception. In a fiery blog post, Christopher Priest lambasted not only the administrator and jury – calling for them all to resign – but the shortlisted novels, including China Miéville's *Embassytown* and Charles Stross's *Rule 34*. Stross, he said grumpily, "writes like an internet puppy". Charlie rushed to design an Internet Puppy t-shirt.

Cries of outrage filled the SF blogosphere, and the mini-controversy even got into the *Guardian*. Some responses were heavily sarcastic about the Clarke shortlist's conspicuous failure to include *The Islanders* by Chris Priest.

If there's truly no such thing as bad publicity, the Clarke Award had a major boost. At the UK national convention over Easter it remained a hot talking-point. The Stross t-shirt (INTERNET PUPPY NO CAN HAZ NOMS) was widely admired. Pundits expected a backlash against Chris Priest, since *The Islanders* was also nominated in that weekend's British SF Association Awards. Would there be a come-uppance? Who would rid us of this turbulent Priest?

The BSFA Award ceremony was memorable, not entirely in a good way. Nominees got front-row seating, where I fretted about the possibility that the *SF Encyclopedia* (now 3.5 million words and just shortlisted for the Hugo) could lose Best Nonfiction to a blog post. Other contenders – for novel, short fiction and artwork – were equally jittery. At least the suspense would soon be over...

Oh no it wouldn't! MC John Meaney opened the show with a stand-up comedy routine. He's a very good novelist, but perhaps not the greatest of comedians; his string of fannish in-jokes, with weird PowerPoint slides, baffled some audience members and enraged others. As I deafly tried to follow increasingly non-PC gags about leprechauns, "babes in SF", hot female authors with smashing looks, and mysterious likening of the heavily bearded Charlie Stross to Osama bin Laden, a

Twitter storm brewed in the dark hall behind. Phrases like "hideous trainwreck" and "Walkout now in progress" were freely bandied.

That now legendary MC performance went on for some forty minutes. Adam Roberts, a best-novel nominee, tweeted from the front row: "When this speech started I was a 46-year old man in reasonable health. I'm now 85 and clinging to life."

Recriminations continued for days. Again the blogosphere became the gibbersphere. A BSFA committee member resigned. The BSFA apologized. John Meaney sort of apologized. Even *Publishers Weekly* took notice. We lived in interesting times.

From my hugely biased point of view, the ceremony ended pretty well. For one thing, the introduction had stopped. This year's BSFA trophies were plastic ray-gun outlines on bases made (don't ask me why) from tatty old SF paperbacks bolted together. The *SF Encyclopedia* won for non-fiction, Dominic Harman for art, Paul Cornell of *Doctor Who* fame for short story (his ray-gun was purple, surely not a comment on his prose)... and, defying all the predictions that he'd shot himself in the foot with his Clarke Award tirade, Chris Priest took the novel prize with *The Islanders*.

Riffing on his advice to the Clarke jury, he told the massed voters: "I suppose you all have to resign now." Then he peered at the underside of his ray-gun trophy and pretended to discover it was "Made for China... oh, Made in China." Rival nominee China Miéville wasn't available for comment, but it got a deplorably good laugh anyway. Naughty Chris.

David Langford was caught on camera pointing the Encyclopedia's death ray at Charlie Stross. Accidentally, he claims.

• *SFX* #223, Summer 2012

Poirot into Space

One of my guilty pleasures, when I need a rest from SF, is reading old detective stories. Sometimes, though, even these contain science-fictional bits. Sherlock Holmes himself meets weird science in "The Adventure of the Creeping Man" – investigating a chap who's hoping for rejuvenation through monkey glands (this was a popular fad of the 1920s) and is influenced to behave in strange ways which might be termed monkey business. "Oook, my dear Watson."

An early Agatha Christie novel, *The Big Four*, sees her regular detective Hercule Poirot battling an international cabal that plans to conquer the world. One of the Four, a French radiation scientist suspiciously reminiscent of Marie Curie gone bad, invents a death ray that wrecks US warships. Another is an evil Chinese genius all too obviously based on Sax Rohmer's Doctor Fu-Manchu. Needless to say, this gang is no match for Poirot's little grey cells, but it was a distinctly offbeat episode of his career.

Near the end of her own career, 43 years later, Agatha Christie invented another world-threatening conspiracy in *Passenger to Frankfurt*. Here the revived Hitler Youth cause widespread chaos but will be defeated (some time after the book ends) by a great scientist's "Project Benvo", aimed to produce a designer drug that makes everyone benevolent and nonviolent. Blimey. This idea of chemically induced nonaggression also features in Michael Innes's thriller *Operation Pax*, where it's treated as a horrific Thing With Which Man Should Not Meddle. Quite right too.

Leslie Charteris injected SF into several stories about his roguish hero the Saint – such as *The Last Hero*, with a nasty "electron-cloud" weapon created by a genuinely mad scientist who gets his just reward: "I shot him like a mad dog." Later Saint adventures feature zombies, giant ants, the Loch Ness Monster, and some very strange inventions... though none as implausible as the antigravity device that doesn't fit at all well into Mickey Spillane's raunchy thriller with the double-entendre title, *The Erection Set*.

Margery Allingham's *The Mind Readers* introduced her long-running sleuth Albert Campion to a genuine telepathy machine invented by schoolkids, using the newly discovered element nipponanium. The really prophetic part involves trawling classmates' minds for exam answers, anticipating the modern tradition of copying your homework from Wikipedia. More telepathic children – whose powers are here the side-effect of a kind of sleeping sickness – baffle Peter Dickinson's hard-headed series policeman Jimmy Pibble in *Sleep and His Brother*. These SF themes creep in everywhere.

Much more common in crime fiction is a touch of the supernatural. Ernest Bramah's blind detective Max Carrados meets a tasty example in "The Strange Case of Cyril Bycourt", where the unfortunate young Cyril is driven half mad by gruesome recurring nightmares of the Black Death – eventually traced by Carrados to the (then) new-fangled electric wiring which carries bad vibes from a generator built over an old plague-burial pit.

John Dickson Carr specialized in impossible crimes, usually committed in locked, sealed rooms. Often it seemed that vampires or other occult forces were the only explanation – until Carr's vastly corpulent detective Gideon Fell (based on G.K. Chesterton of Father Brown fame) explained how the trick was done. But there's one unforgettable Carr mystery, *The Burning Court*, in which after strong hints of witchcraft the impossible murder is duly explained away – whereupon a chilling final chapter breaks the rules of classic detective fiction by revealing that it was $SPOILER all along...

David Langford gazed at the reader through half-closed eyes: "You see, Watson, but you do not observe. You know my methods. Apply them."

• *SFX* #224, August 2012

The Martian Chronicler

Long ago the ABC of international SF fame began Asimov, Bradbury, Clarke. Now they're all gone: Ray Bradbury seemed set to carry on forever but died this June, aged 91. Everyone, from lowly fans to the President of the USA, paid loving tribute. I met Bradbury only once, at a party thrown for him on a rare London visit, and have no scandalous anecdotes – just memories of a nice guy who was patient with his admirers.

The book he's most remembered for is *Fahrenheit 451* (1953), set in a dystopian future America where the problem of dangerous ideas is solved by destroying books. "A book is a loaded gun in the house next door. Burn it. Take the shot from the weapon." The fireman hero tracks down and torches illegal book stashes... until he too becomes an enemy of the system, pursued by the fire department's nightmarish Mechanical Hound. Ironically, this passionate cry against censorship was sometimes banned in US schools by literal-minded loons who assumed that if you write about Bibles being burned you must approve of it. *Fahrenheit 451* was filmed in 1966 by François Truffaut.

After early years as a fan – he published his own fanzine in 1939 – Bradbury began his writing career in the early 1940s with sales to magazines like *Astounding SF*, *Super Science Stories* and *Weird Tales*. He had a flair for the weird and gruesome, usually in nostalgic small-town American settings. Horrid things happen during Halloween party games in the dark ("Then... some idiot turned on the lights"), a man whose skeleton is devoured remains blobbily alive, and the murderous infant of "The Small Assassin" bumps off both his parents at the age of four months. Evocative collection titles include *Dark Carnival*, *The October Country* – commemorating his favourite season – and *Dandelion Wine*.

Readers who never grew up in Bradbury's small towns still felt the nostalgia. Somehow he lent you a chunk of his own childhood and made you feel you'd been there too.

His straight SF included the classic time-travel safari story "A Sound of Thunder". The big-game hunter shoots a tyrannosaurus that was doomed to die anyway, but ruinously changes history by stepping on a butterfly. Somehow one can't help suspecting that the Butterfly Effect in chaos theory was named by someone who remembered Bradbury... He could grab you with a single word. A blistering spaceship voyage "South" to touch the solar photosphere ends with the relieved captain setting his course for cooler realms and savouring the word "North." A foghorn lures an amorous sea monster in "The Fog Horn". In "The Veldt", an early tale of virtual reality gone bad, even unreal lions have fur with a "dusty upholstery smell".

Many Bradbury SF stories were flavoured with what hadn't yet been called magic realism – especially the sequence about a strange, fairy-tale Mars that was assembled as *The Martian Chronicles* (1950) and retitled *The Silver Locusts* in Britain. Despite rocket ships (whose takeoff blast brings a brief "rocket summer" to wintry Ohio), glass cities and shapeshifting Martians, this Mars is steeped in American myth. One expedition is ensnared by a simulated folksy homecoming. The final story hauntingly introduces a colonist family to the natives: their own reflections in a canal. They are the Martians now.

Just about all Bradbury's best genre fiction was written before 1960. He'd long been selling to upmarket magazines besides the pulps, and surprised SF fans with collections including stories about Picasso on the beach or, in "The Fruit at the Bottom of the Bowl", a murderer obsessively wiping away evidence – two more that aren't easily forgotten.

Read his early work. Remember him.

David Langford strenuously denies having scrumped the golden apples of the sun.

• *SFX* #225, September 2012

Jobsworth

Many people are deplorably fascinated by the Australian Poo Machine. Formally known as the Cloaca Professional, this contraption demonstrates what happens to food as it gurgles and peristalses through our digestive systems – from beginning to gooey, smelly end, in strict chronological ordure. I can't reveal which regular column artist begged to illustrate this. Nor which *SFX* editor mused poetically, "Close encounters of the turd kind."

Of course this is relevant to SF. The genre's most sensitive treatment of such end-products must be *The Dark Light Years* by Brian Aldiss, offering the striking definition "Civilization is the distance man has placed between himself and his excreta." In the book, clean-limbed astronauts who believe this maxim are horrified by the alien utods who live far more natural, organic lives – closer to the night soil, you might say – and whose spaceships are veritable poo machines. Things end badly for the utods, who may be peaceful and unthreatening, but... well, yuck.

Iain M. Banks's space opera *Consider Phlebas* opens with the hero about to drown in a rising, malodorous tide of sewage generated by revellers at a lavish banquet given in his honour. James Tiptree's "The Night-Blooming Saurian" features time travel to the dinosaur era, with a special emphasis on coprolites – not the usual fossils but messily fresh specimens. A Piers Anthony story regrettably titled "Up Schist Crick" climaxes with the dilemma of a chap who needs very urgently indeed to take a massive dump but is wearing a kind of skin-tight superhero costume and doesn't know how to take it off. Who said SF fails to address major contemporary issues?

Another such issue is where to locate the training ground for chaos wizards who must practice hurling devastating firebolts. L.E. Modesitt has a cunning answer in his fantasy *The White Order*: apprentice mages are assigned to sewer-cleaning duty, vaporizing revolting blockages while trying not to choke on the stench. Skilled operatives in Barry N. Malzberg's SF novel *The Men Inside* are miniaturized to perform approximately the same task within the natural sewage system of the human intestine, a job description best not contemplated. Returning to fantasy, kids obsessed with Number Twos – like Sam Vimes's precocious son in Terry Pratchett's *Snuff* – have long wondered about *The House at Pooh Corner*, and adults agree that the spinoff *Cooking with Pooh* is the worst cookbook title since James Beard's *Beard on Pasta*.

In Robertson Davies's semi-fantasy *The Cornish Trilogy*, there's a professor who spends his life studying the fascinating internal structure of human stools; even his eventual Nobel Prize hardly compensates for being called the Turd-Skinner. T.H. White's *The Sword in the Stone* introduces the wandering knight King Pellinore who's obsessed with his pursuit of the Questing Beast and always carries samples of this creature's fewmets or droppings to show his friends: "Yes, these are her fewmets." "Interestin' fewmets."

Thus reading T.H. White's Arthurian fantasy explains a warning letter from the Gandalf character in that notorious Tolkien parody, *Bored of the Rings*: "The halberd has fallen! The fewmets have hit the windmill!" Which reminds me that Roger Zelazny's *Lord of Light* – for the most part a fine serious SF novel – introduces a Hindu dignitary called the Shan of Irabek whose mind gets transferred into an epileptic body, all to set up the line: "Then the fit hit the Shan." Some readers never forgave the author.

A final classic of excretory SF is Damon Knight's "The Big Pat Boom", whose visiting aliens offer good money for ordinary cowpats. Instantly a school of cowflop connoisseurship springs up, with artistic Earthlings classifying the natural treasures as queen and even emperor pats (the emperor has a double whorl) and reverently hanging framed specimens over the mantelpiece. Why are those aliens laughing?

David Langford remembers that Pratchett's Vimes had such a deprived childhood that he had to play Poohsticks (invented by A.A. Milne) with real poo.

• *SFX* #226, October 2012

118

The Long Haul

Three point four million words in February. Three point five million in May. Three point six in July. The online *SF Encyclopedia* crawls along towards its four-million-word goal, and meanwhile my home-made spell checker keeps complaining about listings of online books from Project Guttenberg. Or Gutenburg. Reasons of state forbid me to name the contributor who never gets Gutenberg right.

Another of our little helpers has been cribbing his homework. My amazing psi powers can deduce this from the internal Wikipedia links that accidentally didn't get removed. Naughty, naughty!

One Wikipedia idea we actually wanted to steal was a "What links here" list of incoming links for each entry. Too difficult and expensive, according to the *SFE* website designers, so I've written my own script for it – plus a random-entry lucky dip – and am eagerly waiting for these to be installed. *[They're now in place.]*

Project Gubenberg? There's a novelty.

Some of our 13,200 entries (at the time of writing) don't appear in the website's headword lists because they start with funny characters like the ligatured Æ. Finding these is a challenge. Think of them as Easter eggs.

Other peculiar characters lurk in the alleyways. John W. Campbell, editor of *Analog* magazine, invented a special new mathematical symbol ⌢→ for the cover logo, and I had to fudge up a suitable graphic with CorelDraw. Greek crept in when our music expert insisted on mentioning that the SF band Yacht also spelt its name in caps with a Greek delta for the A. The Iceland article infested us with thorns and eths, Þ and ð. An entry for an Egyptian author came with elaborate colour-coding to show which letters should have dots underneath them (which even the learned contributor couldn't manage to insert). But this forces horrible font substitutions in web browsers, too hideously ugly to use: after laboriously working out how to put the bloody dots in I had to remove them again.

My favourite site bug of all is known to insiders as the Hidden

Peril. For weird miscoding reasons, every book title in the author bibliographies containing the word Hidden – such as good old Charlie Stross's *The Hidden Family* – was, in fact, hidden. A blank space in the checklist, followed by the place, publisher and date for this apparently untitled book. How we all laughed! I devised a fix at the cost of many treasured brain cells, but still have to keep watching for this problem. *[Much later: It's gone! At last it's gone!]*

Next: Project Guternberg. Nearly missed that one.

Fortunately we get feedback from our loyal readers, mostly asking why some all-fantasy author – Robert Jordan is the fave rave – doesn't appear in what's supposed to be an encyclopedia of *science fiction*. Others clamour for an entry about their own important selves on the strength of a short-story sale or a self-published ebook. A very few are strangely annoyed to have been included. For me, the most sobering feedback came from an author once famous for tribbles: "I am told that David Langford is one of the most unpopular people in the SF community." I think he didn't like his entry.

On the upside, the editors are madly pleased that despite being a "beta" version still in progress, the new *SFE* has won awards – including the European SF Award as "Best Promoter" of SF. Now we feel like carnival barkers wheedling suspicious punters into the stripy SF tent with grandiose promises about the attractions within... "Ladies and gennelmen, we offer the only genuine stuffed Asimov, Heinlein, Verne and Wells in captivity! Thrill to the hidden mysteries of Time, Space, Fandom, Kipple and Postmodernism! See Women in SF fully exposed! Marvel at the rare Unobtainium! This way to the Egress!"

Onward, towards 3.7 million words and no rest in sight. Dearie me, now our chap has spelt it Project GutenBorg. Resistance is futile. You will be assimilated into the public domain...

David Langford knows that with great power there must also come great irresponsibility.

Later: 3.7 million words in September 2012. 3.8 million in November. 3.9 million in December, 4 million in January 2013, 5 million in November 2015...

• *SFX* #227, November 2012

Forty-Two Boxes

Written for a tiny booklet celebrating Novacon 42 – the forty-second instance of Britain's second regular SF convention, first held in 1971.

To wallow in the utterly bleeding obvious, we're talking about a number made famous by a bestselling genre author. Rule 42, "All persons more than a mile high to leave the court", inspired the 1980 fanzine *Rule 42* from that very very tall UK fan Chris Hughes. Not a lot of people known that. But Rule 42 is also "No one shall speak to the Man at the Helm" (borrowed in vain for the 1993 Eastercon newsletter where I was at the helm). It depends whether your source is *Alice's Adventures in Wonderland* or *The Hunting of the Snark*. One hapless seafarer's lost luggage in the latter epic comprises "forty-two boxes, all carefully packed". (With his name painted clearly on each: / But, since he omitted to mention the fact, / They were all left behind on the beach.) In short, Lewis Carroll was strangely fond of the number 42, having perhaps calculated that it was an interestingly ordinary, even boring pair of digits that worked well in comedy. As we so often wrote in *Encyclopedia of Fantasy* theme entries when memory failed and not a single additional instance came to mind: further examples abound.

113 years after *Alice*, some chap called Adams adopted the number for his best-loved gag. The rest is history. Arcturan Megahistory.

• *The Little Book of 42s*, November 2012

Stainless Steel Harry

Harry Harrison, creator of those immortal SF characters Bill the Galactic Hero and the Stainless Steel Rat, died in August. Newspaper obituaries covered the merely routine facts: his background in comics, his notable steampunk novel *A Transatlantic Tunnel, Hurrah!* published 15 years before the word "steampunk" was coined, his overpopulation novel *Make Room!, Make Room!* (filmed almost unrecognizably as *Soylent Green*, his lifelong fondness for exclamation marks...

Harry had been a larger-than-life presence on the SF convention scene since long before I discovered conventions. He and Brian Aldiss, a notorious double act, had a mysterious habit of hurling (literal) pork pies – one of the strange rites of past fandom.

Conversation with Harry was exhausting and racked you with involuntary spasms of laughter. He seemed to be in permanent fast-forward mode. Critic Peter Nicholls described the effect as "a series of animal imitations interspersed with your actual articulate words, cunningly strung together so as to tease you into thinking you're almost understanding him." Perhaps there was some Esperanto in there; Harry loved the artificial language and used it liberally in SF adventures like *Deathworld II*.

"Frenetic" was always a favourite word. "That book was so GODDAM frenetic!" he said to me about his raucous E.E. Smith parody *Star Smashers of the Galaxy Rangers*. Women got short shrift in the primitive SF series he was sending up, and his final chapter ("Victory Wrenched from the Salivating Jaws of Defeat!") saw two of the male leads locked in a passionate embrace. You couldn't get away with that in the austere 1950s regime at *Astounding SF* magazine, where Harry's interstellar con-man Slippery Jim DiGriz (alias the Stainless Steel Rat) made his debonair debut.

Editors were an *[expletive deleted]* or at least a trial. Once Harry had a tough hero call another character "so young that he still had the mark of the pot on his bottom." A prim American SF magazine changed this to "...still had milk around his mouth from the nursing bottle." In the

UK reprint, perhaps subbed by Mary Whitehouse: "...still had his mouth puckered from his baby bottle." The austere US book version: "...still had diaper rash." It wasn't easy, in those days, to be a potty-mouthed SF author.

At one British convention of fond memory, several chatting SF writers realized with increasing alarm that *none of them had read* various major SF novels like Heinlein's *Stranger in a Strange Land* which they were expected (and indeed accustomed) to pontificate about. What about *Dune?* Harry, exuberantly: "I've never read that lousy thing either." After a few more embarrassing admissions he summed up: "Listen you sods, don't let the fans know! We're supposed to be experts!"

Once upon a time, Harry the practical joker caught me hopping. I was making my way to the first World Fantasy Convention held in London, and saw him waving frantically – even frenetically – from a bistro across the road. Having bought me a drink and squeezed me in at his crowded table, he gleefully introduced me to someone I'd never met but whose prose and vocabulary I'd criticized mercilessly. "I read your review of me," said an expressionless Stephen R. Donaldson. Everything went black and I don't remember any more. Thanks a bunch, Harry.

Now it's goodbye to one of the most energetic people in the SF community. (At the Eastercon where he was guest of honour, attendees were challenged to identify various "Secret Masters of Fandom": Harry was naturally the Secret Master of Dynamism.) Raise a glass of one of Slippery Jim's powerfully unhealthy tipples, such as Old Syrian Panther Sweat...

• *SFX* #228, December 2012

Fifty Shades of Thog

They've tinkered with the Hugo Award rules again. At this year's World SF Convention the definition of Semiprozine – that mysterious halfway house between fanzines done for love and commercial SF magazines – was tweaked to exclude publications with full-time paid staff. Which means the major newsletter *Locus*, with 22 Semiprozine Hugos, is no longer eligible in what they call the "Locus category". Meanwhile the first Hugo for Fancast (fan podcast) was presented, while a proposed Young Adult Fiction award got voted down, partly because YA stories including a Harry Potter novel have already won Hugos without needing a special sandbox of their own.

Amid the frenzy to create as many Hugo categories as possible for good writing, the awards neglect much-loved badness. But the Worldcon had a traditional panel discussion on bad prose, numbing listeners with excruciating snippets of ineptitude, and I was filled with quiet pride to hear from a survivor that the selections were dominated by my own showcase of grot, Thog's Masterclass.

Since the Hugo administrators aren't interested, here are the Thoggo Award winners and some runners-up from recent Masterclasses.

Most Striking Simile. "He picked up his coat from the back of the sofa and moved to the door, feeling distinctly like an ambulant and green soft fruit." (Keith McCarthy, *The Silent Sleep of the Dying.*) "The silence between them was as audible as the twang of an overstrained rope." (Barbara Hambly, *The Ladies of Mandrigyn.*) "The question hung there like an invisible cloud of flatulence." (Neal Stephenson, *Reamde.*) "...the denatured alcohol corroded its way through my GI tract, not stopping until it reached the basement, where my tailbone and testicles resided like an old croquet set." (Joseph Gangemi, *Inamorata.*)

Best Anatomical Peculiarities. "He is forty years old, with a black beard shaped like a spade, a lawyer and a judge..." (Jo Walton, *Lifelode.*) "Shirley's eyes were fixed respectfully on her knees." (J.K. Rowling, *The Casual Vacancy.*) "Her eyes were like a condor's, or some worse star-spawned bird of prey, crimson edged and bleeding into blank holes at the center that seemed to be pinpoint windows into her diseased soul. Kullervo thought he saw *things* crawling around behind those windows." (Emil Petaja, *Tramontane*.)

Best Use of "Literally". "She literally flowed with stories and spunk." (Brad Torgersen, "Outbound".)

Best Scientific Units. "Carlyon, like all Martians, a brown-skinned giant of six hectares high..." (Bengo Mistral, *Pirates of Cerebus*.)

Best Hangover. "Liam gave up trying to scrub his brain awake through his scalp." (Dana Stabenow, "On the Evidence".)

Neatest Tricks. "Her mind boiled coldly." (Felicity Savage, *Humility Garden*.) "Her supple arms drooped to the floor and encircled the lamp overhead. Then her long legs joined in." (Pavel Kohout, *The Widow Killer*.) "My hands are already dirty just from setting foot on this planet." (Brian Herbert and Kevin J. Anderson, *Hellhole*.)

Best Feral Eyes. "...abandoned buildings where the homeless hide and hungry eyes that will take your cigarettes and your wallet." (Joseph S. Pulver Sr, "To Live and Die in Arkham".)

Magical Mystery Metaphors. "Jimmy looked over Nadine's head at Annabeth and Sara, felt all three of them blow through his chest, fill him up, and turn him to dust at the same time..." (Dennis Lehane, *Mystic River*.) "I had too much altar boy in me to seize the bitch goddess of success by her ponytail and bugger the Zeitgeist with my throbbing baguette." (James Walcott, *Lucking Out*.)

My Worldcon panel mole added that the only quoted mainstream fiction to approach Thog for sheer awfulness was, interestingly enough, *Fifty Shades of Grey*. Why isn't Thog a runaway bestseller?

David Langford has the only authentic portrait of Thog at thog.org.

• *SFX* #229, January 2013

More Rotten Cabbages

Tell me the old, old story: SF is still the genre that pundits I've never heard of love to hate. "*Doctor Who* is the most dreary thing," whinged TV presenter Fern Britton on *Room 101*: "I hate sci-fi as it's not real and all these people who are fans think it's real and it's some sort of religion to them." An *Independent* columnist chimed in about *Doctor Who*: "It's over-complicated, over-hyped and it has taken over. It is the McDonald's of telly – all franchise, fries and barely-met expectations. And you can stick that sonic screwdriver in your black hole."

Some folk simply can't stand alien monikers, as in *John Carter*: "I wouldn't trust the sanity of any critic who claimed to understand what goes on in this movie... I haven't any idea of how Burroughs's gibberish should have been adapted. The Therns, the Tharks, Dejah Thoris? You can't speak the names aloud without sounding like Daffy Duck.'" (*New Yorker.*)

David Quantick prefers crime fiction, declaring that "SF is also geeky because it's like a geek – it can't do relationships, its sex is all fantasy and it can build a warp engine but it can't make a cake." (*Guardian.*) Crime author Stuart MacBride nervously calls his SF venture a "near-future thriller" for fear of readers screaming "SCIENCE FICTION!!! RUN AWAY!!!... There's something about a book set in the future that makes them think of aliens, space ships, and pasty teenagers living in their parents' basements...'"

On this vexed topic, it's well known that the Journalists' Code insists that all *Red Dwarf X* reviews must mention its "obsessive fan base, which stereotype would suggest is mainly men in their thirties and forties with a penchant for sci-fi and gaming – see how I'm subtly avoiding the provocative words 'nerd', 'geek' or 'unsuccessful with women' here?" (*Telegraph.*)

Even good SF can't be literature: "Iain M. Banks's novel *Use of Weapons* has a narrative structure that, if it were not a work of science fiction, would qualify it as the most 'literary' of literary fiction." (*Guardian.*) "Lots of its authors, and a slew of its readers, like to think that science fiction sails on the ocean of science, but mostly it just paddles in the shallows of literature.' (*Weekly Standard.*) The real objection is that it shamelessly wallows in the gutters of popularity.

Thus another *Guardian* hack's horror at ebook sales figures: "Kindle-owning bibliophiles are furtive beasts. Their shelves still boast classics and Booker winners. But inside that plastic case, other things lurk. Sci-fi and self-help. Even paranormal romance, where vampires seduce virgins and elves bonk trolls."

Also, just to drive a last nail into the coffin, ebook fans are cheapskates: "... in certain genres (romance, science fiction and fantasy) formerly relegated to the moribund mass-market paperback, readers care not a whit about cover design or even good writing... they just want their fix at the lowest possible price..." (*The Nation.*)

Even SF-loving Nobel prizewinner Paul Krugman plays safe when introducing Asimov's *Foundation* trilogy: "...it's not exactly science fiction – not really. Yes, it's set in the future, there's interstellar travel, people shoot each other with blasters instead of pistols and so on. But these are superficial details..."

Finally, the co-founder of PayPal reckons SF ain't what it used to be: "The anthology of the top twenty-five sci-fi stories in 1970 was, like, 'Me and my friend the robot went for a walk on the moon,' and in 2008 it was, like, 'The galaxy is run by a fundamentalist Islamic confederacy and there are people who are hunting planets and killing them for fun.'" (*New Yorker.*) Why don't I recognize either of those anthologies?

David Langford was quite enjoying A.A. Gill's collected TV reviews until he reached the line "...people who don't like or understand literature read science fiction."

• *SFX* #230, February 2013

Found Poetry

When I started reviewing SF for the Sunday Telegraph magazine in 2011, I naturally hoped for fame and immortality, if not the occasional hundred quid in used notes clipped to page 94 of a review copy. That was Brian Aldiss's helpful Booker Prize tip when he was a judge back in 1981. Current Booker hopefuls should allow for inflation.

For me, major payola so far has been confined to the outsize goodie box containing Cherie Priest's novel *Boneshaker*. Amid a mass of straw, this book came tied up in a double length of white string with a couple of attached bracelet-charms shaped like little bronze scissors. A rummage through the straw revealed nine more charms with a clock-face design, some black iron nuts and bolts, because it's steampunk, and a welcome miniature of gin with a custom label suggesting it came from some entirely different promotion. Who can fathom the minds of publicity people?

This arcane assembly of found objects, all intensely symbolic of something or other, looked as though it ought to be an installation at Tate Modern; and maybe it is. Nevertheless the ploy worked. As a helpless mind slave manipulated by the PR masters of surrealism and subterfuge, I just mentioned the book. The same happened twenty years ago when David Wingrove's Chinese SF epic *Chung Kuo* was launched at a convention with a deluge of promotional fortune cookies containing such uncannily accurate predictions as: "You will report this in your newsletter, Langford, or else."

Somehow my first year reviewing for the *Telegraph* seems very short, maybe because so are the reviews. With only a shade over 50 words allowed per book, it makes the cruel space limits of *SFX* review pages seem vast and cavernous. Then, after all that reading and note-taking to produce a few jewelled sentences, there's the risk that your critique will be vetoed...

When this first happened to me, I was trying to plug Lavie Tidhar's splendid alternate history *Osama* (which later won the World Fantasy Award). No, no, came the stern reply from *Telegraph* HQ, you reviewed that last year. What? Had I fallen prey to the dread occupational disease of amnesia? Actually it was covered by the chap who wrote the column just before I took over, but I still had to do a different book. Then came Yrsa Sigurdardottir's *I Remember You*, surely the finest police-procedural supernatural thriller set in Iceland that I'd read in whole weeks... No: although it contains real ghosts the paper's crime reviewer had bagged that one. Find something else quickly, Langford.

Nearest to hand was a new collection of SF poetry, *Where Rockets Burn Through* edited by Russell Jones. Little did I know that the fickle finger of fate, loosely attached to the long arm of coincidence, was steering me to a mindboggling discovery. On my first random riffle through this volume I found a oddly laid-out prose poem titled "Torn Page from a Chapter on Ray Guns", by Jon Stone. It invoked such high-flown poetic concepts as Isaac Asimov, Stephen Baxter, Arthur C. Clarke, death rays and Robert A. Heinlein. Though fragmentary, the text contained phrase after phrase of exquisitely haunting familiarity...

Indeed, it was all me. I'd become a found object, like an interesting stone or naughtily shaped length of driftwood made into an art installation. The whole poem was "appropriated", as artists like to say, from my column "Ray Guns Forever" in *SFX* #172 from August 2008. This is my ticket to poetic immortality. Or it would have been if the chap whose name is on it had credited his source.

David Langford was soothed by a graceful apology from Jon Stone, who normally gives credit for his depredations but just this once forgot.

• *SFX* #231, March 2013

Podmania

April is the cruellest month, said a poet who was uncannily aware that I'm undergoing one of those fearsome round-numbered birthdays in April 2013. It wouldn't be so grim if, as promised in all the best SF when I was a lad, the occasion were marked by getting a free jetpack pass.

Thanks to the joys of magazine publishing schedules I'm writing in December 2012. (Sudden memories of the A.A. Milne skit for *Punch* magazine in which author and editor thrash out the details of a snow-covered, holly-wreathed, robin-infested story oozing with Yuletide sentimentality like an overstuffed mince pie. Editor's parting words: "Rotten weather for August, isn't it?") It's been a hell of a year.

I've already banged on about the online *SF Encyclopedia*, which hit 3.8 million words in November and seems on course for 3.9 million by the New Year. This has been driving me mad for so long that I only dimly remember what sanity was like. The trouble is that I've somehow painted myself into a corner of total power whereby all new and updated *SFE* entries are plugged into the master text by me, after which the chore of website uploading is passed to skilled technical staff consisting of, well, me. Nearly 1100 new entries in 2012; and either our target of monthly uploads was slightly exceeded or (according to the software record) the year had 207 months. Wibble, gibber.

On top of this general 24/7 insanity and my regular deadlines for *Ansible, Interzone, SFX* and the *Sunday Telegraph*, I inexplicably took on a new project just for the sake of variety. This was spawned by chatter at boozy convention parties, the kind of unreliable venue where someone may at any moment say "Wouldn't it be nice if so-and-so got reprinted?" and someone else, probably me, babbles: "Let's do it right here in the barn!"

So-and-so, this time around, is the late SF author Algis Budrys – whose classic novels like *Rogue Moon* are regularly reissued, but not his award-winning genre criticism. Now the lunatics were on his case. In our copious spare time and a padded cell, the team scanned and OCR-processed the hundreds of "Books" columns Budrys wrote for *The Magazine of Fantasy and Science Fiction*, and – with the blessing of his widow – tried to arrange it in book form using my secret skills of preparing print-on-demand editions.

Again we found ourselves facing Big Numbers (title of a serialized graphic novel that Alan Moore never actually finished). Good news was that the Budrys columns were still readable and witty – you see why he won the Pilgrim Award for life achievement in SF criticism. Less cheering was that they totted up to roughly the same total word count as *The Lord of the Rings*. Surely the SF-reading public wouldn't stand for a non-fiction tome that long? We realized we'd have to do a Tolkien, or a Peter Jackson, and split it into three volumes...

The first instalment is out, to the delight of the two dozen people in the world who are still interested in these things. Long ago Algis Budrys collected his reviews for *Galaxy* magazine in a fat book titled *Benchmarks: Galaxy Bookshelf* (treasured by the two dozen alongside other pioneer SF critical works like Damon Knight's *In Search of Wonder* and Kingsley Amis's *New Maps of Hell*). So with stunning lack of originality, our new follow-up of the collected *F&SF* magazine columns opens with *Benchmarks Continued: Volume I*. We did it! And the *SF Encyclopedia* passed 3.9 million words before Christmas.

Meanwhile, as some cynical non-poet said, there's one reliable way to make a small fortune in specialist POD publishing. Start with a large one.

• *SFX* #232, April 2013

Post-Kindle

The one thing we know for sure about state-of-the-art ebook readers is that a few years down the line they'll have the musty antique feel of VHS, Betamax, punched computer cards or wax phonograph cylinders. What comes after the Kindle and Nook?

Cyberpunk fans would love to think that the next big thing must be direct neural interfacing. The Langford Algorithmic Predictometer isn't quite sure what will be the most fashionable location for a skull-mounted USB port; perhaps we'll all have inbuilt Wi-Fi instead. By feeding data straight into the optic nerve and bypassing all that yucky eyeball jelly, ebooks will display with perfect clarity.

Of course there could be snags. Spammers will be keen to use the same neural distribution channels, and future readers careering along the fast lane of a motorway will need efficient pop-up blockers to screen out all those irresistible deathbed offers from wealthy yet curiously ungrammatical Nigerians.

Worse, will Amazon's famous trick of remotely deleting our Kindle books extend to internal storage inside the head? I foresee a huge court action when, say, a textbook copyright problem leads to a bunch of graduates' entire university education being wiped by an Amazon glitch, leaving the victims with nothing but colossal student debts and – perhaps for the first time in their lives – a completely open mind.

The possibilities for invasive ads are also exciting. Frederik Pohl and Cyril Kornbluth came close in *The Space Merchants*, their 1952 SF satire where advertising agencies *almost* dominate the world:

"They listened to the safety cranks and stopped us from projecting our messages on aircar windows – but we bounced back. Lab tells me... that soon we'll be testing a system that projects directly on the retina of the eye." Or directly into the brain!

All this cyberspace stuff is so 1980s, though. How about biological vectors for publishing? In this version of the future, books could be encoded into the vast DNA storage capacity of a bacterium (giving b-books) or a virus (v-books). Swallow the equivalent of one of those education pills found in early SF, and the genetically engineered biomechanism will painlessly instal its literary payload into your memory cells. This way, lazy readers can avoid all the slog of actually reading classic works like *Moby-Dick*, *Dune*, *The Lord of the Rings* or those *SFX* editorials. *[Crawler – Ed.]* Instead, by popping a single pill, you pass effortlessly into a state of *having read them*.

The danger here will lie in the relentless efforts of self-publishers who'll try to increase the buzz about their work by deliberately infecting people with promotional freebies of their awful prose. Already they're a constant background noise in online communities like Facebook ("Please buy my book! Come to my launch event! Like my Page! Admire my full-frontal naked greed!"). Now imagine such shameless folk entering into an unholy alliance with back-street biolabs. The Langford Predictometer prophesies a norovirus self-publishing vector which can transmit its book payload to new victims, not only by touch but across ten-foot gaps via the established mechanism of projectile vomiting. This will be known as Puke-on-Demand publishing.

Or maybe in 2050 we'll be reading *SFX* on our scrotties, the cutting-edge technotoys that haven't yet been invented...

What goes around, comes around. There's a 1968 Isaac Asimov story called "The Holmes-Ginsbook Device", set in a world of advanced digital reading technology. The title's two innovators devise an ingenious system of printing page images and assembling them into a kind of codex, a physical entity that needs only hands and eyes to read. Of course the inventors are unfairly forgotten when the device bearing their names is shortened by popular usage to "book". Oh, sorry, was that a spoiler?

David Langford, inspired by contemplation of toilet paper, has invented a visionary p-book called a "scroll".

• *SFX* #233, May 2013

Spice Marinas

Another month, another internet publishing scandal. Traditional cries of shock, horror and high-bandwidth digital outrage echoed through cyberspace when the little-known SF ebook *Spots the Space Marine* was pulled from sale on Amazon as a result of Games Workshop's complaint that it infringed their trademark. The author M.C.A. Hogarth was devastated, and said so on her website.

Fascinating though it is to imagine a Games Workshop trademark on Spots ("You can't call our customers spotty adolescents! That would be a serious infringement."), the offending term was Space Marine. Space marines feature in GW's miniatures-based wargame *Warhammer 40,000*, which is trademarked up to the hilt. Therefore, the logic goes, GW owns the term. All Your Space Marine Are Belong To Us.

Naturally there was a chorus of dissent from SF fandom's barrack-room lawyers, some remembering the egregious efforts of the late unlamented Fandom Inc to claim ownership of the word "fandom" without even having trademarked it (though they pretended they had). Hey, Robert Heinlein used Space Marines in *Space Cadet* back in 1948! E.E. "Doc" Smith had them in *First Lensman*, published 1950! Only fanatics remember Bob Olsen's "Captain Brink of the Space Marines" and "The Space Marines and the Slavers", from *Amazing Stories* magazine in November 1932 and December 1936 respectively; but it looks as though Olsen coined the phrase.

Unfortunately this "prior art" argument applies to patent law, not trademark law. (I loved the recent SF twist on the theme when Samsung challenged Apple's patents on tablet computers by citing *fictional* prior art, such as a tablet-like device that appeared in *2001: A Space Odyssey*. This ploy was not successful.) No matter how loudly you repeat that the word "hobbit" dates back to a nineteenth-century list of mythical creatures in *The Denham Tracts* – "boggleboes, bogies, redmen, portunes, grants, hobbits, hobgoblins, brown-men..." – you'll still incur the litigious wrath of Warner Bros and New Line if you produce a film with the dictionary word Hobbit in the title.

Someone did: Asylum's *Age of the Hobbits*, a "mockbuster" epic that cheekily pretends to be about the extinct human subspecies nicknamed hobbits by the archaeologists, was scheduled to launch suspiciously close to the first official Hobbit movie. Warner and New Line contrived to get its public release blocked by a US court order. Hopeful legal arguments about prior art in *The Denham Tracts* (which Tolkien himself may never have seen) were in vain.

I am not a lawyer – and avoid that tiresome abbreviation IANAL since it sounds too much like the geeky little brother of Asimov's *I, Robot* – but I know where to find one. The Scrivener's Error blog, written by a real US lawyer who calls it a blawg and specializes in SF intellectual property issues, examined the case of *Spots the Space Marine* and opined that "nobody should let lawyers anywhere near making judgments about the arts."

Under US law, the Games Workshop trademark covers "board games, parlor games, war games, hobby games, toy models and miniatures of buildings, scenery, figures, automobiles, vehicles, planes, trains and card games and paint, sold therewith", plus "video computer games; computer software for playing games". Ebooks aren't included; mysteriously GW didn't go after the print edition. Though trademark law is sufficiently broken that mark owners almost have to be hypersensitive, getting legally heavy about a non-competing product totally unrelated to games or *Warhammer 40K* is surely over-reaching. Amazon should have ignored the removal request.

Happily for M.C.A. Hogarth, Amazon thought better of it and reversed that decision after her case was taken up by internet pundits and the Electronic Frontier Foundation – whose later headline went, "Trademark Bully Thwarted: Spots the Space Marine Back Online". Our distressed author sold many extra books thanks to the fuss. Games Workshop collected a shedload of bad publicity. The Space Marines were too busy defending civilization to comment.

David Langford fears that applying for a trademark on the word "the" may not be worth his trouble.

• *SFX* #234, June 2013

Dressing Down

Way back in the wooden age of SF fandom, when if you'd mentioned cosplay they'd have thought you meant trigonometry, British conventions didn't have a lavish Masquerade but a tatty Fancy Dress event. People wore hi-tech cardboard boxes over their heads. Aye, those were tough times when fandom were no soft option and we had to read *Battlefield Earth* three times every day, walking barefoot through the snow, uphill both ways... sorry, where was I?

Costumes of yore tended to be improvised and minimal. One ingenious fellow donned a single black glove, transforming himself into Ursula K. Le Guin's *The Left Hand of Darkness*. A group of seven announced themselves as various bodies of water from Windermere to Lake Titicaca, thus almost effortlessly representing the TV SF classic *Lakes Seven*. On a still larger scale, Lionel Fanthorpe's novel *March of the Robots* inspired a twenty-strong protest march with aluminium foil costumes, angry placards ("More Oil Less Toil") and miles of cutting-edge computer tape strewn in all directions. The hotel complained.

Women, in those unreconstructed days, tended to show a great deal of leg; surviving photos from 1950s conventions cast a fascinating, nostalgic light on what was once terribly daring. At the 1979 Worldcon in Brighton, a brave young lady set new standards for British daringness by displaying a huge pair of wings that hardly anyone noticed thanks to the distracting breasts which she also bared to a large audience and, as it turned out, the BBC crew filming the event.

Cheapskate costume gimmicks got several chaps into trouble. I refuse to say anything whatever about my youthful attempt to portray Roger Zelazny's *Creatures of Light and Darkness*, except that black greasepaint takes too much painful scrubbing to remove. My cartoonist pal Jim Barker (www.jimbarker.net), inspired by Harlan Ellison's *Outer Limits* episode "Demon with a Glass Hand", made his own glass-hand prop from transparent resin. Because this stuff gets very hot and smelly when setting, he put it outdoors for the night in a clearly labelled cardboard box... which a panicky cleaner proceeded to report as a bomb. Enter the highly unamused police... Less tragic, though, than the American who qualified for the Darwin Awards with his Dracula outfit's finishing touch: a stake, actually a (steak) knife, hammered into a pine board under his shirt. The board split; the blade went into his heart. Allegedly.

At the 1972 Worldcon, US comics artist Scott Shaw created the all-time low in bad costumes. The principal ingredients were a pair of tights and three full jars of peanut butter, faithfully reproducing the unique, dripping appearance of the comics character Shaw himself had created: The Turd. Awed eye-witnesses would later brag, "I was there when The Turd came out." Under the hot lights of the Masquerade event, it became evident that this one would run and run. The hotel complained. Everyone complained. The debacle was later enshrined in the semi-official Rotsler's Rules for Masquerades:

"7. Parts of your costume should not be edible or smell. Parts of your costume should not fall off accidentally, brush off against other contestants, or be left lying around on the stage."

Some years earlier, UK fan Keith Armstrong-Bridges had also relied on unorthodox make-up, to become a Sirian Dustman. The enemy Sirians in Eric Frank Russell's SF thriller *Wasp* are humanoid but purple-skinned. So at the convention, our man laboriously stained himself with gentian violet for the sake of his art. Only later did it emerge that this wouldn't come off, or only enough to leave indelible purple patches on the bathtub. (Yes, the hotel complained.) Keith had to wait until his outer skin layers wore away. Alas, he died recently, and countless fans duly repeated their favourite anecdote about how he'd once dyed. What a thing to be remembered for.

David Langford has adeptly disguised himself as a shabby middle-aged man.

• *SFX* #235, July 2013

Reviewing Blues

"Be careful what you wish for, because you may get it." So a million finger-wagging moralists have warned us. As a lad, I reckoned my simple wish for more and more books was blameless, high-minded and couldn't possibly go wrong. I hadn't thought ahead to the day when, living with maybe twenty thousand volumes in a big Victorian house, I'm forever fretting about making room for new arrivals.

Free review copies were part of the dream. When I was new to SF fandom, there was a mysterious monopoly deal whereby one enthusiast had persuaded British publishers that he was the official reviews agent for UK fanzines. He cornered all SF review copies and doled them out to editors he approved of. I sent in a humble request but never got anything, apparently because I'd been in the Oxford University SF Group and Official Monopoly Man thought students were poncy elitists.

So I scrounged review copies for my first fanzine by writing to publishers about this "major new journal of SF criticism" in terms that surely made them think, "What a poncy elitist." Unlikely books trickled in. Nonfiction on the healing powers of cod-liver oil; Clive James's first collection of TV reviews (good stuff, but...); a dreadful self-published SF novel by Lord Weymouth of Longleat House in which the human race has evolved into "huge steaming lumps of purple jelly, anchored to metallic plates which are embedded within rubberized constructions of great architectural beauty... And we emit a soft, musical blurping sound for the purposes of communication." Blurp!

Here the page ripples and blurs to indicate the passage of decades during which – thanks to my long book-reviewing stint in *White Dwarf* and other games magazines – regular parcels of freebie genre fiction became part of life. So did the need for a bigger house.

The books still swarm in, burying the doormat in piles of young-adult vampire zombie dystopias with big swords. Some are ARCs, advance reading copies, blazoned with hideous warnings against parting with this priceless rarity. Apparently you must keep all ARCs forever or resort to book-burning. Usually I pass the moral dilemma to Oxfam.

(Peter F. Hamilton's publishers went through a phase of having him sign all his review ARCs. All that wrist-ache and writer's cramp, suffered in the sure knowledge that he wouldn't be getting a penny in royalties from any of those copies...)

In the old days, freebies sometimes came with a gentlemanly note saying "It is particularly requested that no review should appear before the date of publication." The post-Harry Potter era is harsher, with occasional paranoid publicists who ask the hapless reviewer to sign a formal embargo agreement, laden with hideous legal penalty clauses, before being allowed to see the book (hardly ever by an author likely to induce J.K. Rowling-style spoiler frenzy). In these cases I murmur inaudibly yet with much emotion, "If you don't trust me, you can sod off."

Another change that's tiresome for peace-loving reviewers is a switch of (metaphorical) reproductive strategies. Trad publishing used what biologists called the r-strategy: spraying review copies all over the place like frogspawn, in hope that a lucky few will prosper. Now, maybe because of increasingly steep postal costs, some publicists have switched to the K-strategy where each precious volume is cherished like a human child and found the best possible home. In practice this means email exchanges in which a wheedling PR person tries to persuade the surly and uncooperative critic (me) to make a firm commitment to read and review some treasured work before actually seeing the thing. I never know how to answer those emails.

Then there's the reviewing... but that's the easy part.

David Langford gets his headaches from the hard part, which is reading the bloody books.

• *SFX* #236, Summer 2013

Neat Tricks

Do I hear frenzied cries from readers demanding more rancid prose from the literary cesspit called Thog's Masterclass? No, I don't, but that's never stopped me in the past. Take it away, Thog...

As James Branch Cabell wrote in one of his spicy fantasies, the human body is capable of much curious pleasure. In certain writers' murkily visualized prose, it's also capable of feats to amaze a yoga expert. "Babel seemed oblivious to the fact that Korolev's blood had concentrated in his toes." "Two sad brown eyes started at his waist and worked their way up." (Both William Ryan, *The Holy Thief.*)

More versatile eyes: "Sprawling out on the floor of the bar, Elvis's eyes fell on the underside of a nearby table..." (Stephen Bury, *Interface.*) "His teeth would grit, his eyes would bow." "He finished his drink and let his eyes slide away from hers into the empty cup." (Both Doyce Testerman, *Hidden Things.*)

Some eyeballs need a space of their own: "Finally Garth [...] gazed deeply into her dreamy, drunk eyes, and offered to get them a room." (Robert Rosell, *Civitas Island.*) Some may affect your centre of gravity: "Her eyes rolled into the back of her head and she almost took a step backward." (Percival Everett, *Assumption.*)

Hair plays tricks too: "Hairs on her lower leg trembled as if they were on the back of her neck." "... he looked at the white hairs dashing along his forearms and the backs of his hands." (Both Ali Shaw, *The Girl with Glass Feet.*) Does yours have a pet name? "... his Deputy, a portly bald man with a ginger moustache called Bo Sampson..." (Adam Millard, *Dead West.*)

Male body parts are notoriously rampant: "His nipples were standing so erect they looked like little pink pencil erasers." (Nancy A. Collins, *Right Hand Magic.*) Thumbs are detachable: "He reached for her panties and pushed his thumbs inside. She rose up from the beach, and he slid them off and tossed them away." (Brian Freeman, *Immoral.*) So are hips: "The doors finally slid open, and her hips sashayed down the corridor." (Jo Nesbo, *The Snowman.*) And even facial expressions: "He saw that Kate was watching him with an expression that was half puzzled, half irritated. He asked her if he could borrow it." (Paul Bryers, *The Prayer of the Bone*.)

The female rear poses a pretty problem. Which of these phrases of appreciation, from the US and British first editions of the same classic SF novel, is the typo? "Her bottom was good and did not slop too much." "Her bottom was good and did not slope too much." (Brian W. Aldiss, *Cryptozoic!* aka *An Age*.) No, she is not a boat.

Bad digestion moments: "Fegan cursed, bitter anger at the waste rising in him." (Stuart Neville, *The Ghosts of Belfast*.) "His own breakfast came up promptly, and he lost himself in it for a few bites." (Patricia McKillip, *The Bards of Bone Plain*.) Complications while eating shepherd's pie: "Ruben's left eyebrow twitched upwards, forcing a grunt past the plug of mince and potato that sounded vaguely impressed." (Alex Stewart, "Yesterday".)

Contortionists can do this: "'I tasted the heady loam of the spongy earth beneath my feet...'" (Andre Norton & Jean Rabe, *A Taste of Magic*.)

Academy Award for best make-up: "An elderly, uniformed man strolled out of a gatehouse disguised as a cantina." (Harry Harrison and Marvin Minsky, *The Turing Option*.)

Finally... don't try this at home, but here's a nifty trick with kitchenware that many stage magicians would envy. "She threw the wooden spoon at the wall, where it splattered tomato sauce into a Jackson Pollock pattern, turned, and fled for the bedroom." (Sam Bourne, *The Righteous Men*.)

David Langford is in hiding from a mob of outraged authors.

• *SFX* #237, August 2013

Grand Old Man

At age 96 it wasn't unexpected, and he'd stopped writing fiction since his 2004 novel *Lurulu*, but it was still terribly sad to lose Jack Vance this year. Newspapers gave him good long obituaries, so I'll spare you the statistics (three Hugos, one Nebula, SFWA and World Fantasy grandmaster honours...).

One thing that made Vance so special – and highly influential – was his fondness for ornate language dripping with irony. A famous quote from *The Dying Earth* explains the tariff of prophecy:

"I respond to three questions," stated the augur. "For twenty terces I phrase the answer in clear and actionable language; for ten I use the language of cant, which occasionally admits of ambiguity; for five, I speak a parable which you must interpret as you will; and for one terce, I babble in an unknown tongue."

Even angry characters curse in measured tones: "Low-grade assassins will drown you in cattle excrement! Twenty pariahs will drub your corpse! A cur will drag your head along the street by the tongue!" Not an unknown tongue.

Settlers on a watery planet in *The Blue World* are divided into social castes that reveal what kind of transport ship crashed there long ago: Hoodwinks, Swindlers, Malpractors, Larceners, Bezzlers... the last being the priests. Vance loved satirizing religion. The solemn rituals of the Temple of Finuka in *Emphyrio* are, when you think about them, suspiciously like hopscotch; the ultra-pure Chilites in *The Anome* shun women and their contaminating touch, and instead get their jollies from drug-induced "spasms" which – but this is a family magazine.

Vancian space operas usually have simple plots, often driven by obsessive revenge, but glowingly exotic settings and digressions. *Marune: Alastor 933* revels in ever-changing shades of light on a world with multiple different-coloured suns: "the four stars dance a fine saraband down the Fontinella Wisp". On Sarkovy, home of the poisoners' guild, the death penalty (by poison) awaits anyone who throws sour milk over his grandmother. Travel-guide extracts and footnotes – Vance was a major footnoter long before Terry Pratchett – conjure up bizarre, quirky, sometimes demented worlds and societies, especially in the Demon Princes quintet opening with *Star King*. Tourists should beware the food, steamed centipedes, "parboiled night-fish, fresh from the bogs", or worse:

"The chatowsies are fetid, but the ahagaree is ferocious. The pourrain is merely vile. And the lady seems to have washed her dog in the beer..."

Music appears frequently; Vance's title *Space Opera* means what it says. In the mask-wearing society of "The Moon Moth", conversation must be accompanied by appropriate music from one (and it has to be the *right* one) of several small, hard-to-master instruments; getting it wrong means social and even literal death. *Night Lamp* introduces the difficult froghorn, combining a foot-pumped bagpipe, a nose-played "screedle flute" and a brass horn generating "an unctuous disreputable gurgle". Sensation at the Proms!

Another artistic surprise is the punchline of *The Face*, whose megalomaniac villain has been busy throughout the action with a vast revenge scheme, eventually revealed as explosively reshaping the local moon into a monstrous likeness of... but that's a spoiler.

Above all, Vance relished words. Dying Earth monsters include erbs, hoons, bazils, grues, gids and (look it up) deodands. He raided our language for euphonious names, and once called a planet Camberwell: well, why not? The horrified UK blurb-writer, feeling this *wasn't science-fictional enough*, unilaterally renamed it Kammerwelt.

Few SF authors are the subject of books published by the British Library, but here's *Jack Vance: Critical Appreciations and a Bibliography* (2000), of which I'm inordinately fond because (coughs immodestly) it includes an essay by me.

96 years; more than 60 books, including award-winning crime fiction; too many neatly barbed phrases and polished ironies to count. A great career. Thank you, Jack Vance.

David Langford is trying to steer clear of Chun the Unavoidable.

• *SFX* #238, September 2013

E-Overload

My master plan was to have a nice long rest after the Picture Gallery feature for the online *SF Encyclopedia*. The editors wanted to add some tasty eye candy to the vast expanses of text; so the Gallery launched in mid-May 2013 with over 1800 images of first-edition book jackets (plus a sprinkling of surprises – I really must scan those *Doctor Who* fridge magnets that came as an *SFX* freebie years ago) and passed 5000 by 1 July. If you believe the old saw about a picture being worth a thousand words, this added the equivalent of five million words to the 4.1 million of actual entries. Speaking as the sucker who had to write and debug all the upload, display and slide-show scripts, I feel proudly knackered.

Before I could sink into well-deserved apathy, my business partner at that obscure small press Ansible Editions (ae.ansible.uk) remarked that it was time I bloody well got a move on with volumes two and three of Algis Budrys's collected criticism (see April's column). It's not so much the digital typesetting as compiling detailed book indexes that brings on the headaches. At last the collections appeared as tasteful print-on-demand paperbacks from Lulu.com, and it was definitely an occasion for that nice long rest.

Then people started clamouring for ebook editions. For years there'd been demands for an ebook of my least worst novel *The Leaky Establishment*. I kept putting this off owing to technofear and a sense that this wouldn't make me even slightly rich... since the demands, though regular, all came from the same person. But the e-Budrys requests were well into single figures! The customer is sometimes right.

Let Lulu.com do the work, I thought. Alas, their e-equivalent of POD is limited to Epub format, okay for every e-reader *except* the dreadfully popular Kindle. Author friends swear by the ebook publisher Smashwords, catering for every reader known to terrestrial science; but Smashwords imposes a dread and inflexible format requirement for uploaded text. Although I have a reasonably strong stomach for gruesome horrors and nameless abominations, I draw the line at contaminating my computer with Microsoft Word.

"Why not just roll your own ebooks?" someone said, adding that it's just a matter of downloading free software and clicking a few buttons. He didn't mention the days of frustration and further headaches (the pain of migraine is mainly in the brain). In the end I more or less succeeded in rolling my own.

The Langford Method depends on being able to work with plain HTML, as in web pages, the *SF Encyclopedia* and indeed the Budrys collections – these went through an HTML stage on their journey from the original magazines, via scanning and OCR, to printable PDF format.

Once you have a good clean HTML text and a CSS stylesheet with a few suitable format controls, you can feed it into the free ebook software Calibre. This lets you add "metadata" like the book title and author, a cover image and the publisher's name (for me, Ansible Editions). Choose a format such as Epub, Mobi or Kindle AZW3, click a button, and Calibre churns out a shiny new ebook. Marvellous. I must send its author some money.

Then you find the stylesheet needs some little tweaks for nice presentation of things like footnotes – of which Mr Budrys was all too fond. Examples include: "*Don't worry, there'll be a footnote coming along any minute now, but not here," "*I have chosen not to put footnotes in this column," and, after quoting someone's would-be evocative writing: "*Yuck, my reader, yuck!" All these have to look just right, and weeks of obsessive work lie ahead...

• *SFX* #239, October 2013

Take a Dump

The space opera begins with pages of coruscating laser beams, ravening energies, vaporized starships and exploding suns. Great narrative hook, but why all this strife? Reluctantly pausing his interstellar dogfight, our author inserts a hefty essay on recent galactic politics: "Twenty years ago, the ships of the Federation had..." Welcome to the infamous infodump.

Maybe our writer has what she fondly believes is a new hyperspace travel gimmick. Her characters are all familiar with this but it's shoehorned into dialogue anyway: "Remind me, Professor, as though I knew nothing of it, just how the Transfinite Implausibility Woofdrive functions?" Rather like interrupting a thriller car-chase for a lecture on internal combustion engines.

SF infodumps have a long sleazy history. One pioneer was Hugo "Award" Gernsback, whose *Ralph 124C41+* (1911-12) explains high-tech future transport at length *with diagrams*: "'You will understand it better by examining this chart,' and unfolding a plan, he proceeded to elaborate on the finer points of tube construction."

A personal favourite is Mack Reynolds's *Lagrange Five*, with repeated infodumps about a dread super-claustrophobia which doesn't affect astronauts in their roomy capsules but can strike with crippling force when you're cooped up in several cubic miles of space colony. One of its side-effects is to make victims compulsively list the synonyms: "I've got Island fever. I've got Wide Syndrome. I've got... space cafard." Likewise doctors: "'Space cafard,' he muttered. 'So-called Island fever. Sometimes it's named Wide Syndrome.'" Our doctor then helpfully lectures a nurse, who knows all about it, on the subject of space cafard. At last the hero arrives and just for our benefit asks: "What's space cafard?" So help me, they tell him. Again.

Similarly, Anne McCaffrey's cast rehashes its common knowledge in *The Tower and the Hive*: "Had the Hivers but known they had met their match in Jeff Raven and Angharad Gwyn aka the Rowan as partners, they might have quit while they were ahead." (This chap is talking about his own grandparents. Love that "aka".) "And that, of course, brought the entire FT&T organization in at the time of the Deneb Penetration with the Rowan as the focus for the Mind Merge that helped Jeff Raven despatch the Hiver Scouts trying to depopulate his home world. / And why the Mrdinis decided to ask us, through Mother and Dad, to join forces and defeat the Hivers [...] since we could take out a Hiver Sphere without having to resort to suicide missions." Too much information!

But infodumps aren't necessarily bad. Some easily led people take the writing-workshop advice "Show not tell" as unassailable holy writ, but it's more a guideline. Alfred Bester's scene-setting introduction to *The Stars My Destination* is a brilliant, pyrotechnic infodump. Whole chapters of lyrical data-dumping feature in John Brunner's *Stand on Zanzibar* and Kim Stanley Robinson's *2312*. Neal Stephenson's colossal *Anathem* is arguably all infodump, on physics, Platonic philosophy and more – but still a compulsive read despite what Adam Roberts called the annoylogisms.

For a word that seems to have been around in SF criticism forever, the origins of "infodump" are hazy. The *Oxford English Dictionary* SF Project website offers nothing earlier than a 1987 Usenet conversation, and Jeff Prucher's spinoff book *Brave New Words* credits Howard Waldrop as first to use it in print, in 1990. That has to be wrong: "info-dump" is defined as "The incompetent writer's way of revealing the details of his story's setting" in K.W. Jeter's novel *Dr Adder*, written 1972 and published 1984. In that book Jeter says the term comes from a book review in an old SF magazine, but which one? Research continues. If you find a pre-1984 or, better, pre-1972 appearance, there may be a small prize.

David Langford must remind you at length, as though you knew nothing of it, that he writes a column for SFX.

• *SFX* #240, November 2013

Pohl Position

What an astonishing career Frederik Pohl had, one of the longest in SF. It began with a poem in *Amazing Stories* in October 1937, when he was seventeen, and ended with a jokey post to his Hugo-winning blog on 2 September 2013, the day he died at the age of 93.

In between... many things happened. With Isaac Asimov, James Blish and Cyril Kornbluth, Pohl was in that notorious 1938-1945 fan group the Futurians, whose escapades he described in *The Way the Future Was*. Soon he was simultaneously editing awful pulp-SF magazines and writing for them under pseudonyms. After World War Two he became a literary agent and a pioneer SF anthologist while moving to better-class mags like *Galaxy* and *If* – which won three 1960s Hugo awards while Pohl was editor.

It's his fiction that's best remembered. With Kornbluth he wrote the famed *The Space Merchants* (1953), a funny, pointed, prophetic satire in which the massively overpopulated USA is dominated by rival ad agencies. With Mad Men in charge and planning to beam ads directly into people's retinas, contract-breaking is a worse crime than murder and the underclasses are fed on "Chicken Little", an artificial culture of chicken-heart tissue: fast-food science is only now catching up. Customer loyalty gets boosted by lacing junk food with addictive drugs, the Venus colony programme is hard-sold through mendacious TV commercials, and at the Metropolitan Museum of Art our protagonist reverently admires the uplifting classic artwork "I Dreamed I was Ice-Fishing in my Maidenform Bra".

Other collaborations with Kornbluth are well worth reading, especially the very strange *Wolfbane* (1959) – where Earth has been kidnapped by alien robot entities who use people as components in their servo-mechanisms. Kornbluth died young, though, and Pohl did so much more. His stories moved from slick farce and black comedy (as in "The Midas Plague", where automated overproduction leads to Americans meeting enforced user quotas by 24/7 guzzling, swilling and general overconsumption) to thoughtful tales like "Day Million", a jolting evocation of future shock, and two bizarrely different takes on the SF problem-solving tradition: "The Gold at the Starbow's End" and "In the Problem Pit".

Personally I have a soft spot for Pohl's collaborations with another SF golden oldie, Jack Williamson (1908-2006). One example: their 1964 *The Reefs of Space* features fairy-tale asteroid "islands" built by vacuum-dwelling equivalent of coral polyps and crowded with colourful life.

But *Gateway* (1977) is his finest novel. Long, long ago the alien Heechee visited our solar system and abandoned lots of little FTL starships in a tunnelled-out asteroid. Each can take you to an unknown destination, in a gamble vaguely like Russian roulette. Most chambers are blanks; one in twenty crews get rich from Heechee treasures or scientific discovery; three in twenty don't come back. The hero, a chronic loser who became a winner, has a guilt complex the size of Jupiter about how – as slowly and painfully emerges in flashback – he did it. Unforgettable.

Still darker, psychologically, is *Man Plus* (1976), describing an astronaut's cyborg adaptation to survive the gruelling Martian deserts. No *Six Million Dollar Man* wish-fulfilment here, just a steady process of transformation away from human appearance and even – with a computer interface handling his reflexes – human thought patterns. Despite truly nightmarish episodes he does, in a way, win through.

Naturally Pohl collected virtually all the SF awards, not just the Hugo (four times, or seven counting *If* magazine wins) and Nebula (twice) but life achievement honours that lesser authors can only dream about, like the SF Writers of America Grand Master award, the French Prix Utopia, and entry to the SF Hall of Fame. He was always funny, never pompous, and by US standards daringly left-wing. One of the greats. I miss him already.

• *SFX* #241, December 2013

E-Freebies

Buying a cheap e-reader provides new ways to be a cheapskate – besides the traditional sport of writing vindictive one-star Amazon reviews ("WORST BOOK EVAR!") because the publisher priced the ebook 50p higher than you'd prefer. There's masses of free fiction at Project Gutenberg, including stories about which I've been curious for decades, if not curious enough to spend money...

For example, Theodore Sturgeon's introduction to a 1972 collection of his stories plugs the forgotten children's fantasy *The Garden of the Plynck* (1920) by Karle Wilson Baker – who at some stage in her life must have been bitten by a radioactive Lewis Carroll. Among many exceedingly peculiar characters, the story features a pet called the Snoodle whose mother was a snail and whose father was a noodle, a *pedigree* noodle. Though sometimes a fraction too twee, this has enough Carrollian verbal and imaginative weirdness to make it well worth the Gutenberg download. Thank you, Mr Sturgeon.

Also for children and also forgotten, Walter de la Mare's epic monkey quest *The Three Mulla-Mulgars* (1910) gets high praise from John Clute in *The Encyclopedia of Fantasy* as "arguably WDLM's single greatest fiction, and certainly one of the central Animal Fantasies of the 20th century". It is indeed very good, and it's on the virtual shelves at Gutenberg. Thank you, Mr Clute.

Of course you can't win every time. In his autobiography, theatre critic James Agate recommended *Voyages and Travels of Count Funnibos and Baron Stilkin* by W.H.G. Kingston, in which the buffoonish noblemen of the title make grandiose world-touring plans but never – this is the big joke – get beyond Holland. It caused me no pain, but I'm glad I didn't pay certain e-retailers' vast prices like $0.95.

Much more disappointing was John Polidori's *The Vampyre* (1819), the *other* story inspired by the famous writing-party at the Villa Diodati that included Lord Byron and both Shelleys, and led to Mary Shelley's *Frankenstein*. Like many pioneer genre works, *The Vampyre* is fearfully clunky. Its cleverest imaginative touch came from the publisher, who in hope of a scandalous bestseller left Polidori's name off the title page and instead used Byron's.

One of my unsecret vices is reading cobwebbed old crime fiction as a change from space opera and epic fantasy trilogies. The critical round-up *Queen's Quorum* by Ellery Queen is a handy guide, listing the "most important" (this doesn't necessarily mean the best) detective story collections since Edgar Allan Poe set the criminous ball rolling in 1845. Did you know that Baroness Orczy of *Scarlet Pimpernel* fame wrote a longish series in which her eccentric sleuth The Old Man In The Corner solves crimes while sitting in a London teashop obsessively tying knots in a piece of string?

My silliest e-detective discovery is the once highly praised Hamilton Cleek from *The Man of the Forty Faces* (1910) by T.W. Hanshew. The name's an alias, as subtly conveyed when this master criminal taunts Scotland Yard with letters signed "The Man Who Calls Himself Hamilton Cleek". Almost immediately, though, he reforms and turns detective, cracking horrific cases like "The Riddle of the Red Crawl" – a fearful haunting by "a hideous and loathsome creature, neither spider nor octopus, but horribly resembling both". It doesn't take Cleek long to nobble a villain in red spider/octopus costume. "I'd have gotten away with it too, if it weren't for that meddling Cleek."

But Hanshew gets an *SF Encyclopedia* entry because Cleek, besides being rightful king of Ruritania (here thinly disguised as Mauravania), has a genuine superpower! By sheer force of will he can instantly rearrange his face and impersonate people well enough to fool close family members. Apparently his pregnant mother played with a rubber doll that had stretchy features, and by the logic of complete ignorance of genetics this influenced her unborn child. Science has come a long way since 1910. Nowadays he'd have been bitten by a radioactive make-up artist.

David Langford luckily has no room for Cleek's sidekick Dollops the boy wonder, who fights crime with "tickle tootsies" (please don't ask).

• *SFX* #242, January 2014

1 Down: Respect

Newspapers traditionally sneer at science fiction, but the gigantic intellects who set their crosswords include friendly genre fans. Last year I thrilled Chris Priest with the news that the latest *Independent* puzzle by veteran setter Phi used him as a hidden theme, with answers including not only Christopher and Priest but his novel titles Affirmation, Extremes, Glamour, Islander(s), Prestige and Separation. 16 Down was Scintilla, a surveillance gadget in that nifty Priest novella "The Watched".

Displaying the majestic dignity of SF writers, Chris ran all the way to the newsagent to buy that paper. And followed up with an enthusiastic blog post titled "Thirstier Choppers (anag. 11, 6)" which cryptically dropped the name of his one-time reviewer nemesis "Rat Animism (anag. 6, 4)". Go on, you can work it out.

A sadder occasion, the far too early death of Iain Banks, was marked by a crossword memorial from a setter bylined Alchemi. A number of one-word answers, either singly or in pairs, gave assorted Banks titles: Business, Canal Dreams, Complicity, Crow Road, Walking (on) Glass, Wasp Factory and Whit. Not quite as lasting a memorial for our Iain as the Minor Planet Center's announcement that in June 2013, asteroid 5099 was officially named Iainbanks by the International Astronomical Union "and will be referred to as such for as long as Earth Culture may endure."

(See the Asteroids entry in the online *SF Encyclopedia* at sf-encyclopedia.com for several more wandering planetoids that now carry SF authors' and artists' names.)

More crossword fun came with a recent *Independent* offering from Phi, titled "Persuasion" as a red herring for Jane Austen fans. This required solvers to deduce a longish non-English quotation that went round the edge of the puzzle grid, *and* its "translation" as given two letters at a time by extra hints buried in clues. As it turned out, both lines were fresh in my mind because only that week I'd been reformatting my two Discworld quizbooks for Gollancz to release in ebook form.

The quotation, in traditional Discworld dog-latin from Terry Pratchett's *Small Gods*, goes *Cuius testiculos habes, habeas cardia et cerebellum.* The official, bowdlerized paraphrase in the same novel is "When you have their full attention in your grip, their hearts and minds will follow." Just in case "full attention" doesn't seem an entirely accurate translation, Phi helpfully threw in a few special "thematic" clues with no definitions provided, whose answers were Globe, Orb, Pill and Spheroid. A veritable load of balls. Ouch.

Spoiler and subject change alert! A non-crossword puzzle I've also been investigating is whether the plot of UK author Eric Frank Russell's 1955 Hugo-winning comic story "Allamagoosa" was, er, borrowed. Synopsis: a starship in a bureaucratic space navy faces rigorous official inspection. Panic when no one can find inventory item V1098, the "offog", or even remember what kind of gadget this might be. Gambling that the inspector also knows nothing about offogs, the captain boldly has his radio officer build a substitute with plausible dials and blinking lights. They survive their inspection... only to discover the inventory list had a typo. V1098 is actually the ship's friendly mongrel Peaslake, its official dog (off. dog). Dire galactic consequences follow.

Meanwhile, a couple of decades previously, fantasy author and *Punch* magazine contributor Anthony Armstrong wrote many comic sketches of UK army life. One story in *Captain Bayonet and Others* (1937) features an official inspection and another untraceable barracks inventory item, the Spad-Gas. You've guessed it: the armourer fakes a replacement, "a queer bit of metal with odd corners and a couple of tubes". After the battalion has passed inspection, the typo is revealed: Spade, G.S. (General Service).

A fair cop? Maybe not. Russell's biographer insists the original was a 1950s naval legend about a mystery "shovewood", with yet another weird gadget hastily manufactured to replace the inventory's typoed version of an official-issue "shovel, wood". These are deep waters, Watson.

David Langford has begun to suspect this is ancient military folklore dating back to the armies of Napoleon, King Arthur, Julius Caesar...

• *SFX* #243, February 2014

Lessing and More

Another admired writer leaves the party: Doris Lessing died in November 2013 at the ripe age of 94. One tiny career point that wasn't much mentioned in the fulsome obituaries was her guest-of-honour appearance at the 1987 World SF Convention in Brighton. Everyone there was in awe of her. My own tiny fanboy mind had been blown by her SF-ish novel *Briefing for a Descent into Hell*, as I burbled incoherently when I found myself sitting next to the great lady at the Hugo ceremony. I still remember thinking, "Gosh wow, the first person to congratulate me on that Hugo was *Doris Lessing*!" But it's not all about me.

She'd written unashamed SF with her 1979 *Shikasta* – a literary reboot of the traditional "shaggy god story" approach – and its sequels. Moreover, she wasn't afraid to call it science fiction. As the BBC obituarist put it: "By the late 1970s Lessing abandoned social themes for science fiction with her Canopus in Argus series, which she describes as her best work. / In it she outlined a bleak vision of the future with tyranny and natural catastrophes becoming the norm." No realistic social themes there, then.

Doris Lessing's cantankerous attitude to her own biggest award is also legendary. Emerging from a taxi outside her London house one day in 2007, she was mobbed by reporters telling her she'd won the Nobel Prize for Literature and demanding a tasty soundbite. Lessing: "Oh Christ! ...I couldn't care less."

Naturally, writing SF has never been a fast track to Nobel acclaim. The *SF Encyclopedia* entry on Nobel winners is very short but lists Rudyard Kipling (who wrote a lot more SF than you think), George Bernard Shaw (*Back to Methuselah*), Herman Hesse (*The Glass Bead Game* alias *Magister Ludi*) and William Golding (*Lord of the Flies* has an implied background of future global war). Although the Nobel pantheon included one token spaceship (in Harry Martinson's epic Swedish poem *Aniara*, largely unread because it's so very epic and, indeed, Swedish), there were no aliens or galactic empires there until Doris Lessing joyously lowered the tone with her *Canopus in Argos* sequence. Good for her.

Traditional media dissing of genre fiction and its readers continues. Here, in memory of a lady who couldn't care less what the hacks wrote, are some recent examples.

"For those readers who did not get beaten up in high school, *Doctor Who* is a beloved British sci-fi series about a character called the Doctor..." (*New York Times*.)

On tales of catastrophic climate change: "Don't call it 'science fiction'. Cli-fi is literary fiction.' (*Christian Science Monitor*.)

Dialogue from ITV's gay sitcom *Vicious*: "Will there be a lot of single men?" "It's a science fiction fan club event. They'll be single but they'll be disgusting."

Insider view of *The Hunger Games*: "I think my job as costume designer is really to create the vision that the director has, not necessarily the book. Gary (the director) wanted to make a movie that was real, that wasn't a science fiction film." (DVD extras)

On *Game of Thrones* and facial hair: "So it is strange that the programme... is Sky Atlantic's most popular, and has drawn millions of unexpected fans: housewives and historians, as well as the expected men with beards." (*Daily Telegraph*.)

As always, if it's good it's not genre: "*All the Pretty Horses* is no more a western than *1984* is science fiction." (*New Yorker*.)

Once in a while, though, even the horrible old *Daily Mail* can surprise us with a book review like this one from Ned Denny: "Great fun, thought-provoking, highly literate and beautifully written, this is a perfect example of the all-round superiority of 'genre' fiction over the dreary literary mainstream." That's telling them.

David Langford is struggling quite hard to feel superior to the dreary literary mainstream.

• *SFX* #244, March 2014

Outsider R.I.P.

Last November was full of fiftieth anniversaries. Not just *Doctor Who*, but three important deaths on the day before the Doctor's first episode aired in 1963. Thanks to the glare of publicity following the assassination of President Kennedy, no one noticed at first that Aldous Huxley of *Brave New World* fame and C.S. Lewis of Narnia fame had both died on the same day.

Another accidental upstaging happened in December 2013, when the world resounded to reports of Nelson Mandela's death while there was silence about the departure – again on the same day – of Colin Wilson. Even the BBC website, usually pretty quick with death reports, took over a week to catch up.

As a writer and philosopher, Colin Wilson had a strange career. His first book *The Outsider* (1956), an eccentric study of links between creativity and alienation, was an instant bestseller. His huge output included pioneering psychological serial-killer novels like *Ritual in the Dark*, plus many gruesome studies of true crime and gosh-wow reports of the paranormal. 1950s newspapers lumped him together with Kingsley Amis and others as an Angry Young Man, though he was in fact persistently cheerful.

The Outsider led him to H.P. Lovecraft via the coincidence of Lovecraft's first collection being titled *The Outsider and Others*. Like HPL himself and unlike most imitators, Wilson saw the Cthulhu Mythos as science fiction – featuring monstrous, sanity-destroying aliens from other dimensions rather than traditional gods, demons and ghosts. Intrigued, he wrote two Lovecraftian SF novels that reworked the extradimensional nasties in terms of his own home-brewed philosophy.

First came *The Mind Parasites*, in which the "parasites" within our minds are at the same time Cthulhoid aliens, mental cancers, and metaphors for laziness and all the other factors that stop us (well, certainly me) from thinking at peak efficiency 24/7. Clear out all this rubbish with the whirling Dyno-Rod of enlightened thought, Wilson suggested, and psi powers like telepathy and telekinesis inevitably follow. His second Lovecraftian venture, *The Philosopher's Stone*, added immortality to the benefits and provided a vaguely Theosophical history of how the Great Old Ones long ago ruled Earth and created puny humanity before succumbing to their own mind parasites. But they'll be back! Keep watching the metaphysical skies!

This is all cranky fun, as is our man's fantasy *The God of the Labyrinth*, which – perhaps a little tamely – uses the apparatus of porn rather than SF to push the Wilson philosophical agenda. The UK paperback cover, by Discworld artist Josh Kirby, borrowed Arcimboldo's trick of building up a face from smaller objects: Arcimboldo used vegetables but Josh got into the proper, or improper, spirit with a satyr's head constructed from writhing naked bodies. I had to hide that one from my mother.

The philosophy of mental self-improvement even turned up in unlikely nonfiction contexts like the bibulous and obviously well-researched *A Book of Booze*. Wilson once confided that his book of music criticism, *The Brandy of the Damned*, was largely produced to make his record collection tax-deductible. You can't help wondering what boozy research expenses for the later volume were claimed against tax.

Further Wilsonian SF ventures include the A.E. van Vogt homage *The Space Vampires* – dreadfully filmed as *Lifeforce* – and the young-adult *Spider World* series set in a far future dominated by giant spiders against which humanity begins, first with guns and later with philosophy, to fight back. A future children's classic, he reckoned: "They will know me as the author of *Spider World*, in the way that they know Lewis Carroll as the author of *Alice in Wonderland*."

Long ago I worked with Colin on another Lovecraftian project, *The Necronomicon* edited by George Hay: see *SFX* #53. That was fun too. Now (gulp) I'm the last surviving contributor. Am I next on Great Cthulhu's list?

David Langford hopes to pop his clogs on a slow news day when the SF media have nothing else to write about.

• *SFX* #245, April 2014

Badge of Infamy

Once a year I attack the tottering piles of paper in my "paperless" office. This time around, under faded faxes and yellowing 1980s correspondence, I found a tatty rectangular card with the printed legend "Novacon 3" and my name written in by hand. My first convention badge!

Those were the days when affordable badge technology consisted of cutting up cardboard and sellotaping a safety pin to the back of each fragment. The principle of universal entropy then ensured that the pin would sooner or later fall off. In that primitive era, they simply replaced lost badges; at the 2013 World Fantasy Convention there was also a nominal charge of £75. There's progress for you.

My austere white Novacon 3 badge is partly coloured with blue felt-pen, to mark me as a mere Neofan whom experienced con-goers could gently encourage, or avoid like an approaching zombie apocalypse. We neos were also advised to ring a little bell and, from time to time, chant "Unclean! Unclean!"

That reminds me that coloured felt-pens were strongly recommended in Bob Shaw's spoof Fansmanship Lectures, adapting the techniques of Stephen Potter's Gamesmanship and Oneupmanship to fandom. The trick, said Bob earnestly, was to give your badge distinctive colours not used by the convention, thus conveying that you belonged to some important group whose special status was recognized by the con committee. The Secret Masters of Fandom! Nowadays this will probably get you thrown out.

By the time I'd graduated (or sunk) to working on con committees, tatty cardboard had been displaced by the massive Badge Machine. This dread device was forever jamming or malfunctioning, but when in a good mood could take a paper blank with the convention logo and seal it – protected forever by transparent plastic – into a round steel badge with built-in pin. Then the operators would remember that they should have written the member's name on that paper blank *first*.

Now badges are generally rectangular again, with impressive full-colour designs and laser-printed names inside laminated plastic. (Novacon does well here since they have professional SF/space artist David A. Hardy permanently on tap.) Once when I was a guest at Minicon in Minneapolis, there was a panicky "registration party" at which several thousand such badges – delivered in random order by commercial printers – had to be frantically sorted by the committee, volunteers, guests of honour and whoever else could be press-ganged, including the cat.

Breaking the inviolable seal of the Con Fessional, I must now reveal the secret of getting badges right. The important thing is to put the name in large easy-to-read print. Not the convention name, since even the drunkest SF barflies usually know what event they're at, but the name of the actual badge owner.

This is because con attendees like to know who they're talking to: "Oh, *you're* L. Ron Hubbard! I've always wanted to back nervously away from you..." Squinting at teensy lettering can be embarrassing, especially in cases when the badge-wearer may just possibly misinterpret your intense scrutiny of her chest. As that sensitive feminist Isaac Asimov wrote in *Foundation and Earth* (1986), clearly after just such an awkward incident: "Her breasts were a smaller version of the woman herself – massive, firm and overpoweringly impressive."

Which reminds me of the Toronto Worldcon whose badge-holder, with copious storage space for your programme schedule, small change and maybe a lunchbox, was so huge it had to hang round your neck like a bib. I was shortlisted for two Hugos and proudly attached the nomination pins – miniature versions of the Hugo rocket – to the corners of this, er, breastplate. A lady friend promptly told me it put her in mind of pierced nipples. Oh dear.

• *SFX* #246, May 2014

100 Things

Remember Radio 4's "History of the World in 100 Objects"? The US fanzine *Lofgeornost* was inspired to suggest a History of the Future in 100 SF Objects – a great display for some World SF Convention.

There'd have to be a Time Machine (H.G. Wells or the Tardis?) and an iconic Spaceship (*2001*?) or Starship (*Star Trek*?) docking at a Space Station. Also in the Transport department: Flying Saucers, Flying Cars, Rockets, Moving Roadways (see Heinlein's "The Roads Must Roll"), Antigravity, Matter Transmitter, Jetpack/Gyropack, Warp Drive, Space Elevator and Stargate... A.E. van Vogt, as you probably did not wish to know, wrote about stargates in 1942.

A Positronic Robot and its Three Laws are essential, plus a futuristic (and optionally Mad) Computer working as a Universal Translator or issuing helpful information like "???Redo from Start", "I'm sorry, Dave. I'm afraid I can't do that." or "Yes – NOW there is a God!"

The hugest exhibit hall is for Big Dumb Objects, including the Death Star, Larry Niven's *Ringworld* and the Hollow Earth (looks like Earth, but...).

Conversely, one teensy portable display case holds many Nanobots, a bit of that useful Monomolecular Wire that slices through anything but especially fingers, a few Tachyons, the World-Ravaging Plague of your choice and the Incredible Shrinking Man.

For SF handguns, there are too many options. The traditional Blaster, Disintegrator and Stunner can become a single handy package: "Set phasers to Violate Prime Directive!" Larger ordnance includes Powered Armour, Mecha, Cybertanks like Keith Laumer's Bolo "continental siege units" and Doomsday Weapons – paging Doctor Strangelove...

Tomorrow's books: everything you could possibly need to know is in the *Encyclopedia Galactica* from Isaac Asimov's *Foundation* series, and for everything else there's the *Hitchhiker's Guide*.

Future physical fitness is encouraged by Bug-Eyed Monsters and other things from which to run away very fast indeed: Martian Tripod, Triffid, Id Monster, Blob, Alien Grey, Dalek, Sandworm and H.R. Giger. When thoroughly exercised, take a break to enjoy some Food Pills.

Other vital technological gimmicks are Stasis Fields, Cyborgs,

Miniaturizers (enjoy a bacteria-hunting safari!) and Identity Transfer gadgets to allow mind tourism as in Robert Sheckley's *Mindswap*. Justice is ensured by infallible Lie Detectors and total surveillance via Spy-Rays, while magical new Power Sources – tapping, for example, the zero-point energy of space itself – replace fossil fuels at last and provide a fast track to Utopia. Or Dystopia.

There'd be a wide range of entertainment, from the Holodeck and another 57 varieties of Virtual Reality to panes of Bob Shaw's Slow Glass, showing idyllic country scenes from years ago when the light first entered the glass. Avoiding the boring old speed-of-light regulations, bad news will arrive instantaneously by Ansible. Or Ultrawave, or Dirac Communicator. You can even get the news before it happens by investing in a Time Radio.

Laboratory supplies: Green Kryptonite of course, Cavorite, Antimatter (carefully packaged) and Unobtainium. One of the many Drugs that prolong life – perhaps Frank Herbert's Spice (see Sandworm above) or Cordwainer Smith's Stroon, a by-product of gigantic diseased sheep.

In fashion, Spacesuits with Bubble Helmets have a retro charm; and an important survival tip is to avoid wearing Red Shirts.

All visitors to the exhibition will have a chance to guess the nature and purpose of the Utterly Incomprehensible Alien Artefact. There may be an utterly incomprehensible prize.

Catering to the needs of future plotting, we'd need many Clichés, Stereotypes and Infodumps, at least one McGuffin, and a reliable Deus Ex Machina. Since these things tend to be a bit intangible, they can share the large glass case already containing an Invisible Force Field, a Cloaking Device, the Fourth Dimension, and the Pitiless Vacuum of Space.

Oops. The end of the page already and we're still a long way short of a hundred. Must try harder.

You guessed it: David Langford wrote or expanded entries on most of these things for the SF Encyclopedia.

• *SFX* #247, June 2014

Heads We Lose

As long ago as *SFX* #3 in 1995 (has it really been nineteen years?), I grumbled about the strange belief that science fiction authors are in the business of predicting the future. No, not really, not any more than thriller writers habitually track down serial killers or romance writers are lured by their own irresistible tales of true love into hapless serial bigamy. SF isn't about *the* future but *a* future, convincingly argued (we like to hope) but only one of billions of possible routes through Jorge Luis Borges's famous Garden of Forking Paths...

The traditional canard that SF is all about prediction usually heralds a two-pronged attack from genrephobes. Heads they win: book X didn't get the future right, so it's no good. Tails we lose: book Y pinpointed a coming trend, but has now served its purpose like a discarded booster rocket and now (a worthless husk) need no longer be read.

This grubby gambit was trotted out again in the recent "Which Books Should We Stop Calling Classics?" online symposium at Flavorwire, where literary pundits were encouraged to lead their barbarian hordes into the Library of Fame for some exhilarating ethnic cleansing. The novelist Katherine Bucknell immediately put the boot into SF: "For me, science fiction classic is an oxymoron. What could possibly go out of date more rapidly than a book imagining what will happen in a future time or place?"

Her idea of what SF readers like and talk about is even stranger: "The discussions I hear about science fiction 'classics' usually focus on how amazing it is that the author was so close to imagining how things really turned out." I see. *The War of the Worlds* is highly rated, not because it timelessly shows the complacent British Empire getting a taste of its own gunboat diplomacy ("Whatever happens, we have got / The Maxim gun, and they have not") but because so many Martian tripods have since devastated the London suburbs with their irresistible Heat Rays. It happens all the time.

Oops, no: in fact it turns out that Bucknell hurls H.G. Wells into the dustbin of history, along with satirists and adventure writers: "I'm afraid *Brave New World* is the last of Huxley's many interesting books that I would recommend. And I would ditch Jules Verne, H.G. Wells, and the like." End of bizarre polemic.

Of course turnabout is fair play. Using Katherine Bucknell's own ruthless logic, we can sneer at Jane Austen, Charles Dickens, James Joyce and the rest because they failed in the much easier task of predicting the present day or recent past. Historians and genealogists have sadly confirmed that the characters in their books are *all made up*. Conversely, it would seem that H.G. Wells's *The Time Machine* can still be a classic because its "predicted" far future hasn't yet failed to happen. That's logic for you.

Since fantasy is so often about impossible worlds and never-never lands, you can't dismiss the genre out of hand by playing the failed-prediction card. Another approach is required, and "literary fiction" author Russell Banks filled the much-needed gap with his brilliant ploy of Making Stuff Up. Writing in the *New York Times*, he pinpointed the kind of fiction he took care to avoid: "Anything described by the author or publisher as fantasy, which to me says, 'Don't worry, Reader, Death will be absent here.'" Gorblimey.

It is of course notorious that no one ever dies in the wishy-washy Harry Potter saga. Sociologists have proved that rumours of a bony Discworld character who ALWAYS SPEAKS IN DOOM-LADEN CAPITALS are entirely baseless. Only Barbara Cartland rivals George R.R. Martin's *Game of Thrones* for sentimental niceness, especially in the wedding scenes. I need to lie down now.

• *SFX* #248, July 2014

Flash Fiction

As I write there's a *Flash* TV series on the verge of release, and a film about this DC superhero is scheduled for 2016. Gifted with super-speed by the traditional bolt of lightning hitting the laboratory, this was one costumed vigilante who never worried about needing to pee while clad in a skin-tight onesie – a vital problem neglected by comics writers until at last Alan Moore pondered the issue in *Watchmen*. The Flash could undress and dress again in nanoseconds, with a golden shower so swift that no bystander except perhaps Superman could detect the, er, flash flood.

H.G. Wells got there first with "The New Accelerator", published in 1901. No lightning bolts are needed in the lab of learned Professor Gibberne, who brews up a drug to speed human metabolism by a factor of thousands. With a bemused friend in tow, he whizzes invisibly through Folkestone holiday crowds, "going a thousand times faster than the quickest conjuring trick that was ever done" and playing a wicked practical joke on a neighbour's noisy dog...

Only as the elixir is wearing off do our speed freaks realize the hazards of fast-forwarding: "Friction of the air!" Their clothes nearly burst into flame, because they neglected the obvious safety precaution of wearing red asbestos onesies.

A favourite comedy about time distortion is *The Girl, the Gold Watch and Everything* by John D. Macdonald (better known for his colourful Travis McGee thrillers). Just like Gibberne's Nervous Accelerator potion, that high-tech watch tweaks time into overdrive. In one riotous scene the hero's irresponsible girlfriend borrows the gadget and gleefully wreaks havoc on a Miami beach by invisibly removing a great many women's bikini tops. This, incidentally, is a loving homage to Thorne Smith's fantasy *Topper Takes a Trip* (sequel to *The Jovial Ghosts*), where the invisible hands of rowdy ghosts cause similar seaside chaos in France.

Another technological speed-up features in Alfred Bester's *The Stars My Destination*, whose obsessed protagonist gets rewired as a cyborg commando able to switch into ultra-fast action. In one of the sillier episodes of Henry Kuttner's very silly *Robots Have No Tails*, the mad-scientist hero is plagued by an eerie unseen being that steals his food, and eventually turns out to be his own speeded-up grandfather (don't ask: it's complicated). Arthur C. Clarke had a go at the theme in his gloomy morality fable "All the Time in the World", whose antihero has Earth at his mercy thanks to an alien time-accelerator device but can't turn it off since the planet is about to blow up.

Such tinkering with time-flow may be the only way to make the happy days last. In Robert Heinlein's *The Puppet Masters*, our narrator is far too busy dealing with an invasion of mind-controlling alien slugs to get married and enjoy a month-long passionate honeymoon, but nevertheless manages to fit this sidebar action into a single day thanks to the useful drug "tempus" (no doubt a product of Gibberne PLC). At no point, except perhaps metaphorically, do he and his bride catch fire.

Likewise, the ultra-rich youngster who buys Earth in Cordwainer Smith's *Norstrilia* is rewarded in the final chapter by a thousand years of utter bliss with his beloved cat-girl, all compressed by the magic of telepathy into twenty minutes. Which is somehow reminiscent of Richard Matheson's 1959 fantasy "Mantage", where a man's entire life plays out in fast-forward as a Hollywood movie 85 minutes long. "A good length," he thinks at the closing credits, but because this is 1950s Hollywood there are discreet fadeouts in place of the hot bedroom scenes. What a life. All gone in one 85-minute flash.

• *SFX* #249, Summer 2014

The Big 250

Two hundred and fifty years of *SFX*! Science fiction has been through many changes since 1764, when Brian Aldiss was a mere stripling and the year's hot SF novels were *Enrico Wanton's Travels to the Unknown Lands of the Southern Hemisphere and to the Kingdoms of the Monkeys and of the Dog-Headed People* by Zaccaria Seriman, written in Italian, and for English readers the first rib-tickling volume of *A Trip to the Moon: Containing an Account of the Island of Noibla, its Inhabitants, Religious and Political Customs, Etc* by the subtly pseudonymous Sir Humphry Lunatic. Noibla is of course Albion backwards. I am not making this up.

Oh, you said 250 *issues* of *SFX*? I'd better start again.

It's strange to have become the white-whiskered Oldest Inhabitant here, occasionally struggling feebly from an antique rocking-chair to belabour subeditors with my crutch. When I were a lad, magazines with Langford columns had the life expectancy of confetti at thermonuclear ground zero. Typhoid Langford, they called me.

For example, I had a regular news column titled "Fission Fragments" in *Ad Astra*, which was typeset by a million monkeys and occasionally spelt me Davd Largford. I came aboard at issue 9: *Ad Astra* bit the dust with issue 16.

At *Million: The Magazine of Popular Fiction* (a spinoff from *Interzone*, which unkind fans then suggested should be subtitled *The Magazine of Unpopular Fiction*), my merry column "Slightly Foxed" launched in the debut issue and went down with the ship when *Million* hit the Iceberg of Insufficient Sales two years later. By then I'd started another gig in the Brighton-based *Nexus*. After #3, alas, *Nexus* was absorbed into the Brighton-based multinational conglomerate of *Interzone*. The town wasn't big enough to hold them both.

In 1997 came *Odyssey*, where I revived the "Critical Mass" column title I'd used for 1980s book reviews. *Odyssey* indulged me by letting me write quite hefty essays, and paid the price by folding in 1999. "If you must have Langford, keep him to a tight word count" was the message to other editors.

Putting me on the masthead as editor was even more reliably disastrous. *Extro*, the professional relaunch of a Northern Irish fanzine, made me nonfiction editor at issue #2 and never reached #4 – for which I'd commissioned Duncan Lunan to write an article on Comet Swift-Tuttle that he eventually recycled in book form thirty years later. Oops.

What's more, I was a consulting editor for *The Omni Book of the Future*, a bizarre project run from the UK office of the then huge, glossy and high-paying SF/science-fact magazine *Omni* (stablemate of *Penthouse*). For some weird reason *BotF* was planned as a weekly partwork along the lines of *101 DIY Projects You Will Never Finish*, and got killed off before release when market tests revealed that no one *wanted* to buy a partwork that over the years would build into a mighty encyclopedia of, er, SF stories and articles on UFOs. I never got paid for such vital expertise as saying "This Asimov story is one of his worst – there must be something better for the launch issue?" and being told "We're going with that one because we want ISAAC ASIMOV! on the cover."

Then there was the time I destroyed *New Worlds* in its quarterly paperback incarnation, by selling them a Moorcock parody. I've always liked to think the timid publishers axed *NW* rather than risk printing the story.

So I'm raising a glass of champagne to *SFX*, one of the rare robust magazines – *Interzone* is the other – to reach 250 issues despite the curse of a long-running Langford column. Amazing!

• *SFX* #250, August 2014

Hugo Horrors

According to my futuroscope, this issue of *SFX* should appear in the final week of voting for the 2014 Hugo Awards to be presented at Loncon 3, the London Worldcon. Beneath the visible Hugo ballot and online Hugo Voter Packet (of which more below) are seething controversies which – though there's always grumbling – seemed unusually toxic this year.

For starters we had the Wossgate scandal. The Loncon chairs asked TV celeb and SF fan Jonathan Ross to be the Hugo ceremony MC, despite protests from Loncon committee members who'd read the Controversy section of Ross's Wikipedia article and expected trouble. One of them resigned over this.

Sure enough, the Twitter announcement of Ross as Hugo MC generated uproar (Charles Stross: "It's ridiculous and insulting"), some tactful wesponses from Woss – "I'll happily buy the [Loncon] ticket off you and give it someone less stupid." – and a Twitterstorm that within hours persuaded him to step down. All over before most fans knew it was happening.

Next came block-voting complications. One campaign, run by fantasy author Larry Correia, argued that the liberal (in the US sense of "evil commie") SF establishment has long rigged the Hugos against right-wing/military fiction and his own publisher Baen Books. (Reality check: Lois McMaster Bujold, a popular Baen author of military SF, has won five Hugos.) Correia urged his many blog followers to retaliate by nominating a suggested right-wing Hugo slate. Several of these duly reached the final ballot, including Correia's latest novel and a story by the bizarre Vox Day.

Day, real name Theodore Beale, is a controversy-hound who says things like "I consider women's rights to be a disease that should be eradicated." In 2014 he was thrown out of the SF Writers of America for using SFWA's group Twitter feed to spread his racist abuse of an SF author who happens to be female and black. Such charming company for other Hugo nominees.

Another successful Hugo campaign pushed the *whole* of the late Robert Jordan's vast "Wheel of Time" fantasy sequence, which began in 1990. How can this possibly qualify? A rules quirk – a hangover from when novels debuted as SF magazine serials – makes serials eligible in the year of their last instalment, provided no previous segment reached the Hugo shortlist. The final WoT novel, completed by Brandon Sanderson, appeared in 2013. Therefore, the administrators agreed, the entire lumbering behemoth of 14 volumes and 4.4 million words is eligible for a 2014 Hugo as Best Novel. This is the elephant in the room.

Then there was the Hugo Voter Packet disappointment. The freebie download of Best Novel finalists – for Loncon members only – contains the Wheel of Time complete, and three Correia books, his actual nominee plus two prequels; but only "preview" extracts from the remaining shortlisted SF novels by Mira Grant (Seanan McGuire), Ann Leckie and Britain's own Charles Stross. Is this fair?

Alas, it's a publisher policy thing. Tor (WoT) and Baen (Correia) believe giveaways are great publicity, especially with a major award at stake. Orbit UK, which controls the other titles, doesn't. Its boss Tim Holman explained: "There are a lot of different attitudes to the idea of giving work away for free, but we hope most people would agree that writers and rights holders should be able to make their own choice, without feeling that their decision might have negative consequences." A bit weasel-worded, that: Orbit *didn't* let its authors "make their own choice", as they plaintively confirmed in a joint statement on the Stross blog.

Normally, Leckie would be the bookies' favourite: she's already bagged the BSFA, Arthur C. Clarke and Nebula awards. For this year's novel Hugo, though, it's anyone's guess. *[Later: Leckie won, Vox Day placed below "No Award", and there was great rejoicing.]*

During these ructions David Langford, a determined non-campaigner, heard that his own string of Hugo wins was because of "politics".

• *SFX* #251, September 2014

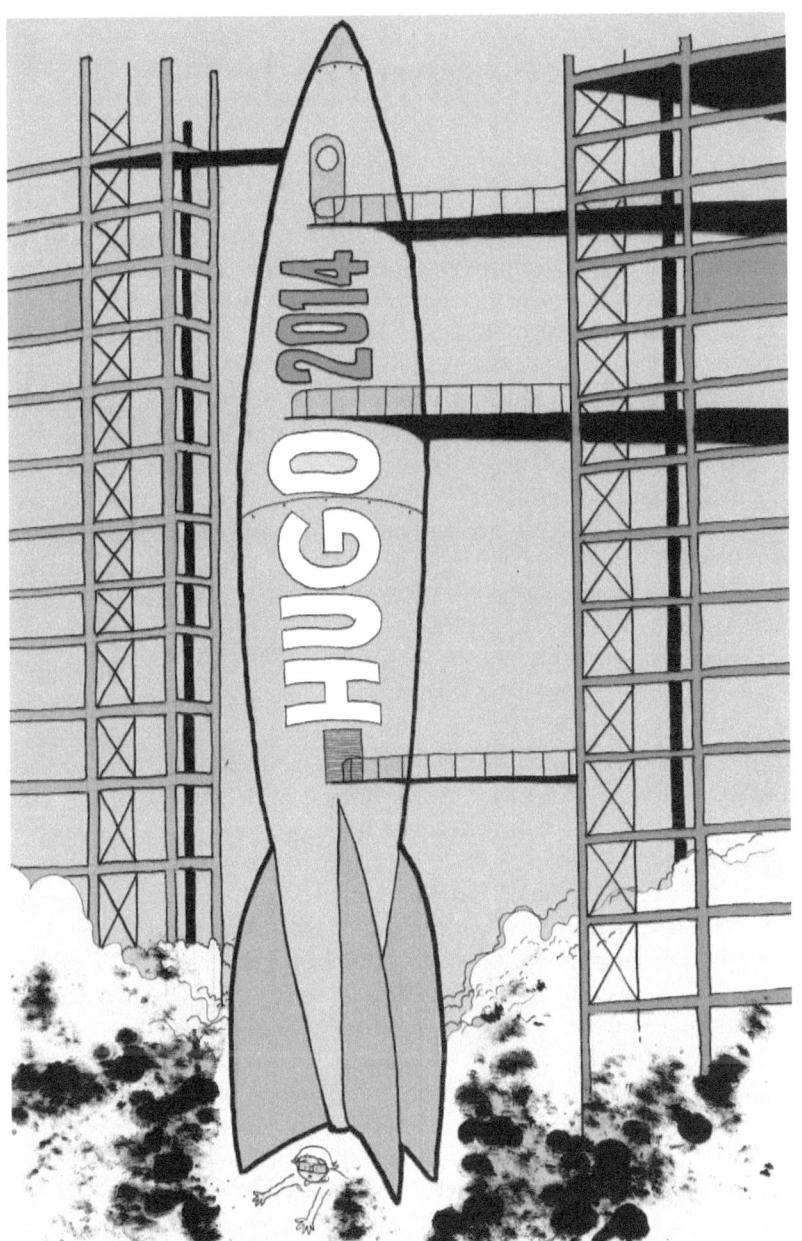

Thogomized!

It's been some time since Thog the Mighty, barbarian hero and connoisseur of barbarous prose, paid a state visit to this page. While he was away, others got in on the act and donned the Mantle of Thog, an almost unbelievably smelly garment from the middens of antiquity.

Famous author Adam Roberts, for example, recently survived a heroic read-through of Stephen R. Donaldson's five 1990s "Gap" space operas, and found rich pickings which he dutifully submitted to Thog. It's a tale of high melodrama and great steaming lumps of emotion:

"Without warning, a tingle ran down Holt's nearly strong spine and tightened around his scrotum." "... he was smiling like a corpse with an orgasm." "Angus Thermopyle laughed – a sound like the pulping of flesh." "With his mouth full of ash and fatality, he recognized that before long he was going to go mad." "His hands thrashed like dying fish at the end of his arms." (All from *A Dark and Hungry God Arises*.)

Overwrought similes, mystifying metaphors: "Wheeling like a blow, he raged." "Angus' heart clenched in a grimace which didn't show on his face." "His aura yowled of furies that didn't show on his face." "Davies looked like his chest was congested with shouts." "The air had grown viscid with mortality." "Nick let out a clenched laugh." "His beard moved like a blade whenever he spoke or turned his head." (*Chaos and Order*.)

In the final volume, people become very excitable indeed: "Indignation and confusion appeared to flush through Chief Mandich in waves, staining his skin with splotches like the marks of an infection." "Her voice ached like Morn's arm." "Min's jaws clenched and loosened as if she were chewing iron." "Smoke seeped out of her hair as if the mind under it had been burned to the ground." "His voice sounded as bleak as hard vacuum." "Standing rigid, as if he were remembering a crucifixion, he shouted." "The sound of knives filled Hyland's voice." "Blaine wore her sexuality like an accusation." "In response he brandished his beard at her like a club." (*This Day All Gods Die*.)

There are other magical phrases ("Anodyne Systems, the sole licensed manufacturer of SOD-CMOS.")... but I should say more about Thog himself, who presides over the tortured-prose department of the SF newsletter *Ansible*. Officially he's a creation of my pal John Grant, whose *The Book of the Magnakai* has the only authentic painting of Thog as its cover art. But Thog gets around. Back in the 1950s, the great US humorist James Thurber reported that his cranky radio would often say "thog, thog, thog" before dying altogether. *Can this be coincidence?*

Gary Larson's cartoon cavemen in *The Far Side* are often called Thog, though also more famously Thag, a name now immortalized in palaeontology – try Googling for "thagomizer". *The Muppet Show* introduced a 9½-foot shaggy blue monster named Thog in its 1970 Christmas special: unlike his green companion Thig, this Thog made several comebacks and was once seen hugging Mia Farrow. There's altogether too much Thog identity theft going on.

Knowing Thog's fondness for eyeball antics, a friend of *Ansible* sent a link to the Nyanglish "English example search" website's coverage of a forgotten crime-fiction hero's eyes: nyanglish.com/jimmie-dale-s-eyes.

Try it! Naturally I wondered what nyanglish.com/thog might reveal, and was boggled by the range of unlikely contexts in which the scourge of the writing classes appears. I don't even *want* to know the source of the sentence "Thog wears a leprechaun costume, while he packs a giant wooden alpaca with potato salad." Truly there are things with which even Thog was not meant to meddle.

David Langford warns the faint-hearted to avoid Thog.org and its "I Feel Unlucky" random selection button.

• *SFX* #252, October 2014

Curiosa Dept

One odd corner of the SF world is "Curiosities", the back page of the venerable *Magazine of Fantasy and Science Fiction*. Here, various old fogeys including me go on about forgotten books that tickle their aged fancy. Here are some unlikely works I've written about there:

C.H. Hinton's nonfiction *The Fourth Dimension* (1904) is arguably even deadlier to sanity than the *Necronomicon*. People have been driven round the twist by its exercises in visualizing 4D space through sets of coloured cubes. With mnemonic chants like "satan, sanet, satet"...

Musrum (1968) by Eric Thacker and Anthony Earnshaw, a deeply weird cult fantasy, features many wise sayings like "A torpedoed cathedral sinks rapidly into the earth." Its central McGuffin, tastier by far than the One Ring, is the Giant Mushroom. Complications include the Second Crimean War.

Lord Dunsany's *The Last Revolution* (1951) is his one straight SF novel, with self-reproducing robots that revolt and threaten English rural life. Luckily they weren't built for the outdoors: just as bacteria nobbled Wells's Martians, the machine horde succumbs to rust.

The Cruise of the Talking Fish (1957) by W.E. Bowman spoofs *The Kon-Tiki Expedition* but turns into SF when the raft crew's pet cats eat radioactive flying fish. This flips them into super-speed, living and breeding in fast-forward until... does anyone remember a *Star Trek* episode about tribbles?

A semi-famous epigram: "You cannot hope / to bribe or twist, / thank God! the / British journalist. / But, seeing what / the man will do / unbribed, there's / no occasion to." Hardly anyone knows it's from *The Uncelestial City* (1930) by Humbert Wolfe, a book-length afterlife fantasy. What's more, a book-length afterlife fantasy *in verse*. I read it for Curiosities so others wouldn't have to. Be grateful.

Leo Lionni's *Parallel Botany* (1977) is a non-fact pop-science book about an imaginary plant kingdom that's unfairly neglected because many examples are invisible. Even if visible, their colours may be an unobtrusive "gamut of blacks", though some cast luminous shadows.

And so weirdly on. Botany by Jorge Luis Borges.

The "real" facts in David Hughes's alt-history *But for Bunter* (1985) were suppressed by the government because "they embarrass the entire century. They make history itself look ridiculous." It emerges that Billy Bunter and his chums at Greyfriars School were all real people (the school rotter grew up as Sir Oswald Mosley); Bunter himself is bumblingly responsible for many twentieth-century disasters including the Great War's death toll and the wreck of the *Titanic*.

Heavens (1922) by Louis Untermeyer is a parody collection spoofing various authors' versions of heaven. Victims include James Branch Cabell, G.K. Chesterton... and H.G. Wells, beginning with a twenty-first-century utopia where "corners and all dust-collecting angles had long since vanished from architecture", and shifting via Time Machine to slightly embarrassing come-uppance in AD 5,320,506.

In John Buchan's only SF novel *The Gap in the Curtain* (1932), various terribly English chaps get one quick glimpse of a newspaper a year in the future. Can they profit from this inside knowledge? There doesn't seem much hope for the two who see their own obituaries, but Time turns out to be a tricky business.

The Devil in Velvet (1951) by John Dickson Carr is an old favourite, with a modern history professor obsessed by a 1675 poisoning case. A deal with the devil takes him back in time for detective work, copious sex and rousing adventure in Charles II's London. Many a swash is buckled.

My first Curiosity was about an Ernest Bramah story, and *F&SF* doesn't let you revisit the same author – so I sadly can't tackle Bramah's *The Secret of the League* (1907), where instead of jetpacks people have strap-on mechanical wings, leading to questions of English propriety: "Hastings permitted mixed flying." And Tunbridge Wells was Disgusted.

David Langford wonders how aged he'll have to be before his own early works qualify as Curiosities.

• *SFX* #253, November 2014

Loncon Overload

So that was Loncon 3, the third World SF Convention in London. Gosh, it was big, and hard on the feet – the London ExCeL venue is close on a kilometre long. This was the first Worldcon to sell over ten thousand memberships; nearly eight thousand people turned up. Were there really 5324 programme events? The numbers ran from 1003 to 5324, but that's secret code for Day 1 Item 1 to Day 5 Item 108. Still, there was a *lot* happening.

Robert Silverberg offered me a vital statistic: "I've calculated that George R.R. Martin's annual income exceeds my total net worth. And I am *not a poor man*."

My one panel appearance was "Evolution of the Encyclopedia of Science Fiction", where we editors shamelessly bragged about reaching 4.5 million words that month. The room was gratifyingly crowded despite eighteen rival attractions in the same time slot. No one hurled rotten tomatoes. That counts as a win.

Finding Charlie Stross's birthday bash and other invitation-only events was a challenge. The Long March to private party rooms went via a huge bare unused ExCeL hall and past four more such vast empty spaces, like parking bays in Iain M. Banks's General Systems Vehicles. Weaklings turned back, but Langford is made of sterner stuff when major issues (free booze) are at stake.

I remember breakfast with Christopher Priest; afternoon tea with Jo Walton; George R.R. Martin plotting horrid butchery of edibles in the fast-food arcade; being accosted by Pat Cadigan with her traditional war-cry "Langford, you dog"; spending too much; event clashes that made me miss the *SFX* party, though later I found our editor downing freebies at the Gollancz do. Sights in the tent-filled Fan Village hospitality area included two Tardises, the Iron Throne and a wandering Hawaiian Tiki Dalek (DO YOU LIKE PIN-A COL-A-DA?) which made it into *Private Eye*'s friendly cartoon coverage.

The *other* SF Encyclopedia panel was a "Reunion" of survivors from the 1979 first edition, before I got involved: mighty critic John

Clute, Malcolm Edwards of Orion/Gollancz – both Loncon guests of honour – and Peter Nicholls, who created the original *SFE*. At panel's end he received a long standing ovation as First Founder... an emotional highlight of the weekend.

Having once enjoyed a free trip to a US Worldcon courtesy of the TransAtlantic Fan Fund (TAFF), I try to support the fundraising auctions and had donated three small stained-glass panels made by the late great Bob Shaw, acquired for peanuts in the 1980s. Would anyone buy them? Halfway through the auction an ashen-faced, panic-stricken auctioneer whispered: "We can't find them!"

This was my cue to run all the way from the auction room (ExCeL Level 3) to the official repository where I'd handed in the stained glass for pickup (Level 0). Then back again with the bag. Puff, gasp, is this what heart attacks feel like? Bob Shaw's creations sparked furious bidding and fetched nearly £800. I'm still boggled.

Despite widespread fears of trouble from block voting in the Hugo Awards (see my *SFX* #251 column 'Hugo Horrors'), the "conspiracy" was a flop. At the ceremony, Ann Leckie's popular *Ancillary Justice* added the best-novel Hugo to its Clarke, Nebula and other awards; our own Charlie Stross's deeply perverse Lovecraftian unicorn story "Equoid" won as best novella, his third Hugo. The most repellently controversial nominee placed below No Award, and Hugo pundits (who shall remain nameless) sighed with relief.

Loncon ended on 18 August with a flying visit from Brian Aldiss, who had been at the first Loncon in 1957 and who turned 89 that day. At the closing ceremony, unforgettably, the entire audience serenaded him with "Happy Birthday to You".

There's more, much more, but I have only this one page.

David Langford thinks the Loncon committee did a bloody good job.

• *SFX* #254, December 2014

Don't Look Now

After the London Worldcon I heard from a nice lady I'd met there, now reading Charles Stross's *Accelerando* (in an ice cream shop, where else?). She wanted to know whether I had anything to do with the book's "neural wetware-crashing Langford fractals". Er, yes, that would be me...

Longer ago than I like to think, *Interzone* published a Langford story called "Blit" that tried to put a new spin on the SF gimmick of information so indigestible that it literally kills you. Way back in Fred Hoyle's *The Black Cloud*, for example, the vast alien intelligence of the title generously makes its wisdom available to puny Earthling scientists – whose brains blow out from data overload.

My take on this, partly inspired by Douglas Hofstadter's *Godel, Escher, Bach*, was a "basilisk" image that leaps along the optic nerve to confront your brain with a program it can't run. Fatal fractals – there are bits of the Mandelbrot set you really don't want to see at high magnification – or Bridget Riley op-art with the dazzle turned up to eleven. In "Blit", terrorists with stencils spray-paint urban walls with a lethal graphic mysteriously called the Parrot.

Years later (see *SFX* #10) I read Greg Egan's nifty *Permutation City* and found one character putting the frighteners on internet spies by typing: "Whoever you are, be warned: I'm about to display the Langford Mind-Erasing Fractal Basilisk, so..." Immortality was mine!

Ken MacLeod gave me another namecheck in *The Cassini Division*, where he called those brain-crashing images "the Langford visual hack". In Ken's book it's more an urban myth than actual fact, and his heroine flatteringly wonders: "What kind of twisted mind *starts* these things?" I couldn't possibly comment.

Good old Charlie Stross namechecked me in *Accelerando* and went on to make my nasties a regular feature of electromagical defences in his Laundry series, with the Langford Death Parrot referenced in *The Fuller Memorandum* and a mention of Cambridge IV (the doomed research facility that developed my Parrot fractal) in *The Atrocity*

Archives. Someone out there on the net stole a sinister-looking, vaguely bird-shaped computer graphic and posted it with a caption that led to this reassuring Yahoo! Answers exchange:

Q. Is the Basilisk photo of the Death Parrot, by Langford real...? Someone go look at it and tell me if you die or not.

A. Yep, it works.

After writing four stories about those killer images and winning a Hugo with the last ("Different Kinds of Darkness"), it seemed wise to stop before the sequence turned into the Fractal Wheel of Time. But owing to unbelievable modesty I have to keep explaining that, apart from the fractals, it's not a new idea. William Gibson's *Neuromancer* has "black ice" cyberspace defences intended to fry hackers' brains. Two earlier examples both coincidentally come from October 1969: Piers Anthony's *Macroscope* – featuring mind-killing "Destroyer" broadcasts from deep space – and the World's Funniest Joke skit in the first episode of *Monty Python.*

Not that Monty Python invented that concept: jokes that make you laugh yourself to death feature in a Lord Dunsany story from 1915 and a comic poem written by Oliver Wendell Holmes in 1830. My own Wikipedia coverage has accumulated some "basilisk" examples which should really be in the useful "Motif of harmful sensation" entry, if that hadn't been deleted for the terrible Wikicrime of Original Research. (Google can still find archived copies.) The TV Tropes site at tvtropes.org – GOVERNMENT SANITY WARNING: this can be addictive – covers the topic under Brown Note, which I'm afraid means what you probably think it means.

When I bit the bullet and wrote a *SF Encyclopedia* article about this theme, I swiped the terminology from my own stories and titled it Basilisks. So there.

David Langford is waiting for Wikipedia to notice the SFE entry.

• *SFX* #255, January 2015

Filmic Factoids

After editing heaps of articles on terrible old SF films, I want to write *The Science of Monster Movies...* in the great tradition of *The Science of Star Trek* and *The Science of Harry Potter*. Some things I have learned:

Radiation makes things big. Nuclear testing creates giant ants in *Them!* (the 1954 classic), cosmic rays produce giant wasps in *Monster from Green Hell* (1957), uranium ore causes giantish spiders in *Horrors of Spider Island* (1959), and a tiny smear of the flesh-eating Blob rip-off in *Caltiki, the Immortal Monster* (1959) not only gets big but uncontrollably *reproduces* whenever a ray-emitting comet approaches Earth.

Radiation also mutates things – fast! Uranium in *The Cyclops* (1957) takes just six months to convert a lost explorer to the title's 25-foot, one-eyed horror. In *Day the World Ended* (1955), World War Three is barely over before radioactive fallout spawns a three-eyed, bulbous-headed monster to menace survivors. Now imagine the script conference where someone asked, "How do we establish that this mutant is whatsername's missing fiancé?" and after much heated discussion they remembered that Hollywood werewolves revert to human form on dying. Death reverses the mutation process! I must have missed that particular biology class.

Radiation works differently on different things. *Island Claws* (1980), made soon after Three Mile Island, sees crabs on the Florida Keys enraged by radioactive leakage from a local reactor. They attack communities in terrifying scenes of stock footage. But thanks to an aspect of radiation known to physicists as "limited effects budget", only one crab becomes traditionally huge. Unable to beat its chest like King Kong, it instead roars and sticks out its tongue, reducing the audience to fear-crazed giggles.

Another principle of monster-movie biology is: "You Are What You Eat". Any animal-derived wonder drug will infect victims with horrid animal traits. Bat's blood spoils your social life by turning you into Batman, or rather into *The Vampire* (1957). Wolf blood serum: a werewolf in *The Mad Monster* (1957). Alligator DNA: *The Alligator People*

(1959). I don't think wasps make royal jelly, but as a beauty treatment it has tiresome side-effects in *The Wasp Woman* (1959). Bee royal jelly: *Invasion of the Bee Girls* (1973)... and so on to the recent *District 9* (2009), where bodily fluid from alien prawns causes the hero to develop a prawnoid arm with Secret Prawn Powers.

This is such a whiskery SF cliché that P.G. Wodehouse spoofed it as long ago as 1926 in a story that opens with film addicts discussing the cliffhanger serial *The Vicissitudes of Vera* (a dig at *The Perils of Pauline* from 1914), in which a mad scientist plans to give our heroine a spinal injection of lobster-gland extract and turn her into a lobster. Because that's what mad scientists do.

Dinosaurs are our favourite monsters; practically every lost realm unknown to map-makers contains a few. For example, they turn up far underground in Jules Verne's *Journey to the Centre of the Earth*, whose 1959 film reveals the surprising fact that dinosaurs looked just like modern iguanas with fins stuck on. This is because... but you're already ahead of me. Dinosaurs are even found on another planet in the singularly unconvincing *King Dinosaur* (1955), where we're firmly told that an ordinary lizard enlarged through the magic of rear projection is a *Tyrannosaurus rex*, crawling on four legs. Couldn't the studio lizard-wrangler have trained it to rear up a bit?

As for lost worlds in cinema... should you ever find yourself in one, remember that they tend to explode. Especially if named Atlantis. An obscure tectonic condition called "fear of anticlimax" means that our explorers can rarely escape to civilization without the lost realm first being destroyed by volcanoes, earthquakes, tsunamis, or preferably all three. This is, frankly, no way to promote lost-world tourism.

David Langford just vanished under a Richter 9 lava tsunami.

• *SFX* #256, February 2015

Wrong Notes

Our local charity shop is closing down, and I rescued a few reference books from oblivion. *Chambers Biographical Dictionary* is bound to come in handy someday... "Are you looking for your own name in there?" my wife asked. "No, no," I lied, quickly paging on to Ursula K. Le Guin. Whose entry mentions the Earth Sea (not Earthsea) trilogy and morphs *Planet of Exile* into *Plant of Exile*. Again I remembered the bit in one of Robert Heinlein's SF novels where the young hero is shocked, shocked when his father casually scribbles corrections in a textbook.

You don't expect textbook standards from newspapers, not now they've fired all the researchers and fact-checkers. A recent *Independent* snippet broke the news that Morten Tyldum is to direct the film *Pattern Recognition*, "Based on the novel *Neuromancer* by William Gibson..." A measure of sanity returned when the following thumbnail synopsis was in fact of Gibson's novel *Pattern Recognition*. The *Indy* obituary for BBC producer/director Michael Hayes credits him with early *Doctor Who* stories and, before that, the 1961 SF classic *A for Andromeda* – or as the headline put it, "the sci-fi series 'The Andromeda Strain'". Duh.

Another Gibson namecheck from a *Sunday Herald* piece on the Glasgow Science Festival: "The whole basis of the internet was famously inspired by William Gibson's book *Neuromancer* and Isaac Asimov, who recently died, 'invented' earth-orbiting satellites in one of his tales." Poor old Arthur C. Clarke, already forgotten.

The BBC website ran a story about that massive flop *John Carter*, "based on the books of Conan the Barbarian author Edgar Rice Burroughs". After the first 5,271,009 complaints, Conan magically became Tarzan.

Our most reliable sources of SF/fantasy disinformation are quiz shows, not covered here (with a nod to *Private Eye*'s "Dumb Britain") for over fifty issues. Put on your tinfoil-lined thinking caps...

The Chase: "In what novel by H.G. Wells does an inventor travel into the future?" Contestant: *"Great Expectations."*

Cash Cab: "What plant is said to deter vampires?" Contestant (after a long pause): "Well, I was gonna say garlic but that's not a plant, is it?" Host: "You've just won ten pounds!"

Ejector Seat: "Which British author wrote *The Jungle Book*?" Contestant: "E.L. James."

The Weakest Link: "In astronomy, a nucleus, a coma and a tail are all parts of which celestial body?" Contestant: "A horse."

The Chase: "Which Irvine Welsh novel features a monologue by a tapeworm?" Contestant: "*Wuthering Heights*."

Two Tribes: "Who wrote *The Ballad of Reading Gaol* after his incarceration there?" Contestant, surely with tongue in cheek: "Gary Glitter."

In It to Win It: "Dame Judi Dench played which character with a single-letter name in James Bond?" Contestant: "I'm thinking D or E. *[Pause]* D!"

Tipping Point: "In the famous equation E=mc², what does the letter E stand for?" Contestant: "Einstein."

While we're veering off into science, *The Chase* had this prophetic foreshadowing of climate change: "What Shakespeare play has the coldest season of the year in the title?" Contestant: "*A Midsummer Night's Dream*."

Pointless: "Which G.O. wrote *Animal Farm*?" Contestant: "I've got George Osborne in my head." What a truly ghastly SF concept.

The Chase: "On what day of the week did Robinson Crusoe find his companion?" Contestant: "Tuesday."

The Weakest Link: "Which 'T' is the wife of Oberon and Queen of the Fairies in *A Midsummer Night's Dream*?" Contestant, surely deserving half marks: "Tinkerbell."

My current all-time favourite is from, yet again, *The Chase*. Host: "*The Nun's Priest's Tale* is a story by which fourteenth-century English author?" Contestant: "J.K. Rowling."

David Langford is not the answer – he's part of the problem.

• *SFX #257*, March 2015

Gathering MOSS

Remember my *SFX 239* column on the joys of creating your own ebooks? Flogging these was a soothing microbusiness, without the hassle of wrapping and posting POD books. Money arrived via PayPal (for example) and books went out as email attachments or website downloads. Sales mightn't be huge, but there was the quiet satisfaction of getting 100% of the profit – rather than the miserable 25% that so many large publishers have decided is an unbelievably generous maximum.

Bad news broke in late 2014, and this simple way of life ended on 1 January. As so often, the problem was Amazon – not directly, but because EU governments hated Amazon's ploy of selling from places like Luxembourg where VAT is low, giving them an edge over registered UK sellers who must charge VAT at 20%. UK microbusinesses weren't bothered because you didn't need to register for VAT until your annual turnover went past £81,000.

Under the new rules, wicked old Amazon must now charge VAT at the applicable rate in the *customer's* country. As noted, that's 20% here. It's a huge hassle to keep track of VAT rates in dozens of EU jurisdictions, but Amazon's accountants have to deal with it.

Unfortunately, so now do tens or hundreds of thousands of one-person microbusinesses selling digital products like SF/fantasy ebooks, Clanger knitting patterns, Klingon recipes, phone apps to generate Langford columns, and so on. The horrible surprise was that although the standard UK VAT threshold stays at £81,000, the special new threshold for EU sales of such digital "services" is... zero.

Right. By selling a single 99p ebook online to a non-UK EU buyer, you're automatically plunged into the nightmare of VAT. You need to sign up at the UK MOSS site (Mini One Stop Shop; how *cuddly* it sounds), apply VAT at the proper rate for each customer's country, and start submitting VAT returns four times a year. It gets worse. You need two non-contradictory confirmations of where each customer lives – PayPal, for example, provides at most one "verified address". You must keep these customer location records for ten years, with tiresome bureaucratic safeguards that dump you into Data Protection Act hell.

It's hardly surprising that after researching the thrills and pitfalls of e-trading under the new "VATMOSS" regime, many SF/fantasy ebook publishers have decided that the best way to deal with the whole ghastly VATMESS is to go out of business. Accountants and lawyers agree this is probably the safest plan.

Alternatives? You can revert to the Dark Ages and make the post office happy by mailing ebooks on CD or floppy disk – because in this Alice-in-Wonderland regulatory world, the identical ebook attracts VAT if it's a website download, but not (unless you're VAT-registered for other reasons) if it's sent by snailmail. You can carry on as before and hope no one notices – but remember the VAT authorities (HM Revenue & Customs) can inflict truly terrifying fines. How about refusing to sell ebooks to non-UK EU customers *[which is what I'm currently doing at my own Ansible Editions]*? HMRC doesn't object but warns that expensive EU anti-discrimination lawsuits could follow. Lastly, you can sign up with a big distributor that takes a huge share of your revenue, such as Amazon, and savour the irony of an anti-Amazon regulation that swells the profits of Amazon.

Frustrated by HMRC advice ranging from unhelpful to contradictory, SF authors and publishers took the lead in pushing back. A Change.org petition to Vince Cable MP, Secretary of State for Business Innovation and Skill, quickly reached 10,000 signatures and brought the useless response "Don't worry, most people won't be affected." Probably he meant "most MPs".

If you sell or hope to sell ebooks or any other kind of digital product online, check for breaking news at euvataction.org/.

[*Later:* I have a longer page of links at ae.ansible.uk/?id=vatmoss.]

David Langford, if transmitted digitally to Hungary, is subject to VAT at 27%.

• *SFX* #258, April 2015

Books About

As C.S. Lewis famously wrote, "If we have to choose, it is always better to read L. Ron Hubbard again than to read a new criticism of him." Actually he said it about Chaucer, but it's an interesting general principle. Sometimes I agree. At other times I prefer a good critical book about science fiction to actual SF, especially if the latter is by L. Ron Hubbard.

Now I don't mean those dire academic volumes with titles like *Some Lesser-Known Aspects of Eighteenth-Century Utopian Fabulation in Albania.* The great SF/fantasy critics are mostly practising writers who praise stories from an interestingly original angle or put the boot in with joyful style and elegance – like Damon Knight with *In Search of Wonder* (1956, but look for the expanded third edition of 1996), Kingsley Amis long before his knighthood with *New Maps of Hell* (1960), James Blish with *The Issue at Hand* (1964), Ursula K. Le Guin with *The Language of the Night* (1979), Algis Budrys with *Benchmarks: Galaxy Bookshelf* (1985), or John Clute with *Strokes* (1988).

The SF criticism in my own home library fills thirteen feet of shelves, so I could carry on listing titles for ages. However, the long succession of names might become a little too like Beachcomber's vital but fortunately imaginary reference work *The Anthology of Huntingdonshire Cabmen.* In these degenerate latter days, there are even several critical collections by me, of which it has often been said... but never proved.

Here are some recommendations from recent reading, one dated 1987 and three from 2014:

Robert Silverberg's *Worlds of Wonder* (the 1987 title) is cunningly disguised as an anthology of classic SF: I didn't buy it when it appeared because I knew all the stories, some by heart. Silly me. What I missed is that each tale comes with an essay from master craftsman Silverberg, taking it apart to show just what makes it a classic. His revealing autobiographical introduction "The Making of a Science-Fiction Writer" is also a must-read.

Similarly, Jo Walton revisits nearly 130 old favourites and ponders why she loves or no longer loves them in *What Makes This Book So Great*, a selection of her many hundreds of thoughtful posts in this vein from the Tor.com blog. She usually has something wise to say. I nodded often – in agreement, I mean, not nodding off – and only rarely shook my head. Her tactful meditation on SF Series That Went Downhill is full of sad truths.

John Clute's latest nonfiction collection – there have been several since that 1988 debut – is called *Stay* and as usual throws you in at the deep end of a deep mind fond of occasional "studiously flamboyant obscurities"... to quote his *SF Encyclopedia* entry, written by one John Clute, who should know. Besides many densely meaty reviews, *Stay* includes five short stories (where else could you find an image like "an entablature of salamanders loosed suddenly into a myoclonic can-can"?) and his 2006 mini-encyclopedia *The Darkening Garden: A Short Lexicon of Horror*. Whose approach to horror is like no other.

Adam Roberts – known to *Princess Bride* buffs as the Dread Punster Roberts – publishes witty, learned criticism at a great rate on his blog Sibilant Fricative (since closed down). For reasons which are deeply unclear, *Sibilant Fricative* the book collects material not from its namesake but from his now-deleted former blog Punkadiddle. Besides being insightful, these reviews include some of the funniest I've ever read: his annoylogistic take on Neal Stephenson's *Anathem*, for example, or the epic assault on all 11 volumes of Robert Jordan's *Wheel of Time*, with extensive quotes from the master's prose. "He sounded like a bumblebee the size of a cat instead of a mastiff." Of course he did.

Someone said it's always better to read David Langford again than to read him banging on about criticism. [H'm. This pithy aphorism seems to need more work.]

• *SFX* #259, May 2015

Bat Durston Lives

Not many people remember the original soap operas – never-ending US radio serials, like *The Archers* but relentlessly commercial and called soap opera because the sponsors mostly tried to sell you soap. (James Thurber has a long, funny survey of the soaps in *The Beast in Me and Other Animals*.) The story quality was low, the cliché count high. Naturally uninspired hack Westerns were soon dubbed horse operas, and in 1941 Wilson Tucker – himself a nifty SF author – coined the phrase "space opera" for the "hacky, grinding, stinking, outworn, spaceship yarn."

Attitudes change: New Space Opera as written by the late lamented Iain M. Banks is ever so highly respected in SF circles. But the Western connection used to be too close for comfort when pulp-magazine authors recycled horse opera as space opera, with six-shot rayguns and radium claim-jumping on the Milky Way's wild western frontier:

"Jets blasting, Bat Durston came screeching down through the atmosphere of Bbllzznaj, a tiny planet seven billion light years from Sol. He cut out his super-hyper-drive for the landing... and at that point, a tall, lean spaceman stepped out of the tail assembly, proton gun-blaster in a space-tanned hand.

"'Get back from those controls, Bat Durston,' the tall stranger lipped thinly. 'You don't know it, but this is your last space trip.'"

That's not the real thing but a cunning spoof. From the 1950s, *Galaxy* magazine ran a regular ad with Western and space-opera versions of the same hack story opening (guess which appears above), plus the strident claim YOU'LL NEVER SEE IT IN GALAXY. Never mind the critics who rudely retorted that you *did* occasionally see it in *Galaxy*, and not just in ads.

In fact there are some good SF westerns, like Bob Shaw's serious "Skirmish on a Summer Morning" or – played for laughs – Poul Anderson's and Gordon Dickson's "The Sheriff of Canyon Gulch", in which impressionable alien teddy-bears adopt Wild West ways, and Howard Waldrop's "Night of the Cooters", where a stray Martian invasion cylinder from *The War of the Worlds* lands in 1890s Texas to bedevil the local sheriff. But mostly it was Bat Durston stuff.

Bat came suddenly to mind, a nasty habit of his, when I read *The New Yorker*'s explanation of how an outright SF novel – *Station Eleven* by Emily St John Mandel – crashed the exclusive "literary fiction" shortlist of the US National Book Awards. It's "set in a familiar genre universe, in which a pandemic has destroyed civilization. The twist – the thing that makes *Station Eleven* National Book Award material – is that the survivors are artists."

If that's all it takes...

"Bat Durston, have you gone plumb loco?" gritted the spacepoke's raw-boned pardner Lefty, scratching his ear with his snub-nosed, six-chambered neutron depolarizer. "What in tarnation you doing there?"

"Reckon I gonna need a mite more gamboge in them thar highlights," drawled Durston lazily, squeezing paint from a space-rations tube on to his big rugged palette. "If art's what them danged National Book Award judges want, then I guess art is what they gonna get."

Smoke curled from Bat's stogie as, narrow-eyed and grim-jawed, he plied his brush with the speed of a striking sex-crazed strooka. Time ambled by like an ornery space-dogie. Outside, space-tumbleweed rolled across great vacuum-prairies, past the floating mesas of the western asteroid belt.

"Shucks," Lefty spat at last, "a five-year-old kid could paint better than that."

Bat grinned a wide, nonrepresentational space-grin. "Right. So I'm figgerin' we're not just fixed with the NBA – this here is a cinch for the Turner Prize!"

David Langford is spurring his Mustang-class star-speedster to head off the greenskins at the pass.

• *SFX* #260, June 2015

20 Glorious Years

This *SFX* comes rolling off the presses twenty years after the first issue, which was dated June 1995, priced at "£3 of your Earth Money" and imaginatively numbered #1. In the light of hindsight, true ubergeeks or William Gibson would have started the count at zero. Somehow, over the decades, I'd mercifully forgotten that my first column drafts were titled "Supercritical" – a quirk which inaugural *SFX* editor Matt Bielby wisely ignored.

Ah, nostalgia. Those were the days when paperbacks cost £4.99, the hot new cover-billed film was *Tank Girl*, Glasgow's first World SF Convention took a full-page ad, the tie-in merchandise spot was headed "Objets d'arse", and readers were carefully briefed on this new-fangled Internet thingy: "All you need to connect to Futurenet is an Internet account, such as Demon or Cityscape, or a direct college connection. Then simply use your World Wide Web browser..." But first, *switch the computer on.*

Reviewers were seemingly in short supply for the first half-year of *SFX.* In those seven issues, besides the first seven Langford columns and an interview with Christopher Priest, I had 53 book reviews. To the relief of all concerned, this glut of me was never repeated.

The first-written review was of Terry Pratchett's *Soul Music* in paperback, Discworld novel #15. Now there are forty of them (with one last Tiffany Aching YA tale to come), this feels like an early book of the series but it certainly didn't then. As I write, the day after Sir Terry's all too early death at age 66, the tributes and obituaries are everywhere. He leaves a big jagged hole in the world.

I was always a tiny bit nervous about reviewing Discworld novels, because I suspected I should declare an interest. Once upon a time I wrote an enthusiastic reader's report on *Equal Rites* for Gollancz, which may have helped persuade them that they needed Terry. But they probably didn't need telling.

That led to many years of reading Pratchett for corrupt personal gain, first for Gollancz and later for Doubleday – going through the early drafts and reporting on plot holes, continuity problems, jokes that seemed to need more polishing or went right over my head... "Langfordization" of Discworld novels became a tradition, continuing from *Mort* through to *Thud!*, but of course I can't take any credit for the results. Mostly it was a matter of prodding Terry to tackle issues he vaguely knew about but hadn't yet got around to. It was fun.

Amazing revelations will not follow, since this tinkering was all in deadly confidence. As our man would add to email when he remembered that I also publish an SF scandal sheet: "NFA,YB!" (Not For *Ansible*, You Bastard.)

I'm endlessly grateful for all the silly conversations at conventions in places as far-flung as Australia; for the introductions Terry generously wrote for my own comic novel *The Leaky Establishment* and my two Discworld quiz books (those were Gollancz's bright idea, but Terry indulgently allowed them to happen); and for the opportunity to write about him in dozens of reference books and, very nearly, an official British Council "Writers and Their Work" booklet. Although it was the British Council's own publishers who approached me about writing this official acceptance of Terry into the UK literary pantheon, he predicted that a backlash of literary snobbery would ensure "that this will wither away"... and he was right.

My jokey prediction in the September 1998 *SFX*: "A few decades hence, perhaps Sir Terry Pratchett will celebrate his 80th birthday by launching the First Church of Discworld." Right about the Sir, which followed in 2009. Wrong about the 80th birthday – but how I wish I hadn't been.

David Langford notes that SFX #1 also had an interview with Iain M. Banks. Another good man lost too soon.

• *SFX* #261, July 2015

Puppygate

The 2015 Hugo nominations caused widespread gloom and outrage. There'd been dark forebodings about a shortlist hijacked by politics – gloating hints on Facebook – and a news embargo broken by the unexpected tweet "Guess Who's A Hugo Nominee?"

Last year's Hugos suffered a bloc-vote campaign from conservative US authors claiming discrimination against their favourite military action-adventures. This made them sad; their "Sad Puppies" (SP) slate promoted their own and their buddies' work, boosting some titles onto the Hugo shortlist though not to final victory. Worldcon voters chose otherwise.

The *next* SP campaign realized the best strategy was to allow those pesky final-ballot voters no choice. There's a huge spread of nominations for each category, with thousands of Worldcon members' preferences scattered across hundreds of possibles competing for just five slots on the Hugo ballot. The SPs concocted a complete slate of five nominees for (almost) all Hugo categories, and instructed their supporters to vote the straight ticket chosen by the Central Council.

It worked. Using these morally dodgy *but* legally permissible tactics, a modest percentage of the electorate can indeed dominate the ballot. As first announced, slate choices completely filled both Editor categories, Related Work (nonfiction), Short Story, Novelette and Novella, with only two non-slate finalists for Best Novel. One novelette was later ruled ineligible.

More complications! SP associate Vox Day had created a variant "Rabid Puppies" slate which additionally, shamelessly, pushed himself and stories from his own small press Castalia House. Despite VD's publicly expressed racism, misogyny, neo-Nazi sympathies and general obnoxiousness, RP was even more successful than SP, with seven Castalia stories on the 2015 Hugo ballot. Not bad for a hitherto unknown publisher. Apparently VD has many supporters in games fandom who bought Worldcon memberships and nominated as instructed. Just why is a mystery.

Morally dubious, I wrote, but the SP/RPs say it has to be okay since "obviously" leftist "Social Justice Warriors" must have done this for years to deny past Hugos to Puppy-loved candidates. George R.R. Martin, who's watched the SF awards scene since the 1970s, paused work on his latest *Game of Thrones* novel for several long patient posts at grrm.livejournal.com, explaining that they'd got it wrong and there's no secret Hugo-controlling cabal (though the Scientologists tried once). Alas, he used logic. The Puppy response was that GRRM is sadly deluded.

Yes, the Hugo voters' vagaries have created past embarrassments, but it was painful to see so much lacklustre fiction – some very poor – railroaded onto the 2015 ballot by slate-voting tactics. Also depressing is having the Hugos dragged into US culture wars: Puppies claim in public that they're simply promoting exciting adventure fiction with no horrid political subtext, while gloating on blogs that this will make those pinko liberals' heads explode, har har. They love Robert Heinlein but forgot the recent major Heinlein biography in their nonfiction slate – so that was crowded out too. One Puppy nonfiction choice is all political message and no SF, but *the right kind of politics*.

Some people found themselves on the slate without their knowledge, or without realizing this wasn't a friendly recommendations list but an ideological battle plan. At least one refused nomination before the shortlist was announced, and (unprecedentedly) three more afterwards – one too late for the ballot to be changed. Meanwhile Vox Day, sounding increasingly like a B-movie villain with a volcano lair, warns that if he is thwarted he will destroy the Hugos forever.

What could thwart rabid puppydom? Every Hugo ballot category has one choice that no nomination slate can change. In the most rigged categories, many sad non-puppies plan to vote No Award.

David Langford (who never thought he'd write this) is so glad not to be nominated.

• *SFX* #262, Summer 2015

Throne Up

What the papers say: "If you haven't seen any of *Game of Thrones* so far, you might be wondering if it's worth ploughing through 40 hours of fantasy hokum to get you up to speed. It certainly looks, at first glance, like a load of old nonsense comprising bare breasts, fighting, dragons and not much else." (*Daily Telegraph*.) Very familiar stuff – but in fact it's the teaser for a rave review.

The *Neue Zürcher Zeitung* also loves *Game of Thrones*, but wants it kept separate from that greasy Tolkien stuff. *GoT*, they say (in German), is "often erroneously regarded as Fantasy, although there are neither magic rings here nor a fantastical triumph of good over evil."

Meanwhile, US TV host Joe Scarborough explains *GoT* without the prejudice instilled by watching it: "I think there are, like, gnomes, and elves, and hobbits, and people with spikes coming out of the sides of their faces." (MSNBC)

Yes, genre fiction still gets a bad press. When a *Guardian* hack wants to sneer at PUA (pick-up artist) culture, it's instant guilt by association: "They're sci-fi saddos; they're World of Warcraft weirdos."

The *Weekly Standard* tackles unashamed SF hack Jules Verne: "And, of course, for those who still feel obliged to read something semi-respectable but prefer not to trouble themselves with heavy lifting, there is science fiction..."

A more upmarket pundit admits SF may be likable but gives it the thumbs-down for not being lovable: "I'm not suggesting that one can't fully enjoy James Crumley, James Lee Burke, Robert Heinlein, Philip K. Dick, and Orson Scott Card, but I'm not sure one can love them in the way that one loves Shakespeare, Keats, Chekhov, and Joyce. One can be a fan of Agatha Christie, but one can't really be a fan of George Eliot.'" (*Chronicle of Higher Education*.) Come to think of it, I remember Kipling wrote a whole story about Jane Austen fandom.

This review of Michael Faber's SF novel *The Book of Strange New Things* explains its main saving grace: "While the bulk of the book takes place on another planet – a vividly drawn environment with green water, no moon and frequent, spiralling rainstorms – it doesn't read like science fiction, or like any genre.'" (*New York Times*.) What a relief.

Even *Godzilla* is no longer popcorn-fed fun: "Appreciation of a movie like this requires an almost morbid degree of connoisseurship, which may, in practice, be hard to distinguish from bored acquiescence." (*New York Times*.)

Genre-watchers enjoyed the uproar when literary author Kazuo Ishiguro published his f*nt*sy novel *The Buried Giant*, and worried in public about the ghastly stigma: "Will readers follow me into this? Will they understand what I'm trying to do, or will they be prejudiced against the surface elements? Are they going to say this is fantasy?" (*New York Times*.) Ursula K. Le Guin delivered a smart ticking-off: "Well, yes, they probably will. Why not? It appears that the author takes the word for an insult." (Bookviewcafe.com). No, no, Ishiguro retorted: Le Guin is "entitled to like my book or not like my book, but as far as I am concerned, she's got the wrong person. I am on the side of the pixies and the dragons." (*Guardian*.)

Mainstream pixie David Mitchell chimed in: "'Fantasy plus literary fiction can achieve things that frank blank realism can't,' said Mr. Mitchell, who added that he hoped *The Buried Giant* would help to 'de-stigmatize' fantasy. 'Bending the laws of what we call reality in a novel doesn't necessarily lead to elves saying "Make haste! These woods will be swarming with orcs by nightfall."'" (*New York Times*.) As bad as that genre hack Shakespeare whose fairies spout stuff like: "Ill met by moonlight, proud Titania."

David Langford has long studied the arts of the Enemy.

• *SFX* #263, August 2015

Butterfly Mind

Whenever I try to concentrate on writing this page, distractions flood in. Sometimes I wish I had the gall to write a column about writing a column, like that chap Tim Key who regularly used to fill his page in *The Independent* magazine with exciting thematic material like "How I Wrote This Column In A Café", and as his swan song managed to wring two whole columns out of how, presumably through popular editorial demand, he'd no longer be writing the column. But Langford is made of sterner stuff.

Where was I? My SF newsletter *Ansible* is a regular distraction. Every month, dozens if not scores of readers expect their news fix, enlivened by one or even both of my famous jokes. In the recent issue #333, that fine cartoonist Steve Stiles contributed a picture of a cute puppy: "333, Mark of the Domestic House Pet!" But Puppies – see my *SFX* #262 column 'Puppygate' – are a painful subject right now.

Ansible brings me kudos but also some criticism. One SF professional who shall be nameless (and didn't like being named) called it an infantile shitsheet; the *British Fantasy Newsletter* once complained it was "Not nearly as controversial as its reputation belies". Its US rival *File 770* announced: "As a newszine, it is the Emperor's New Clothes", an accolade I was proud to publish.

Similarly, the *File 770* website masthead now carries the blurb "... the 770 blog, that wretched hive of scum and villainy..." – an accolade from John C. Wright, who thanks to Sad and Rabid Puppy rigging of the Hugo nominations had an unprecedented six items (one since disqualified) on this year's Hugo ballot. Which led to much discussion of his works at *F770* and elsewhere, the tone of which you can imagine from his response.

I didn't want to revisit the Puppies controversy so soon, but the whole mess has provoked some interesting debate on reforming the Hugo nominations process to prevent slate voting by an organized minority from dominating the ballot. By tradition you can nominate up to five items in each category – five novels for Best Novel, and so on –

and the five most popular choices appear on the final ballot.

Many reformers suggested variations of the "4+6" plan: *four* nominations per category, with the top *six* becoming finalists. That stops a single slate from sweeping the nominations... but fandom's voting wonks soon deduced that if slates (formerly Just Not Done, Old Chap) become a standard tactic, "4+6" simply divides the final ballot between the two strongest slates.

Are the Hugos doomed to an eternity of party politics? Maybe not! An expert in electoral theory has devised a system that dilutes the effect of slates to ensure minorities can't easily rig the ballot. It's called "single divisible vote with least popular elimination" (SDV-LPE), nicknamed E Pluribus Hugo, and it's been explained at numbing length online. If you're curious, Google is your friend.

Meanwhile, though I should be writing a wise and witty column for *SFX*, I keep being distracted by ebook production chores. It's fun converting my old books into digital form, and even more fun when people buy them. See also taff.org.uk for some digital freebies.

How, you ask, am I dealing with the nightmare of VAT on ebooks as introduced in January and horrifically described in *SFX* #258? Sshh! (Come inside these brackets where no one can hear us. I'm refusing to sell to the EU countries where problems arise. So far I've got away with this.) Vigorous campaigning against a tax regime so unfair to microbusinesses has admittedly produced some response from EU high-ups. Roughly: "Ooh yes, there's a problem but we can't do anything about it *this* year."

Meanwhile it looks as though I'll never finish this damned column.

David Langford used to have a butterfly mind but can't remember where he put it.

• *SFX* #264, September 2015

Looking Backward

There's no blue commemorative plaque on John Wyndham's house, but now he has a memorial in South End Green, London. A nameless alleyway dedicated to wheelie-bin storage and identified as an escape route used in *The Day of the Triffids* now proudly bears the sign Triffid Alley. They missed a trick by not repeating the name in Braille.

Maybe one day there'll be a plaque at 32 Thorold Road, Ilford, which on 27 October 1930 housed the inaugural meeting of the Ilford Science Literary Circle – Britain's first SF fan group! Tea and crumpets were served, contemporary SF was read aloud, and history was made by a turnout of just six people.

No, I wasn't there, but I read the crib-sheet. The history of SF fandom is a deeply arcane subject, and for ages the only references were by Americans – such as Sam Moskowitz's *The Immortal Storm* from 1954, telling in prose of epic clunkiness the story of US fandom from the 1920s until World War II. Which, after Moskowitz's impassioned descriptions of apocalyptic fan feuds and brutal fan-political purges, seemed a distinct anti-climax.

History is full of oddments that escaped the history books, and the SF fan world is especially hard to track because so much early data appeared in low-circulation fanzines which, once their owners died, were promptly binned by a loving family. Much had been forgotten, but in the 1980s UK fan history received a shot in the arm. Young enthusiast Rob Hansen, fascinated by this retro stuff, teamed up with golden oldie Vince Clarke – who'd been active in 1930s UK fandom, dropped out in 1960, and twenty-odd years later returned with his vast archive of fannish documents and photos still intact.

The curtain is here lowered and raised again to skip over years of numbing research that spawned Rob Hansen's *THEN: A History of Science Fiction Fandom in the UK*, published as four hefty fanzine-format volumes from 1988 to 1993. Various tidied versions have been online since about 1995, and this year saw an ebook. Rob is currently working on a much expanded edition. Meanwhile, though less carefully preserved than L. Ron Hubbard's works (which the Scientologists once planned to inscribe on 1.8 million stainless steel plates preserved in time capsules, to kick-start post-holocaust rediscovery of the remainder shop), the information in *THEN* shouldn't easily be lost again.

One surprise was the revelation that British fandom had mislaid an entire national convention. According to the official record, three 1950s Eastercons were held at the George Hotel in Kettering (still shamefully denied its rightful blue plaque). Rob discovered a fourth, plunging the historical sequence into chaos because the 1971 "Eastercon 22" suddenly became the twenty-third Eastercon. Numerical sanity was only restored by Jesuitically declaring the 1951 convention to be a special international event, listed among Eastercons *but without a number*. Phew, that was a close one.

Another blue-plaque candidate identified in *THEN* is 88 Gray's Inn Road, London, home of The Flat – a short-lived SF powerhouse where Arthur C. Clarke and two fan friends lived at the end of the 1930s, and hosted the first meetings of the British Interplanetary Society. One of the Flat denizens, SF author William F. Temple, wrote a whole novel about their bizarre domestic life, eventually published in 2000 as *88 Gray's Inn Road: A Living-Space Odyssey*. It's fun.

Personally I thought *THEN* got really exciting in the 1970s volume when at last my own name turned up; but not everyone regards this as the climax of The Decline and Fall of the Fannish Empire. No blue plaque for Mr Hansen, whose greatest accolade was to be mistyped in Brian Aldiss's autobiography: "the historian of fanzines, Rob Hanson". Way to go, Rob.

David Langford had a sevagram once, but the multiverses fell off.

• *SFX* #265, October 2015

Plutocracy

When the *New Horizons* probe beamed back detailed pictures of Pluto, the NASA team decided to name one dark feature after Cthulhu. Will the International Astronomical Union approve this? Guidelines for place-names on Pluto mention underworld gods, but Cthulhu is more your unspeakable underwater abomination... Also allowed by IAU naming guidelines are "Writers associated with Pluto", opening the door to Disney scriptwriters. Meanwhile, working maps of Pluto's companion Charon are dotted with names from *Alien* (Ripley Crater), *Doctor Who* (Tardis Chasma), *Star Wars* (Skywalker, Vader Craters), *Star Trek* (Kirk, Spock, Sulu, Uhura Craters) and other SF. For Lewis Carroll fans, there's Alice Crater.

While Pluto was in the news, the IAU also announced new fame for J.R.R. Tolkien on official maps of Saturn's moon Titan. Here mountains and hills are named for Middle-earth's mountains and characters: Mountains of Moria (Moria Montes), Gandalf Hills (Gandalf Colles). Straits or channels get the names of characters in Asimov's *Foundation* series. Well, why not?

Meanwhile I rushed to titivate the Pluto section of the *SF Encyclopedia* entry "Outer Planets". SF pulp master Stanley G. Weinbaum was an early adopter, publishing a Pluto story just five years after its 1930 discovery: "The Red Peri", which is on safe ground when predicting the dwarf planet is airless and very very cold. If *New Horizons* goes on to detect mobile crystalline life, Weinbaum will instantly become a famous prophet. On the other hand, photos from Pluto of a gigantic Stonehenge-like structure built from ice will mean the glory goes to Kim Stanley Robinson, author of *Icehenge* (1984).

E.E. "Doc" Smith's *First Lensman* (1950) casually mentions that his frigid-blooded alien Palainians colonized Pluto well before Columbus reached America. Wilson Tucker decided that our base on Pluto would inevitably be named after its discoverer Clyde Tombaugh, and wrote *To the Tombaugh Station* (1960). Lots of authors since 1930 used Pluto as the starting or finishing point of a grand tour of all the planets, a prospect even more gruelling than crossing the USA by Greyhound bus. Donald A. Wollheim invented some interesting Plutonian facts in *The Secret of the Ninth Planet* (1959):

"Originally it revolved around another sun, some star which was light-years away. How it tore loose from that star we'll probably never know – the star might have simply become too dim, their planet might have been on a shaky orbit, an experiment of theirs might have jarred it loose..." ("Don't drop that lump of experimental antimatter, Glxpmf! Aargh, too late.")

On the NIMBY principle of conducting dangerous research as far as possible from politicians, Pluto struck some authors as a good place to put those pesky scientists. Thus in Robert Heinlein's *Starship Troopers*, cutting-edge science happens at "Starside R&D" on Pluto. In Roger McBride Allen's *The Ring of Charon* the scientists are dumped on Pluto while the Hugest Particle Accelerator Ever Built surrounds its companion Charon. What could possibly go wrong? An unfortunate side-effect is the sudden vanishing through a wormhole of some planet called Earth.

My favourite Pluto story is Clifford D. Simak's "Construction Shack", where the mini-world turns out to be just what the title says. It's made of metal, and it's hollow, and inside are the very blueprints used by the long-ago builders of our solar system. These reveal to awestruck human visitors that there was supposed to be another planet between Mars and Jupiter, but something went wrong (rising damp? insecure foundations? too much sand in the cement?) and it somehow ended up as a mess of little asteroids. Construction industry practices haven't changed much in the last 4.6 billion years.

David Langford dimly remembers that in animated cartoons, Pluto was the implacable nemesis of Bopeye.

• *SFX* #266, November 2015

Puppy Kicking

This year's Hugo Awards at Sasquan, the World SF Convention in Spokane, were *unusual*. Never before had Dramatic Presentation been handed out, or suckered out, by a Dalek. Never before had Best Novel been presented (via pre-recorded video, but never mind) by an astronaut on the International Space Station. And never before... but first, some background.

After a troubled summer in SF circles, Sasquan's permanent reek of smoke from raging US wildfires seemed appropriate. In *SFX* #262 (see the column 'Puppygate') I told how "Sad Puppies" and "Rabid Puppies" factions gamed the Hugo nominations to swamp the final ballot with their choices, and guessed there'd be widespread voting for No Award. Since then, record numbers had paid $40 for Hugo voting rights. No one knew whether the surge was pro- or anti-Puppy.

Anti, as it turned out. "No Award", which had taken Hugos only five times since 1953, was announced five more times in one evening – for Novella, Short Story, Related Work (nonfiction) and both Professional Editor categories. These were the Hugo slots entirely filled by Puppy nominees.

Elsewhere, from the fan awards to Best Novel (Cixin Lui's *The Three-Body Problem*, the first ever Chinese winner), Puppies were generally smacked with the rolled-up newspaper of placing below No Award. The only winner from the slates, for Best Dramatic Presentation, was *Guardians of the Galaxy* – which voters clearly reckoned was worthy on its own merits.

Was this cruel? It was hard for Pup nominees to sit through cheers of relief at each "No Award" (though they could have refused the tainted nomination, as some principled folk did). Very few Puppy works had award-winning quality, and many were downright awful. The Sad slate was mostly cronyism, with Sad leader Brad Torgersen listing his buddies without worrying about old-fashioned criteria like actual quality. The Rabid slate added naked self-promotion: Theodore "Vox Day" Beale, the Arch-Rabid, unashamedly stuffed the ballot with work from his own small press Castalia House.

That apart, what are the Puppies' aims? The official ideology varies from day to day, with goalposts not so much motorized as fitted with faster-than-light drive. Essentially, Puppies Want Hugos and have been unfairly deprived of them by a tiny, evil cabal of Social Justice Warriors (SJWs) who for many years have controlled the award by causing Worldcon members to vote for PC works they don't actually like – no actual evidence here, but THE PUPPIES KNOW IT – and thus prevented nomination of Puppy-favoured SF.

What Puppies say they like includes media tie-in SF, which was nevertheless mysteriously omitted from their slates, and military SF... unless it's by the very successful military-SF author John Scalzi, who understatedly refers to Beale as RSHD (Racist Sexist Homophobic Dipshit) and is Puppy Public Enemy #1. Scalzi, it must be understood, writes *the wrong kind of military SF*.

What Puppies hate also seems to include girlies who write acclaimed military SF. Especially Ann Leckie, whose *Ancillary Justice* won the 2014 Hugo but is irremediably bad because told from the viewpoint of an embodied AI who doesn't understand gender and calls everyone "she". This is just too yucky (the technical US critical term is "girl cooties"), and proves that Leckie's Hugo victory resulted from the SJW conspiracy. Likewise, presumably, her wins of the Arthur C. Clarke, BSFA, Locus and Nebula awards – pretty much a clean sweep of the top SF honours. As in Jorge Luis Borges's story "The Lottery in Babylon", the conspiracy is everywhere and controls everything.

Weirdly, the Rabids hailed Cixin Liu's Hugo win as their triumph because (*after* pushing him off the ballot with slate tactics; he got in only because someone withdrew) Beale decided he liked the novel. Meanwhile some of the Sads sneered at Hugo voters as Commie fellow-travellers with sinister reasons for supporting a "Chicom" author. O America.

The 2015 Worldcon business meeting passed some measures against ballot-stuffing, but these need ratification in 2016 to take effect in 2017. Expect another year of shenanigans, with those who dislike slate voting again being abused as SJWs and Puppy-Kickers. What jolly fun!

• *SFX* #267, December 2015

Double-Takes

A long time ago in a publishing industry far away, magically gifted beings known as copyeditors would often save authors from serious prose embarrassment. Alas, too many copyeditors fell prey to the Dark Side of Downsizing, and writers now need to take more care. Or their favourite sentences are showcased in my SF newsletter *Ansible*.

Can you imagine these noises? "He walked in and heard a sound like a tomb." (Lee Child, *Tripwire*.) "An eerie soundless shriek of terror ripped from the convulsed shroud." (Terry Brooks, *The Sword of Shannara*.) "The sound of Eddie's voice had been an injection through the ear." (William McIlvanney, *The Papers of Tony Veitch*.) "...a noise so soft and invisible it wouldn't mean anything unless you knew what it was." (John Burnham Schwartz, *Reservation Road*.)

Did these chaps consult a dictionary? "Luckily, the wall beside me was irregular with protuberances, and I was able to pack myself into one of them." (Hugh B. Cave, "The Door of Doom".) "Rugolo glanced at the greenness carpeting the plain, which he had taken to be a variety of grass or moss, forms of verbiage common on many worlds...' (Barrington J. Bayley, *Eye of Terror*.)

Is this what Orwell meant by doublethink? "*Who is this man?* he stopped himself from thinking, yet the thought stayed with him." (Arne Dahl, *Misterioso*.) "Too weary to attempt subterfuge, John relied again on a false story to gain entrance." (Martin Caidin, *The Long Night*.)

How many people can do these tricks? "Under his beard, Torin frowned." (Keith R.A. DeCandido, *Dragon Precinct*.) "Arcadia's head moved sharply back of itself." (Isaac Asimov, *Second Foundation*.) "...slowly a crimson flush spread around his ears. Eventually his earlobes, unusually large and awkward, were illuminated like traffic lights." (Anne Holt, *Death of the Demon*.) "A hand took his, pressed it firmly, looked him straight in the eye." (Neil Gaiman, *American Gods*.) "He rose to his spare elbows." (Charles E. Gannon, *Fire with Fire*.)

Know any pets like this? "Like a cat scenting an approaching storm, she had left with a pair of suitcases..." (Chris Fowler, *Soho Black*.) "His ginger hair with its generous dashes of grey sat on his head like an electrified cat." (J.D. Robb, *Strangers in Death.*)

From *Miss Manners' Book of Extreme Etiquette*: "But one does not scream with a beer barrel tap inserted deep into one's jugular vein..." (Jack Oleck, *The Vault of Horror.*) One certainly does not. One has standards.

Whose eyes can do these tricks? "Dorothy's eyes were turned inward to her long-buried memories." (Debra Ginsberg, *The Neighbors Are Watching.*) "The eyes follow me down the street, pinching the back of my neck."' (Veronica Roth, *Insurgent.*)

Cruel and unusual punishment? "If they were captured wearing the enemy's uniform, they would probably be tortured to death before being shot." (Giuseppe Filotto, "Red Space".)

Powerfully evocative similes and metaphors? "They stared at me, squinting as if I were holding a supernova." (Catherine Asaro, *Undercity.*) "...a face pink and stern as frozen strawberry custard." (Ayn Rand, *Ideal.*)

What would doctors make of these symptoms? "Not for the first time, a cold fist appeared deep within her stomach." (Becky Chambers, *The Long Way to a Small, Angry Planet.*) "His brain began to sway on its base, as the landslide of possibilities unreeled before it." (A.E. van Vogt, "Juggernaut".)

Without comment: "Connie had a wry, compact intelligence, a firm little clitoris of discernment and sensitivity...' (Jonathan Franzen, *Freedom.*') "Daniel sat back, steepling his long fingers across his waistcoat. He bought them from a little shop in Brixton Market." (Paul McAuley, *Something Coming Through.*)

Enough, enough!

David Langford is, as usual, fleeing a mob of outraged authors.

• *SFX* #268, January 2016

Untrue Names

Bob Shaw once explained his struggle to find the perfect name for the hero of his next SF novel. A name that would express every nuance of the guy's personality and subtly imply his whole life story, so once Bob had hit on the one true name it became unnecessary to write the book. I don't know how long Neal Stephenson spent struggling through this agonizing process with his novel *Snow Crash* before realizing that the only possible name for the hero, or protagonist, was Hiro Protagonist.

Stephen R. Donaldson is especially fond of fantasy monikers with over-the-top appropriateness. Not just Lord Foul, but a Gollumish figure with the gigglesome name Drool Rockworm and a noble seafaring giant called Saltheart Foamfollower. Conversely, I rather liked Jack Vance's SF tale *The Anome* with its mysterious, enigmatic character known as Ifness.

Elsewhere in SF we meet a dark invader called Darth Vader, ultimate superbeings called Ultans (Bob Shaw on a bad day), mysterious entities called Mysterons (*Captain Scarlet*), a large world called – by its alien denizens, who presumably know Latin – Terromagna (Captain W.E. Johns of Biggles fame), a naughty-boy character called Malenfant (Stephen Baxter) and tyrannical rulers called Tyranni (Isaac Asimov).

One critic friend objected to Vonda McIntyre's story title "Of Mist, and Grass, and Sand" for being *too evocative*. Lovely title, he whinged. "Conjures up a whole landscape. And then you read the thing and Mist and Grass and Sand are just three bloody snakes." Sorry about the major spoiler there.

There was a similar sense of vague letdown when I read Bruce Sterling's nifty novel *Schismatrix*. Obviously a schismatrix must be a woman who goes around causing schisms. After waiting for half the book for her to turn up and start schisming, I learned that in the jargon of this interplanetary future the whole fragmented Solar System was a *matrix* of *schisms*, geddit? Oh dearie me.

Some authors pick names that give typesetters a hard time. A favourite example from E.E. Smith's Lensman space operas is the occasionally mentioned planet Alsakan. Inevitably, every other reference got corrected to the more plausible "Alaskan". I found myself thinking that since this far-off world was known only for exports of Alsakan tobacco, it might have been wiser to call it Vriginia.

It was similarly easy to misread the name of the dire continent-wrecking Monster From The ID in Clive Barker's *Everville*, the Iad Uroboros. The capital I kept coming across as lower-case L, introducing a lad called Uroboros and leading to distracting thoughts that Uroboros Lad must be a reject from the Legion of Superheroes (because his only superpower was an amazing ability to bite his own bum). Just like that fiercely independent fellow Stand Alone Stan who was in fact the title of a fantasy novel by Phillip Mann, in which the something that stands alone is in fact a stone.

Would-be comic names can lead us into even grimmer territory, as when L. Ron Hubbard attempted biting satirical wit in his truly awful *Battlefield Earth* by introducing a character called Arsebogger. Only slightly more subtle, from Brian Aldiss's *The Eighty-Minute Hour*, is the actually quite nice fellow Devlin Carnate. Not to mention a Croatian lady named Myrtr Tjidvyl.

Some authors definitely need the assistance of Baldrick in *Blackadder*, who as you'll remember suggested a cunning alternative when his master announced his terror-inspiring pseudonym: "I shall be known from now on... as The Black Vegetable!"

David Langford told them again and again that people would misread the middle letter of SFX, but did they ever listen?

• *SFX* #269, February 2016

Crash!

Things in life which are no fun at all include returning from a convivial SF convention (Novacon in Nottingham, since you ask) and exhaustedly trying to catch up on writing deadlines – only for the computer to murmur "I'm sorry, I can't do that" and, pausing only for a brief chorus of "Daisy, Daisy", to die a horrible death.

Of course I have lots of backups (he said unconvincingly), but the time it takes to get it all together on a new machine is... well, the great crash was a week ago and everything is still what in the technical jargon of computer geeks is termed higgledy-piggledy.

Losing access to my vast email archive, even temporarily, is like being in one of these novels that start off with the famous cliché of lumbering the hero with amnesia: Philip José Farmer's *The Maker of Universes*, Colin Kapp's *The Patterns of Chaos*, Robert Silverberg's *Lord Valentine's Castle*, Roger Zelazny's *Nine Princes in Amber* and many more. From the writer's point of view this is dead convenient, since rather than organizing infodumps of background data ("Tell me again, Professor, as though I knew nothing of it") they can let readers follow the protagonist on the journey of learning what he needs to know – or rather, what the author wants readers to know.

Gene Wolfe has an interesting twist on amnesia in his *Soldier in the Mist*, whose hero Latro's recent memories keep vanishing overnight, forcing him to write down everything he might need to know in the days to come. The novel consists of what he writes.

Some characters, like Latro, lose their memories through the traditional knock on the head; I'm not sure there's any medical justification for the handy plot device, much older than SF, that they can be instantly cured by an equal but opposite knock on the other side of the head. Others suffer insidious memory edits inflicted by bad guys or Men in Black. I couldn't help cheering when, on being told by an extra-terrestrial that he knows too much and must suffer memory erasure, the hero of Lloyd Biggle Jr's *All the Colours of Darkness* is grumpily unsurprised: "Aliens *always* erase the memory. We have a substantial literature on that subject."

Something else that occasionally erases minds is Knowledge Too Awful to Contemplate – a problem for any H.P. Lovecraft character who even glimpses the Great Old Slimy Ones or Donald Trump.

On the other side of the coin from all those unfortunates with amnesia are the lucky sods who remember *everything* in excruciating detail. The hero of Robert Heinlein's YA *Starman Jones* soon loses the valuable books of astrogation data he inherited from an uncle, but it's okay because he read them once and can recall every figure, every decimal point. SF has many other characters with photographic memories, like the Microfilm Mind in Charles Harness's *The Paradox Men*, the Mentats in Frank Herbert's *Dune*, Severian in Gene Wolfe's *The Book of the New Sun* and Brutha in Terry Pratchett's *Small Gods*. But one author thought this particular superpower wouldn't be a blessing. The mental prodigy of Jorge Luis Borges's "Funes the Memorious" performs amazing feats of memory but is deeply dysfunctional, lost in a blizzard of tiny details. Can't see the wood for the trees.

All the same, I could use one of those clever chaps to help restore my computer data.

David Langford's latest proof that SF has conquered the world is a restaurant review in The Independent *that sensuously reports: "A helping of kale lay over the chicken like a drunken triffid."*

• *SFX* #270, March 2016

Random Reading
The Prodigal Returns

The main reason for the long hiatus in Random Reading instalments since the August 2011 issue of *The New York Review of Science Fiction* lies in what students of morbid psychology have yet to identify as Langford's Paradox. This states that the more one devotes oneself to toiling on vast and authoritative reference works, the less time is available to keep up with the genre about which one is being so allegedly vast and authoritative. The online *SF Encyclopedia* was launched at sf-encyclopedia.com in October 2011 with 12,230 entries totalling 3.2 million words, quite a bit more than the 1993 print 'edition's 6,571 entries and 1.3 million words. Though not myself a hugely prolific contributor (John Clute, author of over 6,000 solo entries and 2.2 million words of the current *SFE*, here modestly polishes his fingernails), I've overseen its growth to more than 16,500 entries and 5.1 million words... and although it would be exaggerating to say that every word has left its scar, life has been somewhat crowded.

Ongoing challenges include trying to compensate for various eccentricities in the expensively designed *SFE* website. Some of these must remain state secrets, but one personal favourite is that a search for the well-known skiffy magazine *If* reports no hits at all. Apparently the word never appears among those 5.1 million. Well, of course it does, but I deduce that the search engine looks for interesting keywords and ignores particularly boring parts of speech like "if", "this", "on" or "Sad Puppies". This led to the epoch-making experiment of searching (with quotes around the phrase to supposedly force an exact match) for "If This Goes On" – a Heinlein title, as you well know, Professor – and getting hits for hundreds of entries. None of the first ten pages of results seems to include any of the five entries that actually mention this title. It is eerily plausible that these are the exact same results produced by a search for just "goes". For God's sake don't tell our competitors.

Still, the work has its compensations. There's a treasurable scene in

Robertson Davies's novel *Leaven of Malice* where the small-town newspaper proprietor, having been roundly abused by a local bigwig, pulls the fellow's draft obituary out of the files and spends a happy hour lovingly re-editing it. Now that the bean-counters at Future Publishing have marked the twenty-first anniversary of my column in their glossy media magazine *SFX* by conveying that they can no longer afford such luxuries as "star writers", the *SF Encyclopedia* entry for that publication may be in need of a little reworking...

The "As Others See Us" department of my SF newsletter *Ansible* regularly reports horrid things people say about the genre ("Like most science fiction, this is a pack of lies meant for babies." – Sam Biddle, Gawker.com, January 2016) and nervous attempts to free approved work from the taint of genre: "Though there are extra-terrestrials, *We Are the Ants* by Shaun David Hutchinson (*The Five Stages of Andrew Brawley*) isn't really a science fiction novel." (Shelf Awareness, February 2016, which further confides that this YA book "blends existential despair with exploding planets.") Thus an unexpected good word is always a treat. The collected *W.H. Auden: Prose: Volume III: 1949-1955* (2008) reveals that, when invited to write for *Publishers Weekly* about the best-produced books of December 1950 in various categories, Auden took as his solitary fiction choice *The Cometeers* by Jack Williamson (Fantasy Press, $3). Though a certain faint cattiness can be detected in the commentary: "My choice comes from a field in which one would least expect trouble to be taken, namely science-fiction. In this case paper and type are such that no parent need worry about the eyesight of his twelve-year-old son even if he reads in bed."

The Plain People of NYRSF: Were you planning to discuss any actual genre books?

Myself, unconvincingly: I was coming to that.

Gilbert Adair's *And Then There Was No One* (2009) is the third of his "Evadne Mount" mysteries in the manner of Agatha Christie, or at least of her titles: the first two were *The Act of Roger Murgatroyd* and *A Mysterious Affair of Style*. Both were apparently more or less straight pastiche, with crimes tackled by detective novelist Evadne Mount, who seems not a million miles distant from Christie's own fictional crime writer and possible self-portrait Ariadne Oliver. This third book gets all postmodern – which was indeed Adair's trademark – with Adair himself meeting Mount at a Sherlock Holmes festival in Meiringen,

Switzerland, where the main tourist attraction is the Reichenbach Falls. A reading at this event provides the opportunity for an inset Holmes pastiche, "The Giant Rat of Sumatra", before the inevitable murder. Literary gags and red herrings fly thick and fast; the story eventually heads determinedly up its own po-mo orifice. Deconstructionism, after all, inevitably implies The Death of the Author. Quite fun actually.

After Alice (2015) by Gregory Maguire of *Wicked* fame is yet another follow-up to Lewis Carroll, in which Alice's barely mentioned friend Ada follows her into Wonderland / Looking-Glass territory and has differently frustrating adventures amid sub-Carrollian verbal quibbling and logic-chopping, all leading to a revisionist finale. I liked the delayed-drop revelation of Ada's personal Jabberwock, but overall the story – though worthily written and even dealing in racial issues – seemed essentially unnecessary.

In *The Annihilation Score* (2015), Charles Stross's latest "Laundry" tale of covert occult ops, our usual viewpoint character Bob is displaced by his partner Mo – her narrative voice being pretty much the same – as the world or at least Great Britain continues to slide downhill to the Cthulhoid apocalypse coded CASE NIGHTMARE GREEN. The latest twist is that side effects of the increasing thaumaturgic noise level are generating assorted UK superhero figures whose antics need to be contained by the frightful power of bureaucracy. There is yet another finale in which a Dread Portal to Very Bad Things (this time around it's the King in Yellow) is unwisely opened, in a more public place than ever before. Lively enough, but disbelief is sometimes rather hard to keep suspended.

The strange title of *Coriolanus, the Chariot!* (1978) by Alan G. Yates pertains to a cabal of unsecret planetary masters who with varying degrees of plausibility embody fused Shakespearean and Tarot archetypes: Prospero the Magician and so on. The SF premise of far-future theatrical "plactors" who shapeshift into perfect representations of their roles seemed vaguely interesting, but rapidly moves into unpleasant territory. Once treated with the "ambiology" potion and becoming a were-thespian, one can not only learn to change oneself but may be remotely transformed by any sufficiently strong-minded auteur. Our protagonist's first audition involves his being painfully reshaped into a woman solely in order to be brutally raped. This lesson learned, he presently plays a nasty tyrant and throws himself into the part by committing an equally brutal rape. Offstage, with his will-power now boosted by such ordeals, he humiliates an unsympathetic instructor by causing him to grow such gigantic, muscular (yes, that's what it says) breasts that they burst through the fabric of this unfortunate's jerkin. Eventually, through further triumph of the will, our man breaks into the inner ring of dramaturges or "playtors" who run this nonsensically sadistic show, and it is indicated that he is no longer – if he ever was – a nice guy. There's nothing like ending a sour story on a sour note.

Lastly, a little unfinished business. In a Random Reading instalment mysteriously titled "The Spad-Gas and the Offog" (*NYRSF* December 2009), I mused that the central device or "offog" of Eric Frank Russell's story "Allamagoosa" (1955) might well derive from Anthony Armstrong's army barracks sketch "Captain Bayonet and the Spad-Gas" (collected in book form in 1937). Like the offog, the spad-gas is a missing inventory item which nobody knows what it is and for which a plausible fake is substituted, all because someone long ago mistyped what should have been Spade, G.S. (General Service). But John L. Ingham's indexless bio-bibliography *Into Your Tent: The Life, Work and Family Background of Eric Frank Russell* (2010, with no index) has an alternative theory! Ingham, foe to indexers, is convinced that the seed of "Allamagoosa" was a 1950s naval legend about a mystery "shovewood", with yet another weird gadget hastily manufactured to replace the inventory's typo for – in this case – an official-issue "shovel, wood". These are deep waters, Watson. The true source must remain a riddle wrapped in a mystery inside an enigma. Did I mention that *Into Your Tent* annoyingly lacks an index?

• *The New York Review of Science Fiction* #331, March 2016

[The above column will have given an embarrassing hostage to fortune if for absolutely inescapable commercial and bibliographical reasons it turns out that *The Last SFX Visions* is published without an index. The whirligig of time, as Shakespeare so memorably said, bites Langford in the bum.]

Ten Year Hitch

It's that time of the decade again, when starry-eyed fans begin to mutter about bringing the World Science Fiction Convention back to this country. London in 1957 and 1965, Brighton in 1979 and 1987, Glasgow in 1995 and 2005, London Docklands in 2014... and now there's a feeling in the air that the stars will be right in 2024 for either the awakening of Great Cthulhu to devour our puny human brains or (much the same thing as far as the organizers' brains are concerned) yet another UK Worldcon.

From modest beginnings like the inaugural 1939 New York event with 200 people and London in 1957 – the first in Britain – with 268, these fan-run events have become biggish business with terrifying budgets and many thousands in attendance. Prospective committees need to spend significant chunks of lifetime preparing their bid and wooing the sceptical voting membership with wild parties and wilder promises. The crunch point comes with the site selection vote at the Worldcon two years before your target year. In 2015, Helsinki was chosen as the 2017 venue, to general Finnish rejoicing. After that, New Orleans and San José (California) are the rival bids for 2018, and at Worldcon 2016 in Kansas City the voters will confirm that There Can Be Only One. So far the only hat in the ring for 2019 is Dublin.

Britain in 2024, whether or not an opposing bid emerges, will need to persuade the voting members of the 2022 event. This, according to worldcon.org/bids, is currently a toss-up between Chicago – a plausible venue that's hosted many a past Worldcon – and Doha, Qatar, a concept that frankly makes my sense of wonder blow a fuse. Especially when I remember some of the Worldcon community's more *interesting* people and practices in the light, or the murk, of Qatar's human rights record.

If 2024 seems a long way off, that's because it is. For less delayed gratification there are British UK conventions all the year round. This year's national event – the annual Eastercon – is called Mancunicon, and readers deeply versed in the subtleties of linguistics will deduce that it's in Manchester: for full information see www.mancunicon.org.uk. 2017 should be making history with the first ever Welsh Eastercon: Pasgon in Cardiff, whose details have been leeked at www.pasgon.org.uk. *[Since cancelled, alas.]*

For my own part I have fondish memories of being on various UK con committees, one an Eastercon; of chairing a long-ago Eastercon bid that went for a hyper-expensive central London venue and mercifully lost; of organizing Hugo trophies for one of the Brighton Worldcons; and of almost entirely missing three conventions (two of them Eastercons) because I spent the weekend in a stuffy room full of equipment, editing and publishing the several-times-daily con newsletter. When I gaze bleary-eyed on these past glories and feel the urge to have another bash at convention-running, I dose myself liberally with whisky and lie down quietly until the feeling passes away. It's your turn now. Anyone's turn but mine.

The Plain People of SFX: How, oh how, can I join the exciting discussion about planning a 2024 UK Worldcon?

Myself: This may be one of those terrible secrets of the universe with which humanity should never meddle, but if you insist: send a grovelling email to FutureUKworldcons@googlegroups.com. Just don't blame me if you end up with one of the tough Worldcon jobs like disposing of the bodies after a guest appearance by George R.R. Martin.

• *SFX* #271, April 2016

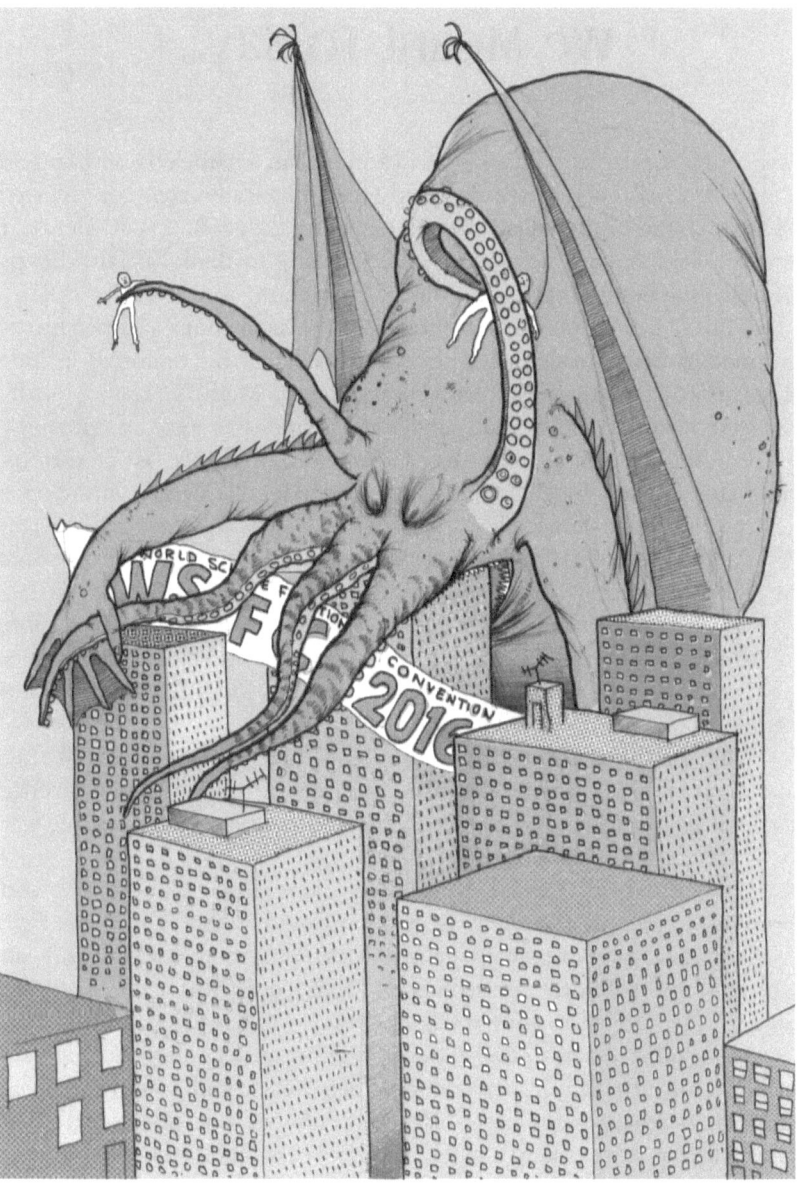

We Meant To Say...

Reporting the lamented death of David Bowie, chameleon of pop and Man Who Fell To Earth, a flustered Heart FM Radio presenter blurted "David Cameron has died" before her hasty revision "David Bowie, I mean David Bowie." It would be very wrong to think SF fans' hearts lifted a little before they sank with the correction.

Those newspaper "corrections and clarifications" departments sometimes have a touch of genre relevance. *Guardian* examples include Tintagel's "tavern traditionally known as Merlin's Cave", sadly corrected to "cavern", and advice to emphasize text in email by surrounding it with Asterixes. Correction: "Asterix is a cartoon character created by Rene Goscinny and Albert Uderzo. The device referred to is an asterisk..."

At the end of 2015, a *Pasadena Star-News* roundup collected some SF/fantasy gems:

The New York Times on the author of *Charlotte's Web* and *Stuart Little*: "Correction: An earlier version of this article misidentified the number of years E.B. White wrote for *The New Yorker*. It was five decades, not centuries."

The Brighton *Argus* on futurology: "*The Argus* would like to apologize for suggesting that the director of the Brighton Science Festival believes the '21st century will be remembered for a terrible war between mankind and goats.'"

Alas, the best *Star-News* discovery came from a satire site and brought a grumpy complaint from its claimed source *The Prague Post*. "Last week's column mistakenly misidentified a source. The European Commission president is Romano Prodi, not Buffy the Vampire Slayer." Definitely too good to check.

The online *Baltimore City Paper*, reporting on a comics-themed cafe called Bamf after an *X-Men* sound effect, clearly had a storm of geek complaints... "Correction: An earlier version of this post stated that Nightcrawler says 'Bamf' when he teleports. It is the sound that happens when he teleports. *City Paper* regrets the error." And so it bamfing well should.

Wall Street Journal: "The Minotaur is a monster in Greek mythology that is part bull, part human. A travel article in Saturday's Off Duty section mistakenly called it a one-eyed monster." That would be a Cyclopsotaur.

Slate: "In a March 2 'Future Tense' blog post, Torie Bosch misspelled the science fiction award won by writer Bruce Sterling. It is of course the Hugo Award, not the Huge Award." This is traditional: I fondly remember a 1970s fanzine description of the top sf awards as Huge and Knobbly.

The *Independent*'s Mini-Me paper "i" is flaky at astronomy: "In yesterday's report 'Copernicus and Galileo: now stars in their own right', we said Copernicus had demonstrated that the Sun goes round the Earth. It has been pointed out to us that this is wrong and, in fact, the Earth goes round the Sun. We are sorry for the mistake." Nobody expects the Spanish Inquisition!

The *New York Times* had more important matters on its mind: "An earlier version of this article misspelled the name of a creature in the *Star Wars* universe. It is a wookiee, not a wookie."

The Sun: "In an article on Saturday headlined 'Flying saucers over British Scientology HQ', we stated 'two flat silver discs' were seen 'above the Church of Scientology HQ.' Following a letter from lawyers for the Church, we apologize to any alien lifeforms for linking them to Scientologists."

And a million netizens who shared Simon Pegg's alleged tweet – "If you're sad today, just remember the world is over 4 billion years old and you somehow managed to exist at the same time as David Bowie." – need to know it's not by Pegg and wasn't originally about Bowie. Good line, though.

David Langford regrets that in his column on Shapeshifters, this word appeared with the F missing throughout.

• *SFX* #272, May 2016

Balderdash

Not a lot of people know that Hugo Gernsback, the SF magazine pioneer after whom the Nebula Award isn't named, liked to publish little spoofs of glossy US journals as substitute Xmas cards. His 1945 effort, copying the design of *Time* magazine but subtly called *Tame*, was dated Christmas 2045 and reviewed the first century of the Atomic Age.

In this 2045, maybe thanks to a long history of radioactive fallout, normal Earthlings are bald and an actress with hair is promoted as a weird throwback. *Tame*'s cover shows a bald secretary thinking correspondence into her "mindwriter" machine...

Did this inspire Arthur C. Clarke's *3001: The Final Odyssey*, in which baldness is among the bare necessities for working with future technology? Hair gets in the way of the Braincap interface that lets you use Clarke's amazing Thoughtwriter and (unless you have huge powers of concentration) send rambling messages full of asides like "Sorry again – trouble with Thoughtwriters – hard to stick to point–"

H.G. Wells made his baldy prediction long before Clarke or Gernsback, in the 1893 essay "The Man of the Year Million". This scientifically imagines Future Us as big-brained and big-eyed, with shrunken body and limbs overshadowed by that mighty hairless intellect. Wells's own Martians in *The War of the Worlds* are like this only more so, and the tradition carries on to other bad baldies such as the Mekon. Not to mention ambiguous ones like the Alien Greys of UFO folklore, who come in peace but work in mysterious ways by erasing memories and investigating our inmost secrets with terrifying rectal probes. Ask Whitley Strieber.

In comics, another famously wicked bone-dome is Superman's glabrous nemesis Lex Luthor, whose entire life was warped by premature hair loss. His vaunted scientific genius is somehow unable to come up with the kind of solution imaginable even to the rudimentary mind of Donald Trump.

Fortunately for the fate of civilization as we know it, some bald chaps are on the side of the angels, like Professor Xavier of the X-Men ("I am Professor Charles Xavier, and my superpower is the ability to say these lines with a straight face.") and Captain Picard of *Star Trek: The Next Generation.* Not to mention *most* of the psi-powered Baldies in *Mutant* (1953) by Henry Kuttner and C.L. Moore, where those gifted with the power of telepathy are marked from childhood with hairless pates so ordinary folk can persecute them. Perhaps the furious mental activity of all that thought-transfer just naturally fries your follicles.

All this brings us to the terrifying real-life prediction made by US psychic The Amazing Criswell, who played himself in the legendary *Plan 9 from Outer Space.* His "sensational bestseller" *Criswell Predicts* offers a definitive scenario for the future, including:

"I predict one of the most horrifying things to befall any woman. I regret to predict that women will lose their hair. I predict that scientists will try to prove that the cause of this falling out of the hair is due to the gaseous fumes polluting the city's air."

Yes, apocalypse looms in St Louis, Missouri, with "law suits, divorces, murders, desertions and even massacres... male hair dressers will be murdered... beauticians will be beaten, slashed and shot. Divorce courts will be swamped with irate husbands seeking freedom from their bald-headed wives." Surely not if they look anything like the shaven ladies in *Star Trek: The Motion Picture* (Persis Khambatta) or *Dune* (Francesca Annis).

Fortunately Criswell calculates from the small print of his horoscope that after three grim months, "new hair will be grown as mysteriously as it disappeared." When will this horror begin? The scheduled date of our psychic's infallible 1968 prophecy is, er, February 1983.

David Langford wishes his wife wouldn't say "getting a bit thin on top, dear".

• *SFX* #273, June 2016

All Good Things

Twenty-one years ago I wrote in *SFX* #1 about Harlan Ellison's long delayed anthology *The Last Dangerous Visions* (breaking news: still unpublished). I've been in every single issue since then and hoped to make it to the next gloriously round number of #300, but the harsh realities of modern publishing say otherwise. *[Which is about as close as I could come to saying in print that I didn't jump ship but was pushed. See the introductory Author's Note.]*

So Thog, my connoisseur of Differently Good Prose, offers a farewell banquet of weird SF anatomy. His favourites – so tasty! – are eyeballs:

"Franklin left his eyes on the floor, took half a step backward." (Kelli Stanley, *City of Dragons*.) "His eyes fixed like grappling hooks on AAri's face..." (Rachel Pollack, *Golden Vanity*.) "... his eyes felt as if they had tendrils growing out of them, crawling like ants across the floorboards." (Sheng Keyi, *Death Fugue*.) "Eyes like anguished talons were clutching hers." (Charles L. Harness, *The Rose*.) "Her eyes have the puckered sheen of day-old ripe olives." (Ed Bryant, "Their Thousandth Season".)

Brains: "The human's brain began to function once more; he could almost feel it sweating." (Poul Anderson and Gordon R. Dickson, *Earthman's Burden*.)

Stomachs: "The pessimism of the twentieth century has been a massive burp of indigestion; but the stomach ache is passing." (Colin Wilson, *The Philosopher's Stone*.) "Worry [...] ate inside him like a ferret trying to burrow out of his middle." (Robert Jordan, *A Crown of Swords*.) "Maybe her stomach knew what it was doing when it threw up her toenails." (Mike Shepherd, *Kris Longknife: Unrelenting*.)

Big Hair: "His unruly shock of red hair towered six feet above the floor..." (Edmond Hamilton, *Captain Future and the Space Emperor*.)

Lungs: "But at least in space I can breathe..." (E.E. Smith and Gordon Eklund, *Lord Tedric*.)

Rear End: "Her buttocks were fresh-baked loaves; they were ivory eggs, they were the eggs of the lonely phoenix. They were a fist." (Ron Miller, *Silk and Steel*.) "He felt once again the desire to bite his own backside in fury." (Andrzej Sapkowski, *Blood of Elves*.) "There has to be a natural limit to how long anyone can spend like this, in a black aluminum suppository lodged in the asshole of the earth." (Garth Risk Hallberg, *City on Fire*.)

Faces: "His dark face was pale." (Terry Brooks, *The Wishsong of Shannara*.) "Her face had the fragrance of a gibbous moon." (Ron Miller, *Silk and Steel*.) Plus a cheesy grin: "... I said through grated teeth." (Ioanna Bourazopoulou, *What Lot's Wife Saw*.)

Hearts: "His heart didn't have the strength to do much of anything, except pound, and beat, and maybe squat in his mouth..." (Gordon Eklund, *Space Pirates*.) "Phrgg felt as an intelligent blood corpuscle would feel when caught in the circulation and fed unceremoniously through a palpitating aorta!" (John E. Muller, *Dark Continuum*.)

Legs: "The wind was shrieking, and so were her legs." (Kelli Stanley, *City of Dragons*.) "Her legs were quills. They were bundles of wicker, they were candelabra..." (Ron Miller, *Silk and Steel*.)

Naughty Parts: "Breasts like bronzed mangoes." "...her tits look like soft blue balloons." (Garth Risk Hallberg, *City on Fire*.) "The nipples rose like mercury with her heat." (Ron Miller, *Silk and Steel*.) "But when she took the warm shaft in her hands, she found that she did not know how to call upon its strength." (Stephen Donaldson, *The Runes of the Earth*.) Oh, sorry, that was actually the Staff of Law.

Lastly, adapting the words of a famous fantasy character: *though twenty-one years is far too short a time to spend among you – this is the END. I am going. I am leaving NOW. GOOD-BYE!* (Puts on the Ring and vanishes.)

• *SFX* #274, July 2016

Also available from

Sibilant Fricative ~ Adam Roberts
Witty, incisive, refusing to conform and and pulling no punches, this is a masterpiece of literary criticism.

"*Sibilant Fricative* is undoubtedly one of the finest collections of essays that genre criticism has ever produced."
– *Jonathan McCalmont, BSFA Vector magazine*

Rave and Let Die ~ Adam Roberts
Continuing in the same vain as *Sibilant Fricative*, here masterful reviewer takes on the Herculean task of assessing the genre output for an entire year in literature and beyond.

Winner of the 2016 BSFA Award for Best Non-fiction

Lifelines and Deadlines ~ James Lovegrove
James Lovegrove is the *New York Times* best-selling author of more than fifty novels and novellas.

James also writes nonfiction, his reviews and articles having appeared in numerous venues in print and online, including a regular review column for the *Financial Times*. This volume gathers the very best of his work.

Steel Quill Books, an imprint of NewCon Press.

IMMANION PRESS
Purveyors of Speculative Fiction

The Lightbearer by Alan Richardson (May 2017)

Michael Horsett parachutes into Occupied France before the D-Day Invasion. He is dropped in the wrong place, miles from the action, badly injured, and totally alone. He falls prey to two Thelemist women who have awaited the Hawk God's coming, attracts a group of First World War veterans who rally to what they imagine is his cause, is hunted by a troop of German Field Police who are desperate to find him, and has a climactic encounter with a mutilated priest who believes that Lucifer Incarnate has arrived...

The Lightbearer is a unique gnostic thriller, dealing with the themes of Light and Darkness, Good and Evil, Matter and Spirit.

"The Lightbearer is another shining example of Alan Richardson's talent as a story-teller. He uses his wide esoteric knowledge to produce a story that thrills, chills and startles the reader as it radiates pure magical energy. An unusual and gripping war story with more facets than a star sapphire." – Mélusine Draco, author of "Aubry's Dog" and "Black Horse, White Horse". ISBN: 978-1-907737-63-3 £11.99 $18.99

Dark in the Day, Ed. by Storm Constantine & Paul Houghton

Weirdness lurks beyond the margins of the mundane, emerging to dismantle our assumptions of reality. Dark in the Day is an anthology of weird fiction, penned by established writers and also those new to the genre – the latter being authors who are, or were, students of Creative Writing at Staffordshire University, where editor Storm Constantine occasionally delivers guest lectures. Her co-editor, Paul Houghton, is the senior lecturer in Creative Writing at the university.

*Contributors include: Martina Bellovičová, J. E. Bryant, Glynis Charlton, Storm Constantine, Louise Coquio, Elizabeth Counihan, Krishan Coupland, Elizabeth Davidson, Siân Davies, Paul Finch, Rosie Garland, Rhys Hughes, Kerry Fender, Andrew Hook, Paul Houghton, Tanith Lee, Tim Pratt, Nicholas Royle, Michael Marshall Smith, Paula Wakefield, Ian Whates and Liz Williams.*ISBN: 978-1-907737-74-9 £11.99, $18.99

Immanion Press
http://www.immanion-press.com
info@immanion-press.com

www.ingramcontent.com/pod-product-compliance
Lightning Source LLC
Chambersburg PA
CBHW030113260626
47156CB00008B/2641